# *Winter's Flower*

by
*Dr. Ranae Johnson, Ph.D., MRET*

Published by **Rain Tree Press**

**Rain Tree Press**
C/o Rapid Eye Institute
3748 74th Avenue SE
Salem, Oregon 97301
503-399-1181

This is the story of
Kelton's journey through Autism
expressed in the writing and poetry
of his mother, Ranae Johnson.


This book is dedicated with love
to all who make the journey
on the path of growth.

# My Gratitude

To God...who is always there with Love.

To Kelton...who taught me that we are healed in our desire to heal others.

To my Mother...for example of faith.

To my husbands...who all tried to help in their own loving ways–but especially to Joseph who could love so much another man's children.

To my children and family...who have been the greatest traveling companions I could ask for.

To my friends, this list is long...each touched my life with love, caring and encouragement.

To Diana...for her love, encouragement and help.

To my sweet daughter, Lynell...for hours of typing.

To Kevin...for art work and other help.

To Sonja...for sharing her talent and love.

# Preface

Early morning dawn varnished the distant mountains. Hypnotic colors bathed the awakening town, as I watched the golden orange sun creep higher in the sky, I felt a Oneness; I was light merging with the light that cast about the countryside.

I was flooded with a deep gratitude for all the beauty around me; the vast Oregon greenness, the growing, living abundance–each bore the signature of God, each an extension of his creation. My tears were of joy. Miracles! Why had it taken twenty years for me to discover that miracles are natural?

I had been touched–touched deeply by Kelton. I saw his face before me– saw his eyes that flashed with anger one moment and softened with love the next. From behind the invisible wall enclosing him, I was privileged to glimpse his reality and his perception of life, and to recognize the lessons he taught–to accept him as he is–to see him as he could be–to never give up.

Kelton lives in a world of different realities than the ones we know. I remembered the thousands of hours of working with him, of writing notes and letters, searching out doctors, of testing, of fighting labels, praying endlessly and searching within myself. The answers were within, but I had been too full of fear to find them.

Kelton was eight years old, when we finally received the answer that would explain his strange and often violent behavior; Kelton suffered from infantile autism. We had heard so many different opinions about his condition from physicians and psychologists. *They* had said he was severely retarded, brain damaged, incapable of speech. *They* had said he was unreachable and untrainable. Even with professional training available, it would be a futile effort, and *they* recommended we institutionalize him.

I had contacted parents of autistic children in my effort of finding a support group and to learn from their experiences. When I discovered the methods that were used at that time in dealing with autism, I knew I would never subject Kelton to that kind of barbaric treatment. I had concluded that the children were mere subjects of experimentation, and the so-called treatments were nothing more than the practices of the snake pits from the dark ages: electric shocks, drugs, striking, behavior conditioning and chaining to bedposts. Kelton would never suffer the indignities the medical community had devised. Trapped in a body that could not communicate was a beautiful spirit, a child of God. I was determined that our child, conceived and born in love, would live with love. I also knew that first, I had to heal my own hurt and bitterness.

Our family became a solid unit of courage and love, determined to overcome self-pity and self-appointed martyrdom, and face with courage the day-to-day pressures of living with an autistic child. Kelton would be treated with dignity due any human being. Within our family circle we would create our own program of training; we all would become his teachers. We rocked when he rocked, jumped when he jumped, flapped when he flapped, and took part willingly in his own precise rituals in order to contact him.

We became a family with a common purpose and goal: to reach a small boy lost in another world–a child who had the power to shut off the world around him, remain unresponsive, and who would erupt with sudden bizarre behavior with the force of an active volcano. We had to learn to look beyond the behavior and see the boy inside.

It has been a long and rough journey, and for part of that time my traveling companions were denial, anger, guilt, frustration and loneliness; overpowered by the lack of support and adequate resources, I lived in fear– not unlike the constant drop, drop, drop of the Chinese water torture–that they were right and all we did was for naught.

I found my sanity in trusting God, and in my own initiative and courage. I realized that I was capable of adapting to whatever came along in life. From my experiences with Kelton, I continually learned and grew as a person. I knew I had to be positive and strong in spite of the events in my life. Success rested on the far side of failure. At first I failed to hear the spirit with the intent to  understand until I learned to listen to my inner voice.

There has come a time when images and fears have passed, and I have come to know what I am. I thank Kelton for starting me on that journey. I have forgiven God for giving me an autistic child; I have forgiven myself for all the wrong attitudes and illusions I had about failure and suffering, and I opted for joy, love and the appreciation of this beautiful child.

When Kelton and my life touched on this earth, it taught me to give up guilt and center my life on God. From his higher form of reference I learned a deeper discipleship.

> *"Come unto me, all ye that labor and are heavy laden,*
>     *and I will give you rest.*
> *Take my yoke upon you and learn of me: for I am meek*
>     *ad lowly in heart;*
> *An Ye shall find rest unto your souls.*
> *For my yoke is easy and my burden light."*
>                                      (Matthew 11:28-30)

# Introduction

Autism is a childhood disorder syndrome characterized by a lack of social relationship, and communication abilities, a resistance to change, and a variety of persistent compulsive rituals. There is no specific test to help diagnose autism. Autism is not defined or diagnosed by its symptoms.

Autistic babies are *good babies* and prefer to play alone. The infant may often be fascinated with sights or sounds around him, or he may create his own amusement by watching his fingers move and wiggle, or scratch steadily on a bed sheet for hours at a time. He can be completely absorbed by rocking himself or banging his head. These infants show little curiosity of what goes on around them and rarely explore their environment.

Some children are late to walk. Others exhibit early motor development which manifest in unusual movement, such as walking on tiptoes, spinning, running, rocking, twirling, or jumping–which acts they perform with maddening persistence over and over, hours on end. These children are also fascinated and occupied with moving objects.

Autistic children do not relate to the people around them. They prefer to play with some object of their choice, and find comfort in routine. The children's ability to converse is severely impaired. Interference with or change in their environment or activities can be upsetting and brings on a temper tantrum.

Autistic children take comfort in rituals–from eating and dressing, to driving down the same road, and they do not tolerate deviations from norms. They may scream at something as common as taking a different route on the freeway, mix the peas and mashed potatoes on their dinner plate, or change into a new pair of shoes.

Some autistic children develop a strong attachment to a particular toy or object–clothes, shoes or even food. A five-year-old I know carried a telephone book with him everywhere. Older autistics often have unprovoked temper tantrums and may execute aggressive attacks; some even hurt themselves.

Autistic children have trouble receiving information and responding verbally. They often have the ability to speak but chose not to communicate. Pronouns, If used at all, are reversed. To the question: "Do you want to eat?" the child responds: "You want to eat."

Occasionally these children demonstrate special abilities. They may have accelerated motor development, such as early waling or other skills that require balance and coordination. Autistics may demonstrate particularly keen memory acuity–memory for details or rote skills such as memorizing poetry and names. They can be talented in music, proficient in mechanical aptitude, or able to put together difficult jigsaw puzzles.

The experts do not know the cause of autism. What they do know is that 15 out of every 10,000 children are born with this dysfunction.

It was a popular belief for quite some time that autism was the result of negligent Parenting. We know differently today.

The most frustrating aspect of raising our autistic child was the fact that no one would listen to us. We lived with Kelton's condition 24 hours a day, but according to the medical community, we didn't know anything! When I asked the doctors if any of them had ever had an autistic child in their family, the answer was always No! Very few doctors had ever worked with a child afflicted with autism. The physicians knew only what they had read about the problem. Until the middle 60's special education was available only for children with intellectual and sensory impairment. Today, there are special services available for a larger range of disturbances, in many states autistic children are still lacking training facilities, work programs and adults housing.

Most autistics are not capable of functioning on their own then they get older, and have little or no language development. The majority of autistics end up in an institution. Unfortunately only a few have found their way out of autism.

☆ ☆ ☆

Planted with love–but how to crack the seed?
First comes the bitter bite of frost,
Then the stiff unwillingness to grow.
Still, you are my planted flower.
So we wait for the sun, watching,
Caring for the new shoots of growth form your lonely world
Formed by continued tests and labels.
The rainbow always lies just beyond the garden.

Father, let not this flower stay in the bud too long;
For the gift to grow is there, competing with conflict.
Needing the warmth of stability and acceptance.
But had not the root accepted this soil of love,
where would be tomorrow's bloom?

☆ ☆ ☆

## 1

$A$s we parked the car near the field where a special baseball game was under way, we could hear the exciting shouts of
encouragement from the spectators. "Run, run, run." their voices
yelled loudly, imparting a sense of urgency and enthusiasm to the
players.

We hurried through the crowd that had gathered to watch
a baseball game being played by a team of special players—each
one was handicapped in some form or another. Our son, Kelton,
was one of the players. Kelton had fought his way out of autism,
but was functionally retarded.

The day was perfect. I glanced at the cloudless blue sky
and felt the warm sun on my face. The smell of french fries and
hot dogs hung in the clear summer air. I felt elated. My spirit soared
as I saw the pleasure and the pride on the faces of the young
people, who had more to over come in life than winning a ball game.
But this was their day. It was their time to compete and to share—
win or lose. They were competing in a Special Olymipics softball
game. It was a day of triumph for them.

My eyes spied Kelton in his green shirt, standing a little apart from his teammates, moving when they moved, his eyes on the field. He looked happy. His eyes were bright, his sandy hair had turned a darker brown, and he had lost some weight since I last saw him. His shoulders were broad and he stood taller than the others in his group.

A young girl approached and said something to him. He reached in his pocket and came up with some change. The girl took it, and, with a quick nod of her head, hurried away.

"Kelton," I called to him. He turned toward the sound of my voice, recognized us, smiled, quietly said "hi," and walked toward us.

To Joseph's question whether he had his turn at bat, he replied with a brief "no." We were glad we had not missed watching him play.

Kelton turned away from us to watch the next player who had come up to bat. Our eyes followed the young girl's struggle to reach home plate. Nothing, but nothing came easy to these valiant people; every step, every move, anything new presented a hurdle to be overcome.

A cheer rose from the crowd as the girl took a swing at the ball, which, rather than being hurled from the strong arm of a pitcher, sat on a tall tee, like a big golf ball. She swung the bat and missed the ball.

"Try again," her coach shouted. "You can do it."

"Come on," yelled the crowd cheerfully.

"Hit it!" Kelton said, laughing. The young girl swung again, this time knocking the ball down the field past the pitcher.

"Get the ball!" Kelton said encouragingly in his quiet voice, as her team mates cheered her on with loud shrieks of run - run - run.

I smiled as I watched Kelton's excitement, realizing that at last he was involved with the events around him. Each change, there was growth, each small achievement was a golden moment for us.

I walked closer to my son and asked who his friends were. Still speaking echolalia, he repeated my question and then in his typical laconic way he replied : "Your friends Heidi and Mike."

Joseph and I greeted the young people and inquired if they were enjoying themselves. Mike told us that he had hit a home run, and had lots of medals and ribbons at home in his drawer.

"Are you all on the same team?" I questioned.

Heidi explained that she and Mike were on the B-Team and Kelton was on the D-Team, because he wouldn't run the bases. We laughed and joked with the kids for a moment, and shared in the pride and pleasure of their accomplishments. We watched them run off to take their turn in the game, found our seats and joined the other spectators in the stands.

Just then one of the players rushed up to Kelton and said breathlessly: "You better hurry, Kelton. D-Team is supposed to play now."

Kelton walked away with him and we sat down to watch the game.

Dedicated to their task, volunteers and coaches cheered, praised and encouraged tirelessly, until their voices were hoarse. The simple joy on the players' faces as they hit the ball was a touching and rewarding sight.

Kelton came up to bat and I stood up to get a better look at him. He walked slowly to the field, picked up the bat and glanced up to see if we were watching. I waved and he waved back.

"Hit it hard, Kelton!" I yelled, but he didn't hear me; he was waiting for the pitch.

The first ball fell short. He whacked hard at the next pitch, and the ball whizzed through the air, as Kelton stood by watching it sail high and far. He smiled, pleased with himself, when the crowd cheered.

"Let him run the bases," I pleaded all to myself.

"Run, run," everybody shouted, "run to first base."

Kelton set out walking.

"Run, Kelton!" his coach screamed, jumping up and down, but Kelton continued to walk. His coach was so excited, he touched Kelton's arm, which is a violation of the rules, and the umpire yelled, "Out!"

Kelton would have been out, anyway. Even so, everyone cheered. He had hit what could have been a home run. It just wasn't important to him to run the bases.

That's Kelton. I wondered silently if he'd ever conform to the rules of our world? Slowly and painfully, Kelton, my winter's flower, had come a long way. Who knows what miracles are in store for him.

## 2

"Ranae, Ranae."

Faintly I heard a voice calling my name. I struggled to leave the deep darkness of unconsciousness. The voice became closer and louder:

"Wake up Ranae. You have a boy. A big boy! He weighs 11 pounds and does he ever have a set of lungs."

Slowly I responded. My eyes rebelled against the intrusion of the bright light in the sterile white room. With an effort I fought my way back to the real world. I was in the maternity ward of the LDS Hospital in Provo, Utah and someone was telling me: "It's a boy!" I looked up at the face bent over me and recognized my doctor smiling at me as he repeated the wonderful words: "You have a fine healthy boy; Ranae. He's perfect! I was more concerned with you. Four days of labor was too much. You've dislocated your pelvic bone during delivery, and you're going to need some help around the house for a while." He gave me a gentle, reassuring pat on my hand, and left me in the care of the nurses.

I was weak from 96 hours of hard labor and still groggy with the fading effects of the anesthetic. But when a smiling nurse handed me my bundled up newborn and settled him gently into my outstretched arms for the first time, the pain was forgotten. Joy filled my heart, and love rushed in to embrace this new life as warmly as it had done with all of my children.

We named the strapping baby boy Kelton, and added his newborn snapshot to our gallery of baby pictures.

I thanked God for my healthy and beautiful son.

My husband, Jack and I were already raising three wonderful and healthy children: Sharlene was seven, Vern five and Lynell was our delightful two-year-old. Kelton made four. The kids took their new baby brother into the family circle, anxious to help, eager to please and ready to play with him.

The year was 1961, and the place Provo, Utah. Jack was attending Brigham Young University taking a degree in business, and we were the typical young couple struggling to get the man of the house through college, take care of the needs of a growing family and at the same time still have some fun.

I had been married before, and Sharlene and Vern were from my first marriage. Their father was killed in an automobile accident when the kids were little. Jack and I found each other at BYU, and were married soon after we met. Jack was a gentle, kind and sweet man. We loved each other very much, enjoyed our children and didn't mind working hard towards a bright future.

Kelton brought a lot of love into our home. The children gladly helped caring for him in the months to come while I got my strength back. Sharlene was like a little mother to all the children, and I depended on her for a lot. The younger children loved Kelton as well and tried to play with him.

Kelton was a good baby; he lay quiet and content for hours in his basket. He cried only when he was hungry. He developed his coordination early, sitting up at three months, crawling at four and a half, and by ten months, this lively baby was running all over the house. He was an independent little guy. Strangely enough, he didn't like us to hold him and cried until we put him down. Some times I felt a gnawing at my heart. He was too quiet. But quickly, I pushed the worry away, grateful that my youngest demanded so little time of me. He would make up for it later; I was certain.

Kelton smiled a lot when we played with him, but he preferred being left alone to watch some object, preferably something in motion. One day, a swinging branch outside the bedroom window held his attention for over an hour. Jack and I were amazed that it took so little to keep him entertained. Unlike the other children, Kelton wanted to be left alone with his bottle. He had become strangely attached to it.

Worry crept into a corner of my mind. He was so different from my other children. I banished the nagging worry, easing my mind with the thought that no two babies were alike, and the fact that Kelton was a healthy child was most encouraging, yet I couldn't get over that eerie knowing that there was a noticeable difference between Kelton and the other children.

He never cooed nor made an effort to talk. When we showed him objects, he never looked directly at them. We tried to teach him things with little blocks and simple toys to no avail. Finally we decided that he was developing in his own special way— a view shared by our doctor, who seemed less concerned than we were.

The days flew by in my busy life. Kelton's brother and sisters grew up happily chasing after Kelton. Our house was always a buzzing beehive of activities with the coming and going of members of my family. I had been the oldest girl of fourteen children, and was used to sharing my space and thoughts with someone. I helped raise two of my younger brothers and sisters. My youngest sister, Karla, spent a lot of time in my home. You might say that I raised kids all of my life. But never one like Kelton.

Our next surprise came the day Kelton got on his feet and walked. He was a little over 10 months old. Unlike most toddlers, he neither wavered or lurched, never missed a step or succumbed to the law of gravity and plopped on his bottom. He required no help, never clutched at things for support or steadied himself by grabbing at one of us. He just walked, as if he always had been on his little feet.

About that time we bought him a puppy and named her Ginger. When we first brought the little dog home, Kelton stared at her for a long time. Ginger dashed about the house sniffing this and that, wagging her tail, and getting acquainted.

"Puppy!" I said to Kelton, took his hand in mine and guided him to touch the dog. He pulled away, but stood by quietly and watched the puppy in deep concentration. Ginger made a bee line for him and jumped playfully up on him. Startled by the sudden friendly contact, Kelton lost his balance and toppled over. The puppy bounced all over him, licking his face and hands. Kelton's body tensed up for a moment, but the puppy paid no attention to his resistance and continued lavishing her puppy love on the little boy. From that moment on, child and dog were always together. A deep love formed between them and they were in each other's company all the time. We never saw one without the other.

We had moved to the pastoral town of Orem, just north of Provo, and found a comfortable house with a small orchard in back. The quiet country setting gave the children lots of freedom and room to play. I loved the spacious bright house with the large windows, the big kitchen and a basement for even more room. It was a perfect place for our active and growing family.

The kitchen window framed what soon came to be a familiar sight: two-year-old Kelton exploring the orchard, with Ginger running circles around him. Our little boy still preferred being alone, and except for the company of Ginger, he never looked for anything from anyone of us. Why was he so different? As regularly as I questioned the odd behavior of our two-year-old, I always assuaged my fears with the fact that he was such a healthy toddler, never ill, independent and content as long as we left him alone.

He was big for his age and completely self-sufficient. We never had to toilet train him. He watched his brother Vern, and trained himself. He used the bathroom with the door closed, threw away his diapers and had few accidents. We never taught him anything that had to do with his person. It seemed that he had come into this world with a knowing others had to acquire.

I had visions of his becoming a hermit or a scientist sequestered in a remote place, doing his own thing, needing no one.

Jack was still going to school when we decided to go to Texas to check on a business opportunity in the motorcycle industry, which, if it panned out, would dictate a move to California. Jack worked toward a degree in business, liked sales, and the idea of importing and selling Italian motorcycles appealed to him.

My widowed mother lived close by and would take care of our children for the two weeks we planned to be gone. She was the dear and loving grandma all our children adored. Although Lynell, our three-year-old cried bitterly, begging to go along with us, she adjusted to our absence quickly. But Kelton cried and screamed during the entire two weeks we were gone. It was the first time I had been away from him for a longer period than running a few errands. When we returned, my poor mother was exhausted from the ordeal of taking care of a screaming child. I was baffled because I knew how well she got along with children of any age, and I also knew that Kelton liked her.

Kelton settled down quickly and was fine as soon as things went back to normal. It was apparent that he was unaccustomed to my mother's ways of doing things. He simply did not like change, I decided. Little did I know then, how important my observation would be and how this discovery would be the key to

Kelton's behavior pattern which would help us develop effective teaching and training methods.

But as time went by, we became increasingly concerned that he had not started to talk and he didn't like to be held. He would just lay there, for hours at a time. He wouldn't look us in the eye. His fingers would be in constant motion scratching at the sheets.

I was angry with the doctors because they did not listen to me. I was just a mother, one of those hysterical creatures with a wild imagination. What did I know? I felt I had become a permanent fixture in the doctor's office and a broken record on top of it, as I kept insisting that there was something different about Kelton—he was not at all like my other babies.

The doctors kept saying that all children are different and suggested to give him time; more time. When he was almost two years old I took him for a checkup with our pediatrician, who assured me that all was well with Kelton.

"I've examined him thoroughly, Ranae. He's fine and healthy except for a hernia in his navel which needs to be repaired," he said. "I would like to put him in the hospital, do the surgery day after tomorrow and get it over with."

Jack had decided in favor of the import business and we were going to move to California. It was just as well we would take care of Kelton's surgery on familiar ground.

We took our little boy to the hospital at the appointed time, but the day came and went without surgery being performed. Kelton fought against the anesthetic. His temperature climbed, his lips were parched, his eyes distant and glazed. He screamed with fear without stopping. He squirmed and thrashed about; he bounced and threw himself violently against the sides of his crib, accompanied by his horrible howling.

Jack and I stood by helplessly. We were embarrassed and worried at the same time. Kelton refused to let us hold him, and acted as if we were all monsters. He exerted an enormous strength for such a young child. Today, I believe that he was allergic to the drugs that he had been given and his violent behavior the result of extreme discomfort.

I spent the night at the hospital by his side. The next day things went better. The doctor was able to sedate him and perform the operation. Our boy came through it with flying colors, and we took him home, thankful that the nightmare was over.

Kelton's personality changed after his ordeal at the hospital. He no longer ran outside with his puppy, but sat and rocked himself on his wooden horse. He rocked for hours at a time, or sat and slowly turned the pages of the Children's Encyclopedia. He never cried, he never asked to be entertained. We wondered if the change in his behavior was the result of the unhappy experience at the hospital.

He loved to play in the water, and spent a lot of time in the bathtub. Every day he repeated the same ritual at about the same time. He filled the bathtub with water, put his toy boats and rubber duck in the water, climbed in and stayed there for hours at a time. He needed little attention and even less help.

Kelton was two-and-a-half years old and seemed to know exactly what he was doing, and where he was going. He watched for cars when he crossed the street, and would not get into an automobile with anyone except Jack and me. Yet when we tried to question him or tell him to do something, he appeared to be in another world. He refused affection, screamed and ran away if we came too close. If we wanted him to move, we had to physically position him. If we wanted him to do something, we had to take him by the hand and guide him to carry out the command.

Each day was a puzzle. Each day a gnawing reminder that there was something wrong with our son. I wished I knew what. I felt as if I had a great and deep wound. But when I showed my wound no one could see it, and when I talked about it, no one heard me.

## 3

Moving any size family cross-country is not an easy undertaking. But our little caravan made it safely over the mountains, and we wasted no time settling into our new home. We had made the difficult decision to leave Ginger, the puppy, behind, since our new landlord did not permit pets on the premises. Kelton cried bitterly for two days. When he stopped crying, he acted as if it never happened, but never liked a dog again.

The house was comfortable, and I especially liked the big, fenced backyard which gave us complete privacy and a safe place for the children. We were only a half a mile from the beach and took the kids to play and picnic every chance we got. Even Kelton soon adapted to our seaside outings.

I came to love California quickly. I enjoyed the people and their lifestyles, I liked the shops, the warm climate and the ocean with its sandy beaches and pounding waves. I never wanted to leave.

The older children were in school, only Kelton remained at home with me. He was his own astonishing and puzzling self. He never asked for anything, he still did not talk. When he wanted to drink milk, he went to the refrigerator and turned on the spigot of the milk carton, and filled his own bottle. He loved the suction motion when he drank, and had put up a terrifying battle when we first tried to get him used to the cup. Later on, when we finally did take the bottle away from him, he did not touch milk for years.

He was still an independent little guy. His independence took on new dimensions as the weeks passed. He dressed himself, and preferred his own company.

On his third birthday I prepared a party for him. He refused to have anything to do with it. He never looked at the cake or the pretty decorations, and systematically broke every toy we had given him. We wondered at his strange behavior, looked at each other in dismay, and worried.

Since Kelton was such an unusually healthy child, we had no reason to take him to the doctor. But we did find a pediatrician in Huntington Beach for the children. He was nice, liked children, and—no different from his colleagues— assured us calmly that there was nothing wrong with our son. All the child needed to catch up with the others was time. Just time.

My frustration and anger rose to a new level as yet another member of the medical profession refused to listen to my observations, and regarded my fears as blowing off steam by just another over concerned, stressed and worried mother. But I knew better, I had to deal with it every moment of my life.

Jack understood little about children. He was overwhelmed and confused with the problems of raising Kelton. His fledgling business required a great deal of attention, and Jack gladly escaped into his work. He was a wonderful person and I could not find fault with him. He just didn't know what to do, and most of the time I understood.

One evening, we both worked on the business books. We had locked up the house for the night, and I had asked the children to put Kelton to bed. I had addressed no one in particular to take care of the chore, and assumed Kelton had been tucked in for the night. Two hours went by when we decided to go to bed ourselves. As always, I checked on the children.

Kelton's bed was empty.

We searched the house and grounds frantically and carried the search to the neighborhood. Jack went knocking on doors. One neighbor confessed that a small boy had turned up at his place, and when the child did not respond to questions, the good man felt it was his duty to call the police. The police had come and taken Kelton to the station.

Partly relived, but still shaking, I called the police station and asked if our little boy was there.

The woman who answered the call, said curtly: "We don't have your boy here."

I didn't realize then that the woman had set herself up as judge and jury and brought in a guilty verdict the moment I identified myself as the mother of the lost child.

"But that's impossible," I cried terrified, "my neighbor just now told me he had called you and that the police had picked him up and brought him to this station."

"If you'd watch your child, he wouldn't be lost," she lashed out further.

Her hateful words stung deeply. I controlled my anger and explained the unusual circumstances. She finally relented and admitted that Kelton indeed was there and we could pick him up. Still furious with her, but relieved to have located our little guy, we drove off to retrieve him.

It was late when we arrived at the police station. A cold and impersonal air greeted as we walked through the front door, looking for the place where Kelton was held. The overwhelming stillness in the building sent shivers through me. The morgue couldn't have been more quiet.

"My poor baby," I thought to myself, "He must be as terrified as I am."

We walked down several hallways and came into a small foyer, where a policeman sat leaning back in his chair with his feet propped up on the desk before him—fast asleep.

He quickly woke up and became alert when we told him we were looking for our three-year-old son. After I described Kelton and the clothes he wore, the officer led us to a glassed in room where Kelton sat quietly on a padded bench, eyes glazed over, swinging his legs.

"Kelton, are you alright?" I asked, my arms reaching out, eager to hold him.

He pushed me away in his remote matter-of-fact way, and marched out through the doors without a glance back. His odd behavior hurt as much as a blow to my stomach.

"This hasn't upset him much," the police officer observed.

But I knew better. Kelton had delayed reactions to events and it would take days or even weeks before he would feel the effects of his escapade. On the drive home he was quiet and unresponsive to my questions, and as far as I could tell, happy. He never did anything a 'normal' child did. Why couldn't the doctors understand that?

The older children had waited up for us and were glad to see their brother. We tucked our little explorer into bed. Exhausted, we gladly called it a night.

Jack and I lay awake a long time, talking about our strange little boy, wondering what lay ahead of us. I had a feeling that it had just begun. I was terrified and had no idea what to do.

I spent the next days hovering around Kelton to prevent him from running away again. We installed a chain lock on the front and back doors. With the six-foot stone wall enclosing the back yard, we felt we not only could keep an eye on him, but we were reasonably certain that we could keep him confined.

Were we ever wrong!

Many summer days and evenings were spent with frequent searches for Kelton, knocking on doors and followed by countless trips to the police station. We remained mute under the accusing glances of neighbors and the policemen, and bore helplessly their silent tongue lashings and unspoken reprimands.

What kind of people must we be not to watch over a little boy who was wandering around the streets day and night? Didn't we care? Were we so irresponsible?

The fascinating fact was, if left to himself, Kelton would find his way home with the unerring sense of a homing pigeon. The problem arose when someone stopped the little wanderer, and when unable to elicit a response, would turn him over to the police. He was undisturbed when the officer placed him into a solitary cell. It was not a punishment for him, after all, he lived in solitary wherever he was.

Yet it would break my heart to see this tiny boy of mine sit content and unruffled—no tears streaming down his face, no wailing for his mother—in this sterile, glassed in observation cell, swinging his legs, swinging his legs.

It didn't take very long for Kelton to learn to avoid the police. He made his way home at all odd hours, unmoved by our worries and unconcerned about punishment.

He also learned to vanish from friendly helpers. No sooner would one of his kind rescuers reach for a telephone to call the police, and Kelton was gone. Surprised and chagrined—no more than we were—the would-be rescuer had lost his subject before rescue could take place, and was scratching his head wondering just how did it happen? How did the kid disappear from under his feet? We, too, were wondering the same thing.

Locks didn't keep him in, nor did walls. When watchful eyes wandered for a split second, so did Kelton. Amazing. Confounding. Frustrating and maddening.

I was panic-stricken when I thought of all the things that could happen to a three-year-old boy. I felt like buying a leash. In spite of our efforts and watchfulness, Kelton continued to explore the world around him.

Somehow he was never hurt, lost, or exhibited any signs of being afraid. He may have been lost for us, but he could always find his way home. No matter what size a shopping mall or store, Kelton would unerringly find his way to our car, one of hundreds in an overflowing parking lot of look-alikes.

The hectic summer passed quickly; fall saw the children back in school and occupied with their activities. Before I knew it, it was time for the holidays. We started our Christmas preparations and went all-out to make it a special time for Kelton. We baked cookies, decorated the house and trimmed a big tree, but Kelton paid no attention to any of the goings-on. In a setting of festivity and gladness, with his brothers and sisters eagerly unwrapping their gifts and exclaiming joyfully about each one of them, there was Kelton, rejecting all his toys, books, and clothes, eventually destroying them all. Our attempts to make him happy were futile.

"I guess Kelton is fighting for his independence at the age of three," I remarked one day to Claudia B., whom I had met at church. I had told her about our experiences with our son and mentioned my concerns and fears. Claudia was not only a good friend but a good listener, and I had found a compassionate and sympathetic ear.

Claudia was a psychologist who happened to operate a pre-school in her home.

"Bring him to my school next Monday," she suggested. "He may be bored. Maybe he just needs to learn!"

Claudia was almost six feet tall and a dynamic woman. She was about my age and had two children of her own. And I believe that Claudia's offer to take Kelton in her school saved my sanity. I had him at her door on that Monday morning right on time and my son started pre-school. I had gained a few precious hours of freedom to get things done, to read a book, to relax.

On his second day of pre-school, Kelton walked in our front door an hour after I had dropped him off at Claudia's house. He had run away from school and walked the ten blocks home. A phone call soon followed from a frantic teacher, who was glad to hear the runaway was safe.

Despite Kelton's screams, I took him back to pre-school and this time I stayed with him till the end of the pre-school day. Luckily, he had discovered the swing in the yard. Fascinated with motion as was his pattern, he enjoyed swinging so much that he was upset when it was time to leave.

Kelton could try the patience of a saint, but Claudia stuck to her guns. She took him out to the playground and insisted he watch the children play. She listened to his screams, but never stopped working with him. For a long time, he kept to the sidelines watching, or hiding under a table.

He participated in art class and started painting. He used only one color at a time, and he filled every inch of white space on the page. We were thrilled to see him do something new and different.

To our delight he was getting used to going to school. But I was still bothered by his refusal to accept a hug or be cuddled and touched.

"The more I try to hug him the more he rejects me!" I told Claudia. "He wants to be left alone. He doesn't want anybody to talk to him, he wants no music, no TV. And I worry that with all my energy going to Kelton, the other children will eventually suffer."

"Do the best that you can do and keep trying!" she encouraged. "He does the same thing to me at school. If someone touches him, he yells."

"I feel like such a terrible mother when my own child suddenly goes rigid and screams just because I try to pick him up," I replied.

"Well, maybe the doctors are right. Maybe he just needs space and time," she said in an effort to comfort me.

As Kelton withdrew more and more from everyone, the fear within us grew and took on unmeasureable proportions. And with the fear grew my helplessness, my anger and frustration. No one believed me there was something terribly wrong with Kelton.

Even my mother didn't hear me. She insisted that Kelton had something wrong with his hearing. She spread the story of his deafness around the family circle and even suggested the child could be blind. I resented my family putting labels on the child. We had his sight and hearing checked. He was normal; he could see and hear as well as the rest of us.

When I looked at him, I saw a strong, well-built nice looking pre-schooler, big for his age with sandy hair, chubby checks and bright eyes that defied the very thought that he had a problem. But his behavior belied his 'normal' looks.

Sometimes Kelton would scream for no apparent reason. Although he didn't respond when we called him, he would appear at my side at the slightest whisper when we made plans to go somewhere. He still would not look us in the eye. But he could get himself up the slick trunk of the banana tree and toss down the fruit. No one else could get a leg up on that tree, much less climb it.

We began to make the rounds to different doctors and specialists. No one could find anything wrong with him. That left us with our problem unsolved, a mountain of medical bills and a tidal wave of frustration. Nobody had an answer for Kelton's strange behavior.

During that summer I was not well. I was a bleeder at that time and was in and out of hospitals getting blood transfusions. I bled after I had a tooth pulled and I bled when I cut my finger on a little knife. I was rundown.

Our family talked little about Kelton. We all knew there was something wrong, but nobody talked about it; it might be too terrible. I hurt on the inside, and the pain never went away.

One day, eleven-year-old Vem was playing basketball on the driveway with a friend. Kelton joined the boys, watched for a moment and started jumping and waving his hands. He continued the jumping and flapping for half an hour. We tried to distract him, but nothing we did or said could stop him.

"Stop it! Stop, Kelton, come in and eat dinner," I said.

He didn't respond. When I picked him up, he went stiff in my arms and started to scream. I carried him into the living room and as soon as I put him down, he started jumping up and down and flapping his hands all over again. The activity became an obsession with him and in spite of our attempts to distract him, he continued to bounce and wave for the rest of the evening.

"Kelton has found a new way to irritate us," remarked Vern, and I had to agree with him.

Then one day, I noticed Kelton's eyes had changed. Once clear and focused, they now were glazed. He wouldn't look at things when we asked him to do so. He seemed to be escaping yet further into a world we could not enter. We fretted and worried. We wondered and puzzled and wished we could help him— but we didn't know how. Nobody else did either.

The older children cooperated in our efforts to help Kelton. We all tried to communicate with him, to make him ask for things, to point at things. But he would rather go without than speak. After a while, when there was no response to their efforts, the children left him alone. It was easier to leave him to himself than to hear him scream in protest. He continued to jump, to rock on his horse, and wave his hands whenever anything excited him. He kept moving but it never got him any where.

*Kelton,*
*You must not rock alone*
*With nowhere to go*
*Your glazed stare matches*
*The rocking horse.*

*Back and forth, back and forth*
*Hours on end*
*I'll rock with you for a while as*
*You must not be lost*
*Along the way.*

*The silence helps us*
*Set aside our fears*
*Pass into a new awakening or healing*
*Clear our mind for the seeding*
*Plant the question*
*How to find each other?*

*Tomorrow after tomorrow*
*Is too late, too far away for help*
*We must harvest the answer early.*

*I'll rock with you today child*
*But we can't linger here*
*Too long.*

## 4

One bright California Sunday, we had just returned from church when the phone rang. Kelton was in the kitchen with me when I answered it. With my back turned for just a brief moment, he took the opportunity, and away he went. We had no idea how he got out. His quick getaways would become more and more of a nagging puzzle. At the same time we were astonished at his Houdini-like talent. We dropped what we were doing including our plans for Sunday and went searching for Kelton

"If we'd just go ahead and cook dinner, Mom, he will show up," said Sharlene. "He always does."

We looked in all the usual places, but he was not to be found. How can a little guy go so far so fast, I wondered as the usual panic washed over me?

This time Kelton had wandered into a different neighborhood. He had stopped to pick some flowers from the yard where two elderly ladies lived, and played with their cat. The ladies became alarmed that such a small child was roaming around alone.

They gave him milk and cookies, and tried to keep him in their house. When they attempted to pick him up, he screamed loudly. The two women tried to talk to him to no avail, He only looked at them in silence. Frustrated and concerned, they called the police. Kelton, upon hearing the familiar call, looked for a chance to slip away. By the time the police arrived, Kelton had disappeared.

"Must be the same kid that's always running away!" said one policeman.

"Yeah, he's getting quite a record," remarked another.

The police and several neighbors joined us in our search. Kelton seemed to have vanished into thin air, while my heart bounced around between a terrifying panic and a strange wonder at the antics of my child.

When I voiced my fear, the children reminded me, "He always comes home, mother," they said.

"But he's so little!" I cried.

Sharlene gave me a reassuring hug. "I know, Mom. I'm a little scared too. But I just know he'll turn up. He knows something we don't know."

Sharlene was nine years old by then, quite grown up for her age and my best helper. She started to prepare Sunday dinner with an efficiency that belied her young years. I was so proud of my children ... if only Kelton would...

Evening came. We were about to sit down to dinner, when the front door opened and Kelton appeared—unharmed, unruffled, unconcerned. He had gotten hungry and came home to eat.

"I have aged considerably today," I thought to myself, as a prayer of thanks left my heart.

Before going to bed that night, I went into his room and saw him sleeping peacefully. I wondered how I would survive this child-traveler passing through my life. How could I understand the world he lived in? Quietly, I left his room and went outside. I gazed at the evening sky sparkling with stars and knew I would continue to fight the battle—one day at a time.

A few days later, we took the children to the beach. As much as we loved our beach trips, the outings bore witness to our frustrations of bringing up Kelton. The entire family shared the responsibility of keeping an eye on him. We took turns watching him.

A little girl approached Kelton with a friendly greeting. When he did not respond, she walked away. A young woman said a cheery hello to him, and left in a cloud of his silence. People would stop to chat and were greeted without his friendly reply. Children all around us were playing, chasing balls, chasing each other, but Kelton seemed unaware. He sat motionless and looked at the sea. He was alone.

Seagulls circled and landed near him, rose to dip and soar, their shrill cries piercing the air. I saw it then. He was one with the gulls, diving and swooping, sailing on the updrafts and winging into the wind. Kelton did not see himself as trapped inside a limited body. He was as free as the gulls. There were no sounds for him but the thunder of the ocean, the gulls in flight and the song of the wind.

Two lovers walked in front of him, barefoot and holding hands. They spoke to him, but his eyes were glazed and far away.

"Is he all right?" they asked.

"Yes," I said. With the unanswered questions on their faces, they turned to go. The waves came in and washed away their footprints from the sand.

"He is acting out his life as best he can," I thought, wishing I could join him in his world for even a moment.

Kites rose and fell on the offshore breeze. People spread their blankets, soaked up the sun, scolded their children, ate their food, and moved around Kelton just shaking their heads. "Poor child," they said, and gathered their own children close, as if his silence might somehow infect them.

Although he sat still, I knew Kelton's mind was busy, flowing with the coming and going of the tide, the cresting and crashing of the waves and the flight of the seagulls. His eyes never left the scene before him.

As I sat at a distance observing him, I visualized what he must be experiencing, and I merged my earthbound body with the sea birds in their exuberant flight, and for a precious moment I experienced freedom from the force that bound me to the earth.

I glanced back to where Kelton was sitting. I was startled out of my meditation.

Kelton was gone.

"Where's Kelton?" I screamed with accustomed panic burning in my chest.

Jack looked up sharply, "But he was just here," he yelled, and quickly called to the children, organized search teams and sent them off in all directions.

"Meet back here in one-half hour!" he reminded them, then left immediately to alert the beach patrol.

I ran up and down the beach, searching the face of every young boy. Wild images of Kelton drowned or kidnapped accompanied me in my hunt for our son along with my breathless prayers.

"God, where is my little boy?" tears flowed down my cheeks. "Please keep him safe!"

I scrambled up a sandy hill to get a better vantage point, hoping I could spot him. I was numb with fear. My throat was dry and my face stiff from dried tears. I looked down at the beach. The people reminded me of ants hurrying around, oblivious to my panic.

Like clockwork, half an hour later, we reassembled, but no one had seen Kelton.

"How could he have just disappeared like that?" Vern questioned.

"But he always just disappears like that!" Sharlene reminded us. "I know, I have that problem almost every time I watch him!"

"Let's keep trying to find him," Jack encouraged us.

"We will meet back here again in another half-hour. Let's get going!"

I stood looking at the ocean, pleading with God to end this nightmare and to help us find Kelton. Jack came up behind me and took me in his arms, comforting me with his love.

"Don't worry, honey. You know he always shows up," he reassured me.

"But he's so little. He's just a baby," I cried. "I try to trust God to watch over him, but I'm afraid most of the time."

"I know," Jack said, "so am I."

The beach patrol drove slowly up and down the stretch of beach with Vern standing on the fender ready to identify his little brother.

Hours later, exhausted and aware that other children needed to go home, we returned to the spot where we had parked our car. There, in the back seat, all done with his adventure and ready to go home, sat Kelton, looking at us as if he wondered what had kept us this long.

"Looks like he knew where he was all the time," the beach patrolman said.

His words triggered an explosion of thoughts in my head. Kelton wasn't lost in his mind. I'm the lost one. I know I'm lost when I try to communicate with him. I'm lost when I get the blank stares from doctors—lost as one day blends into the next without any answers or help.

"I'm glad we found him, mother," Lynell patted my arm.

"He's still lost," I thought numbly. "Only his body is here. His spirit is somewhere we cannot be."

I was torn between gratitude for his safety and frustration and fury for the anguish as I stared down at my young son who was content to ride home in the car, as long as no one touched him.

I spent the rest of the day quietly going about my chores, worrying and wondering just what the future held in store for all of us, including Kelton.

Although we tried to force Kelton to accept our lifestyle, our way of things, he did not respond. He still didn't like interruptions. He hated to have the TV or the radio turned on. He disliked it when I talked on the phone, and would always take advantage of that moment to get into something. I would turn around and find flour on the floor or strange things in the dryer.

Everything in life has a beginning. The beginning of Kelton's preoccupation with locks took place one evening in Jack's offices. Jack was working late that night, and since his car was undergoing repair, I had to pick him up and took all the children along. It was an adventure for them to go to the shop and see the latest motorcycles. Excitedly, the children wandered all over the store looking at everything until Jack was ready to leave.

"Get in the car, kids," I called. "We're ready to go." Everyone piled into the car as Jack locked up the shop.

"Where is Kelton?" I asked.

"I thought he was with you," Vern replied.

My negative reply activated all our fears.

We piled out of the car like a bunch of tumblers at the circus, and Jack unlocked the office and turned on the light. There stood Kelton confused, with tears rolling down his cheeks— one of the few times he cried tears—and then he began gasping with built-up panic. I soothed him as everyone climbed back into the car for the ride home.

From that moment on, Kelton became lock-conscious and did not tolerate any kind of lock. He went about checking for locked doors. Somehow, he opened closed doors, even unfastened padlocks, employing his strange, unaccountable Houdini-like gift, a fact I never revealed to anyone. The child especially liked combination locks, and could figure out the combinations in seconds, no matter how sophisticated or complicated.

While it all was disturbing and worrisome, it was also a challenging mystery and my mind worked overtime trying to solve it.

In the meantime, we continued to make the rounds of doctors, psychologists, psychiatrists and clinics, looking for answers to Kelton's problem. Nobody ventured an opinion, come up with a diagnosis or offered an uneducated guess. In their eyes, Kelton was a fine healthy child, who, not unlike Einstein, was late to talk. If in fact he did strange and wondrous things that could not be found in a medical model, they were not the concern of the medical profession.

We watched helplessly as our child withdrew from us more each day.

My widowed mother and her three youngest children had moved to California. Mother had hurt her back and was no longer able to work. The house she rented was just a few miles from where we lived, and a much bigger place than ours. It also had a lovely fenced back yard and a large banana tree stood tall in the front. In order to help out mother, we combined households and moved our family into her larger home. There were ten of us under one roof, which made for a lively household. Since we were all used to large families, no one considered it a hardship.

The situation unsettled Kelton. There were more people around now, a new house, different routines and more noise. It was all too much for him. He regressed for a while as the changes descended on him, withdrawing until such time he could accept the new system.

Kelton turned four that June. Once again we showered him with enough gifts and attention to please a celebrity. Once again he rejected everything. He did not eat the cake, ignored his gifts and stayed outside until the whole affair was over. He tore up his new shirt and all his birthday toys disappeared mysteriously.

Nobody understood his behavior, and played make believe that all's well. I often felt he was above the "worldly" things, but how could I prove it. All I tried to do was to make this child part of our family and keep our family together.

I was not registering a complaint nor did I feel abandoned, but just the same I was alone and felt that loneliness all the time. There was no one to turn to, no one to support me.

I started an ironing business to help with the expenses of our crowded household. I bought an automatic ironer, placed a few ads in the newspaper, and soon had a steady clientele. My mother took over the cooking, and everyone else pitched in with the household chores which freed me up to do my ironing.

The house ran smoothly in spite of Kelton's disruptive episodes. He now had a new obsession. As I sat at the ironer, which was controlled by a knee-operated lever, Kelton sat beside me and watched the clothes move through the large roller.

One day I went to answer the doorbell and turned off the ironer. I had just gotten to the door when I heard Kelton scream. I dashed back to the family room and saw Kelton's hand caught under the roller. I ran to the machine and hit the operating lever. The roller raised, releasing his hand. The back of his hand was badly burned. I applied cold soda water as a quick first aid, and rushed him to the emergency room at the hospital where nurses took care of his hand properly.

His hand healed quickly, and Kelton never tried to iron clothes again. He developed a great respect for the ironer. There were other accidents to follow, fortunately we always managed to get to him in time. Perhaps someone special was watching over him?

Kelton had a daily routine. Each morning he went to the garage. There he put all the fruit jars on the shelves, arranging them according to size—the smallest jam jars on one end, next the quart jars and on to the two-quart jars. Then he came into the kitchen and ate breakfast. After that he watched the clothes tumbling in the dryer and played for hours in the bathtub, or sat by me while I ironed.

I did not always remember how routine-bound Kelton was. On picnics and outings I carried water in plastic Clorox bottles that I had scrubbed clean of its former contents. Kelton used to get a kick out of the gurgling water when he tipped up the bottle to drink from the big gallon jugs.

One morning I heard Kelton scream in pain. I jumped up and ran to the garage. At first I couldn't see what was wrong, but when I picked him up, I smelled Clorox on his breath and realized that he gotten into a full bleach bottle thinking it was filled with water.

I carried him to the kitchen and forced milk down his throat and he vomited. I took him to the doctor and was relieved to learn that there was no damage done. Well, we won another round!

When we got Kelton a cat, he seemed frightened of it at first, but soon played with it. One early morning we woke up from a persistent and pitiful meowing. The frightened animal was caught up on the roof. We got out the ladder and removed the cat from its high perch wondering how it got there.

But somehow, several times that day, the cat ended up back on the roof. I had gone outside to look for my boy and I caught my little son in the act. I was shocked. Kelton was pitching the cat on to the roof while laughing hysterically. I stopped him at once, but was secretly surprised at the strength he must have to toss a fully-grown cat high into the air and with precision aim, on to the steep roof. The cat soon learned to protect itself, and boy and cat became good friends after all.

About this time, two of my teenage cousins, Scott and Terill, came to live with us. Kelton didn't like having more new people around, and started bugging and annoying Vern and Scott. He took their things and either broke them or hid them. Kelton always reacted negatively when the world got difficult. Life was not peaceful. Sometimes he ran away or withdrew, other times he screamed. He did not like change and his erratic behavior was the proof.

We had been in California for a year and a half when we were able to buy a large, two-story house on a quiet cul-de-sac not far from where we lived. We were all excited about the move and the fact that we would be in our own home was a good feeling. The cousins went back to their mother, and, with fewer people around, Kelton was less destructive.

This time Kelton did not display withdrawal and added remote behavior when the move into the new house was completed. But strangely enough, he stopped eating everything except peanut butter sandwiches for a long time.

We loved California more and more the longer we lived there. People were friendly and progressive. Within an hour, we could be in the mountains enjoying a snow-clad winter scene; we were five minutes away from the beach. We could catch a Broadway show, or take the family and friends to Disneyland at the drop of a hat. It would always be novelty to go to the beach on Christmas Day, and to be living just around the corner from where movies were made, and the stars had their homes.

Claudia had closed her pre-school and we had to find a new school for Kelton, She had accomplished quite a bit with him in that year. He took part in school activities, and once Kelton even let her hug him without screaming. He loved puzzles, and put them together amazingly well. But there were some things Kelton had learned that were less attractive.

He threw rocks in the neighbor's yard, and ran along the top of the brick wall, which scared them to death. I'm sure they were glad to see the nursery school close.

We enrolled Kelton in a private nursery school. Mary, his teacher, cared about Kelton, and in turn our son liked her. Few people could make that statement. Mary became a source of support and brought me many helpful ideas and sound suggestions for dealing with Kelton.

Established routines were etched in his mind and he followed them rigidly. He still did the same things every day, in the same order. He wanted the clothes dryer going so he could watch it revolve, he checked to see if the jars were in a row, he made sure all the toys were in order on the shelf. He was upset if I took him along on an errand and disturbed his rituals. We constantly introduced him to new and different experiences in every manner possible, but he fought us all the way.

The next episode took place a few days later. Every day for two consecutive weeks, he threw everything from the top shelf of his closet on the floor, and would climb up on to the shelf and stay curled up for thirty minutes at a time. When I spanked him for throwing things on the floor, he put everything he had tossed out on the bed and climbed back on the shelf.

Next, he went into his sisters' room, and repeated this unpopular closet clearing act. A constant state of war existed between Kelton and his siblings, as he continued to use their things, and eventually ruin everything he laid his hands on. It seemed that the whole world belonged to Kelton and he did not understand the right of individual ownership.

Only when he got sick from drinking Sharlene's perfume did he keep away from their rooms and leave their stuff alone for a while.

Much of my time was spent keeping peace in the family. Through all Kelton's antics and the battles between the kids, Jack stood at the sidelines in his gentle quiet way, willing to do anything, to ease the problems, if he only knew how. I worked hard at avoiding my feelings. I was afraid if I'd let go, I might not find my way back to my troubled world.

One way of introducing fresh ideas into his life was buying him educational toys. He never liked any of them, until Jack came home with a set of Lincoln Logs one day. Kelton liked the logs and let his father help him build the first house. After that, he would sit for hours building houses. As I watched him, I realized he displayed an amazing sense for construction and architecture in the way he put the logs to use. We knew how much he liked things in motion, and found all kinds of wind-up toys for him, which kept him interested and occupied for a while.

One of his favorite games was to throw the ball over the house, run around and get it, then throw it back again. He would repeat the routine for hours at a time. He liked doing everything he could by himself, anything that permitted him to be alone. He would run away when his father or other people came near him avoiding close contact at all costs. Jack tried hard to relate to his son, find a way to reach him, but was rarely successful at being accepted.

Sometimes Kelton stayed by my side when I did my housework, just watching as I moved about from one room to the next. He decided to help with the laundry when I wasn't looking. He loaded the machine with clothes, and poured in too much soap and too much bleach.

When he turned the machine on and the tub filled with water it overflowed. Soapy water came bubbling out of the washer, turned into a small river of white foam as it ran through the kitchen into the family room What a mess it made!

Because most of his activities became his obsessions, we were concerned that this might be his latest and kept a close watch on the laundry room. He required little sleep and was up before the kids, prowling through the house and we were never sure what we would wake up to find. Sometimes I felt I lived in a powder keg on top of an active volcano ... waiting...waiting.

With the laundry room obsession on a momentarily hold, Kelton gave his attention to the attic. One early morning we were awakened by something banging on the heating pipes in the house. We discovered Kelton in the attic hitting on the pipes, enjoying the noise. Everyone wondered how in the world the child had managed to enter the attic. The only access to the attic was a trap door in the hall ceiling. The trap door was open and Kelton was in the attic. Neither a chair nor a ladder had been placed in the hall under the open trap door to reach the opening in the ceiling.

How did he get up there? We didn't know. What we did know, was the fact that nothing was safe from him and we couldn't possibly predict what he would do next.

We tried to treat him just like other children. When he threw a screaming tantrum, he was sent to his room. When he misbehaved, he was spanked. If we tapped him on his rear with a wooden spoon, he would find the offensive piece of wood later and break it in half. If I spanked him with my hand, he would grab my hand with a strong grip and push it away from him. I suffered great pangs of guilt when I punished him, wondering if I did the right thing, questioning my judgement.

I had observed him jumping and flapping his hands for long periods of time, and decided to join him in this strange activity and began jumping and waving my hands. He stopped screaming and looked at me curiously. I jumped into the kitchen, he jumped after me. It seemed like one way to reach him, to get him out of his trance, to stay in touch with him. The whole family jumped, waved, flapped and rocked. It may have helped us do "his thing" but it brought him no closer to us, as we attempted to see beyond our reality and look at the world through this little boy eyes.

Kelton made no effort to enter our world. He just got on his rocking horse and rocked. Alone. By himself .. all alone.

I wanted to scream—scream at the doctors, at God, at everyone. Why me? Why this? What's wrong? Where's is this going? Is there an end?

We took him to a different psychologist. Each visit was a nightmare, but we kept on with our visits. Maybe, just maybe, we could get some answers from this learned individual. When the psychologist did not come up with a diagnosis for Kelton's problems, nor an effective means of dealing with him, he subjected Jack and me to therapy with astonishing results.

Considering the fact that we brought a screaming child to his office for the counseling sessions, he assumed that he was dealing with a parenting problem and labeled gentle and kind Jack a potential child abuser, which according to the good doctor's opinion, was the root of Kelton's disturbed and erratic behavior as well as a threat to the child's further development. Even though nothing could have been further from the truth, the wild and cruel accusations left a bitter taste in our mouths, and a big dent in our hearts.

It was this kind of unprofessional, uneducated and insensitive treatment we encountered regularly that left me hovering on the edge of insanity and poured salt on my open wounds.

Kelton hated the psychologist and all the people associated with the clinic. Most of the time he screamed in protest as I dragged him to the clinic. He may have known the futility of these visits. When all else failed, we agreed to have a brain scan done on Kelton.

What happened next was a scene straight from the Middle Ages. Kelton was strapped down while the technicians taped needles to his head. He fought wildly against the restraints the entire time throughout the procedure. I was so upset that I was in tears. I was beginning to hate the doctors and the tests as much as Kelton did.

All the tests revealed nothing but normal functions. We went home having learned nothing new or different—exhausted beyond description, upset and angry, and added one more medical bill to our pile of financial stress.

Kelton continued to scream for the rest of the afternoon and most of the night. I had a hard time listening to his endless screaming. I was twenty five years old, and felt I had lived a hundred. Kelton's quiet withdrawal the next day was a welcome relief to us all.

*He lives where he lives,*
*His dreams walk about the town.*
*He has no interest in my dreams:*
*He cannot establish a network*
*From his mind to mine.*
*I try to leave the circuits open,*
*But I am denied.*
*He stands there by himself*
*Holding his thoughts within—*
*Whatever wanders through his mind*
*Stays there; he doesn't share.*

*I look at him.*
*In these few seconds*
*I have lived*
*A lifetime.*

# 5

Alarming, and at the same time amazing, things happened the summer Kelton turned four. Without warning, and as spontaneous as all his acts were, he suddenly decided to take up residence on the roof of our two-story house. We couldn't figure out how he got up there, but he did. He quickly declared the roof his territory, his sacred place—a fact we didn't grasp at first.

When we had discovered his whereabouts, we were more than curious as to how he had reached the roof. We checked and rechecked every possible way to access the roof a four-year-old—or for that matter an adult acrobat—could manage. To this day, I can't decide whether I was more disturbed by his unexplainable Houdini-like talents, or by my raging fear he would fall on to the cement driveway and land on his head. Those were our concerns and fears, but not Kelton's. He moved about the steep roof, foot sure with the ease of a mountain goat.

Every summer morning we woke up to find Kelton perched on the roof ready to watch the day's activities unfold as he listened spellbound to the sounds of the world below him.

Up there he was safe ... there he was above everything... there he was alone.

Each day for weeks, Jack would drag out the ladder, lean it against the house, climb up and bring Kelton down—a stiff and screaming bundle of fury. Even though we watched him like a hawk, Kelton was soon back up on the roof, and he came down only when he wanted to eat. No matter how we kept a constant eye on him, not once did we catch him on his journey from the lofty heights of our roof. There was no end to our puzzlement.

The children were torn between awe and wonder, wishing they had Kelton's nimble ways and felt a bit left out of the fun. Then there were the neighbors. They would have had us all committed if they had their way. I could read their disapproval and their unkind thoughts on their faces, as they judged us unfit parents, careless and irresponsible.

I didn't blame them. What do I say? How can I explain? My four-year old lived on the roof, and we didn't know how he got up there, anymore than we knew how he got down. We never saw him coming or going. They just didn't understand Kelton. But then, neither did we. We just made more room in our hearts for him and lived with his strange antics.

The psychologist knew no more than we did. But, basically, he did not believe us and thought that we were liars and made up stories. In the end, the doctor recommended we ignore Kelton in the hope that the novelty of living on the roof would wear off. We shook our heads fearfully, wondering just what's in store for us next?

One morning as I watched Kelton perched on the roof near the chimney, I decided to join him. I found an old pair of rubber soled shoes, dragged out the ladder and, closing my eyes, I tried to ignore my fear of heights. Getting to the top of the ladder was the easy part, but climbing onto the roof took all the courage I could muster, telling myself to breathe deeply and relax. My body stiffened. I slipped and caught myself as I searched for a foothold, and finally got on to the roof.

The response from Kelton to my appearance on the roof was not what I expected. He was not happy I had invaded his domain. He immediately disappeared over the gable with the speed of a mountain goat. I was left alone to cross the shingles, eyes glued ahead to where I was going, sensing that my safety lay in looking up. Not until I reached the chimney and held on to it for dear life, did I begin to relax.

"Okay, Ranae," I laughed at myself, "what are you doing up here? You have got to be out of your mind." I sat very still, seeing the humor of the past months.

I remembered the time Lynell's friend Mira came to play and was drenched from above by a wildly amused Kelton urinating on the unsuspecting child as she rang the doorbell. Lynell shed tears of embarrassment and anger at her brother's prank and Mira was horrified, humiliated and furious—insulted beyond words. Kelton had done it before, and, God help us all, would no doubt do it again.

Much later, the neighborhood joke to bring an umbrella when visiting the Steele house became a source of amusement and laughter among us. But it wasn't funny at the time. We were all mortified, but no amount of reprimands, threats or punishment stopped Kelton from abandoning his latest and disgusting prank.

At that moment my thoughts were distracted by Kelton running past me bouncing a basketball near the edge of the roof. He looked through me as if I didn't exist. My heart jumped into my throat.

"I'll never get used to your doing that," I yelled, realizing that Kelton had never perceived the fear that bound me, "I wish I could do that!" I called after him. Kelton somehow did not share our fears.

I stood up holding on to the chimney and looked down into its dark, narrow throat. I could make out some articles of clothing Kelton had thrown down. There, stuck in dark silence rested the answer to the disappearance of food, shoes, toys, clothing and other things. Nothing was safe from this child.

Kelton would laugh and giggle as he witnessed our frantic search for missing things, void of any other feelings than his own mirth.

"Kelton," we would yell up at him, "where's my shoe... where's my baseball... where's my..."

We would get a long stick, poke it up the chimney until the missing objects came tumbling down at us. Fortunately we had not used the fireplace, and there was no soot to soil our things.

I smiled ruefully, remembering how I had been dressed for church a few Sundays ago, with one shoe on, and the other missing. With broom in hand, I climbed into the fireplace and retrieved the other shoe from the chimney. As I poked and prodded with the broom handle, a two quart jar of salad dressing came flying down and crashed at my feet, broke into a shower of shards and splattered its contents with explosive force. I never imagined that anything short of a tidal wave could cover such a wide area. There was mayonnaise everywhere—my clothing, my hair, face, the fireplace, the carpet and the furniture. The children, who had been watching the search for my shoe, suppressed their laughter as they scurried beyond the reach of my wrath.

As summer tapered into fall, the neighbors and our family had grown accustomed to the little boy who lived on the roof, and watched with a blend of awe and discomfort as he ran swiftly on the very edge of the roof disappearing around the corner.

Occasionally he would lower himself down the chimney to stand on the pipe inside which prevented him from falling down into the fireplace. It was at just the right height for his head to appear over the edge of the chimney. He certainly displayed a sense of whimsey, and we could tell he loved the reaction of us mere mortals who choked back our astonishment and tried to act as though we saw children going down chimneys every day.

I came out of my reverie and realized what a ridiculous sight I must be perched on the roof clutching the chimney, when a neighbor slowly drove her car down the street and parked in the driveway across the street. She got out of the car and glanced up at the roof—something people had been doing lately. We had become a bigger attraction than a carnival.

" What in the world," she yelled at me, "are you doing on the roof? I realize that you try to share Kelton's experiences but, isn't this a bit much, even for you?"

"Do you think you can help me down?" I laughed, "We may have to call the fire department this time."

"It's lucky for you that I know your situation or I would just call the funny farm to come and get you both!" she shouted back.

Grateful for her sense of humor and lack of judgment, I made it down the roof on to the safety of solid ground where most of us had our being. Even though I was on the roof for a brief time only, I liked the quiet of looking down, not being a part of what's down there, and feeling remote, removed and alone. I could have stayed a long time, I thought.

We watched Kelton for a moment while he was dropping the basketball from above through the hoop which was nailed over the garage door, trying to make a basket.

"Well, at least I don't have so many people frantically running into my house these days because they've just seen a little boy on the roof disappearing down the chimney," I said, "the neighbors must be getting used to us."

"What blows my mind is your attitude to all of this and the way you respond so calmly: 'Oh, that's all right—he lives up there'," she giggled, and then added with a note of seriousness, "The Ericksons came to our house again last night, trying to get us to sign a petition to force you to put Kelton in an institution. But don't worry, they're not getting anywhere."

"Tell them it's better he's on the roof, than running lose around town getting picked up by the police," I laughed in helpless frustration. "Up there, we know where he is."

What could we expect next? They say a life of suspense is the best cure against boredom. I was ready for a little boredom, my frustration had reached beyond the safety line of my patience. Would I be able to hold on? Could I?

*I saw him sitting there*
*Perched on the edge of the roof,*
*Watching the oncoming world—*
*Unaware of time.*
*Measuring the balance of bondage*
*Between his world and mine.*
*Feeling free to decide,*
*Eluding what he doesn't understand.*

*Dwelling in the shadows,*
*Defending obsessions,*
*Playing out rituals*
*Letting his image be distorted—*
*Avoiding the arrival of*
*Kelton.*

## 6

Rather than worrying and creating phantoms as a daily chore, I had to do something in order to help myself stay sane and at the same time further Kelton's development. I started a pre-school in our home because we were unable to find suitable training or education.

I turned our family room into a big school room. I put up low black boards, shelves for books and educational toys, set up tables with benches, I read everything I could about learning disabilities and took psychology classes at Orange County Community College. I modeled my program after the Montessori method, which includes the use of all our senses in most everything taught to youngsters.

I labeled objects in the house with large signs; CHAIR, TABLE, CAR, and so on. Brightly colored letters of the alphabet were placed on the wall at a child's eye level. Every morning we sang the alphabet song, and then sang their sounds. We felt sand paper letters, smelled different scents, explored different sights. Jack built jungle gyms for the kids to climb on, and a big sand box for them to play in. We made the family room and back yard look like a real school.

When everything was ready and school could begin, I passed the word around and on opening day there were eight three- and four-year-olds ready to participate. By the end of the year, 16 children attended classes. There were two boys who resembled Kelton in several ways, yet each boy was different, with his own personality and his own phobias. One boy couldn't tolerate having his feet off of the floor. His mother had to bathe him and care for him with his feet always touching the floor. We worked with him similar to the way we did with Kelton and we were eventually able to get the boy over that habit, much to the joy of his grateful parents.

In each case, these kids had to be forced to accept new things. They wanted to hang on to their routines; they didn't want change. The other boy acted like a little squirrel, hiding objects that he liked. We found things in strange places; yet he could always remember where he had hidden his treasures. He took things home with him that belonged to other kids or the school with the expertise of a full grown jewel thief.

At first, Kelton refused to take part in the activities at school and join the other children in their play. He hid under the table or jumped and flapped his hands. When I made him sit with the other children, he screamed loudly. But I persisted and managed to make him behave.

He persisted and stuck by his guns. He would get up when I wasn't looking, take a child by the hand and open the front door to put him out, like you would put out a dog or a cat. He did that with everybody who came to the house. Hospitality was not his strong suit. He didn't like strangers. I often wondered if he could see inside people, didn't like what he saw, and turned them away? Wonders never ceased with that child.

Once he escorted a church official out the door and locked him out. Jack never left the house without his keys.

Kelton would lock him out regularly, to our chagrin.

I did not charge a fee at the school, I only requested payment for supplies. Several mothers volunteered to help. I don't know what I would have done without the moral support the mothers of our little students gave me. It was wonderful.

The school was open for half a day, five days a week. I kept adding new ideas, games, crafts and methods to teach the children worthwhile things. The public school board of education lent a hand and let me borrow their in-service library.

I had to forget to figure out why Kelton didn't speak or respond, and instead encourage him to communicate with us in his ways. We tried our very best to prevent him from withdrawing and losing him to another world. Kelton had to have freedom to explore and learn. We accepted the fact that in spite of his young age, this tiny person could take care of himself in traffic and would not get lost. Humbly and with love, I finally put Kelton into God's hands for safekeeping and let Him watch over His child.

Because Kelton liked his rituals performed without deviation, at the same time everyday, we had to be extra careful not to use conditioning as a teaching tool. He would latch on to something that fascinated him and turn it into a fixation.

An example of this was his latest irritating habit of smelling everything he came into contact, as he had learned in school. He had become hung up on smelling his food before he ate it. Unfortunately, he also smelled everybody else's food, which led to embarrassing moments when we took the children out to eat. To our chagrin and other people's horror, he smelled the food at the home of friends and at the table of strangers in restaurants. We found ourselves constantly explaining why our little boy acted like a royal food tester or health inspector.

But then, that was nothing new, we always had to explain Kelton. The world just wouldn't accept him as he was. I understood. We had a hard time accepting him as well. But he was our child, and we loved him, and in spite of the hardships, there were wonderful and unforgettable moments. Had he not come into our lives, none of us would be what we are today—more compassionate and understanding of those who are different.

When Kelton was very young, we teamed. We had to do things differently with him every day. We had to cook his food differently, put him to bed at different times, take different routes home, shop in different stores, change his clothes and shoes. At first it disoriented him, but he soon accepted it. It prevented him from becoming stuck on one way of doing things and becoming upset when it was changed.

Forcing change on him proved helpful in his development. We had to watch out not to create too much structure in our teaching or Kelton got dependent on it and wouldn't progress. In nursery school we taught him skills that were necessary for play, he would only accept what he wanted to, which was often only a segment of an activity. In playing basketball he would not learn the rules. He cried or withdrew whenever someone else had a turn at something. He would not wait in line for a turn down the slide or the swing but push ahead and scream. In order to make him comprehend these basic rules, we stood by his side, holding on to him, keeping him in line, listening to his yells of protest, with everybody looking on disapprovingly, until his turn came. It was hard, and nerve-wracking, but it was the only thing that worked. Eventually he accepted the rules. Everything we could teach to make him function in our world was bound to help him in the future. That was the reward for our efforts, exhaustive as they were.

Schools and doctors would not believe that Kelton discriminated between his environments. Skills that he exercised at home would not carry over when we took him to a school or for testing. Many times, I insisted that the officials come to my nursery school to observe Kelton. They were always surprised to see Kelton doing so well when he would not perform the same tasks the day before at the clinic. When Kelton attended school later on, he did not transfer skills from school to home. The school's environment was so structured that Kelton easily adjusted, but he didn't learn. He merely got by, and his potential never was challenged. At home, if he did a task once, we would move on quickly to the next one. The faster we pushed, the more he learned—completely the opposite of the slow method used at school where he was bored and withdrew.

It was important to focus his attention with the precision of a drill sergeant to further his learning. When we moved fast, he had no time to look at the ceiling or be distracted in some other way. It was amazing how quickly Kelton and the other two special children learned when we used the fast track method. We concentrated on teaching the kids to perform, giving priority to their present behavior. Often, we had to stop what we were doing and wait until their aggressive outbursts were under control.

We did not buy in to their negative and disturbing behavior, and used whatever method worked to change their attitudes. We did not use a specific method in dealing with their screaming. That might have conditioned them, which could become a greater problem.

We were on the move like a fast train to fit their speed of accepting new ways. Before I became totally aware of the conditioning factor, I would use social isolation as a method for reducing undesirable behavior and sent the troublemaker to his room. Kelton became quite comfortable being in his room and wouldn't come out. For a long time it was painful to get him to participate in family activities, so for behavior modification we had to take something away from him he liked very much. He loved his boots. We took them away each time he misbehaved. It worked.

These children had no interest in things around them. The environment had to affect them profoundly in some way before they focused their attention upon it. Stimulating the senses was important, and we kept at it all the time.

We threw a basketball through the hoop to get Kelton's attention. By shooting baskets we could teach *up*, *down*, and *through* to him. It also provided interaction with others and made him use eye contact. After a while he would repeat instructions. It was nice to confirm that the child could speak.

Kelton's motor functions were good—way above average. He would get stuck on something he liked, like shooting the basketball, and do it for hours. We would all chant, "Throw the ball up, Kelton—through the hoop—down comes the ball." He loved to hear us sing this song and then clap when he made a basket. He would laugh, clap his hands and jump.

When we discovered he had a difficult time transferring the concepts of *up*, *down*, *through* to other areas. We purchased a play tunnel, crawled through and stood up. We used this showing method of teaching in every situation to demonstrate *up*, *through* and *down* to him and expanded the action to other words like *push*, *pull*, *open*, *pick up* and *go get.*.

We used the same method in the nursery school for all the children, and sometimes I had to force Kelton to participate. We moved fast from one activity to the next, singing as we went. The children loved it and learned quickly; even Kelton caught on, in spite of himself. Although he did not like many of the things we did in school, and sometimes he screamed and fought me all the way, there were many things he accepted eventually.

Just when I thought we might be making some headway, he developed echolalia: repetition of speech.

"Hi Kelton," Jack said.

"Hi Kelton," Kelton echoed.

"How are you?" said Jack.

"How are you?" Kelton repeated.

What to do now? The challenges did not stop but rather escalated the older he got. With that in mind, and conjuring up future problems and phantoms, I wondered how I slept through the nights. I concluded that it was sheer exhaustion which induced sleep and gave me some rest.

Capitalizing on his love of movement, we gave him a reel-to-reel tape recorder, with tapes of children's stories, songs and rhymes. He listened to them for hours and increased his vocabulary, even though it remained echolalia for a while. To this day, Kelton will echo part of the question first before answering when he is under stress.

We recorded dialogue with music he liked in the background. I would say, "What is your name?" Then I would answer, "My name is Kelton Steele."

"How old are you?"

"I am four years old."

I continued this type of dialogue through the whole tape, and Kelton listened to it. I wonder how long it would be until we could estimate results.

It wasn't long after we started the tape recorder routine, when a visitor asked Kelton what his name was, and he responded. They asked him how old he was and he told them—not in complete sentences, but the answers were correct and we could understand him. He did not revert to echolalia with these questions.

It was a great and glorious breakthrough for us. Kelton continued to learn words. His tendency toward echolalia was still strong, and when he would speak he would repeat what was said before answering with words of his own. Most of the time, he merely repeated our words. We had to withhold objects he was fond of from him until he gave the appropriate response.

We tried to use sign language with him, but it didn't work because he quickly picked it up and then refused to speak at all. The challenges for Kelton lay in the learning process of a new skill not in its application. We tried using the typewriter as a means of communication. He loved the click and clack of the keys and their motion, but would never type the letters we called out. He would keep tapping out one specific letter until it filled the whole page.

My basic assumption that Kelton needed role models from his own age group was correct. He learned a lot from the youngsters who attended our little nursery school. His behavior was better, his communication techniques improved and his social skills expanded.

Our training method of applying structure and repetition only in areas we wanted conditioning was effective in teaching Kelton to come into our space. We taught him to cope with our ways and understand this world a little bit more each day. He would be able to communicate with people, and above all, he would understand that he was a worthwhile person. Singing everything we learned, moving around quickly, touching objects, teaching a concept rapidly and going quickly on to something else, caught Kelton's attention and he learned.

After his birthday in June, I tried all summer long to get him enrolled in kindergarten. He underwent a battery of tests and failed everyone of them. Upon my insistence the school psychologist came to observe Kelton at my pre-school. She was amazed at what he was able to do because he had not displayed any of his skills when he was tested on the school  premises.

In spite of her efforts to help us, she was at a loss, because no one had diagnosed Kelton's problem, and the school officials didn't know into which program to put him.

It was through her that we filled out a diagnostic questionnaire by Dr. Rimland, a pioneer in autism, and were able to get two doctors to agree that Kelton was indeed autistic. We had a diagnosis. The other two boys from our pre-school were also diagnosed as autistic. Now we had a name for what was wrong with our child. Perhaps that would open the door to help. I began my own research into autism and read everything I could lay my hands on. Most of the information was repetitious, little was known about the condition and there was no report of curing autism.

Dashed hopes and broken dreams could not get me down. I would continue with the help of my family and friends to direct my energies to work with Kelton. Who knows what could happen?

Kelton had taken hearing tests, vision tests, and EEG's for brain damage, the results of which were normal. He had been tested for schizophrenia and psychiatric disturbances. Some thought he was aphasic or had a psychosis. We never accepted the diagnosis that he was retarded because he displayed a keen level of intelligence. In spite of the dark side it was a relief to finally discover a name for what had been a mystery for so long.

The children were wonderful during these stressful and trying years, and mother and Jack were always there to help and support me. But raising a difficult and disturbing child would leave its toll. Our family went through a lot, with an admirable determination to make the best of it.

"Why am I being punished? What did I do to deserve this? How long do I have to wait for Kelton to be a normal, functioning being? When will the darkness lift? Is there going to be an end?" These thoughts raced through my head, and I knew I had to banish all bitter feelings before they devoured me.

I realized I couldn't open tomorrow's door. The future loomed large and menacing at the edge of my despair. Was this all just a nightmare played out awaiting my own awakening? I had no answers, only determination to go on. Near the end of the summer, Kelton decided to come down from the roof and live in the house again. By this time, the neighbors had petitioned the court to force us to put Kelton in an institution, to no avail. And, I was pregnant again. My fears took on a new meaning–another child. What if there would be something wrong with my next child? The doctor said the odds favored our not having another handicapped child, but I remembered the family in our parent group that had three special children. The possibility was there, and I had to learn to accept it. Fear and worry lived with me for the remaining months of my pregnancy.

After a day filled with Kelton's screams, spilled messes, battles and fusses with too much to do and too little time, the house was finally still. I lay sleepless in my bed for hours, crying, reaching out to God to put my trust in Him and find peace. How many more nights of tears and panic, how many more days of havoc and exhaustion? I got up, put on my robe and stood at the window looking at the pale, pre-dawn sky, my mind going over the nightmare of the past summer. I fell on my knees, "Please God, help me, give me strength, give me hope, give me faith and give me peace."

A warm, comforting feeling washed over me. The tiredness and fear of the long months left me, and I knew He had heard my prayers. He was there. Powerful words flashed in my mind. "After the trial of your faith."

"After the trial of your faith," I spoke out loud. That was the answer. I could go on. I could survive. I then could sleep peacefully.

When the first rays of sunlight came through the window and the shadows of the night vanished, I prayed once more, "Thank you, God, for another day to try again."Tired but peaceful, I went to wake up Jack.

Some of Kelton's antics were not only embarrassing, but made us realize there was no right or wrong in Kelton's world. Everything just *was. It was his to do, his to use, his to own.* He would give the ice cream man a small rock in payment for his popsicle, for instance. He didn't seem to know it was wrong. He would hide a pebble in his clenched fist and hand it to the man. The other kids thought Kelton had a great system. All he saw was an exchange taking place and the objects of the exchange of *things* did not matter.

Out of the blue, Kelton started talking. His first words were: "Want a peanut butter sandwich."

We were thrilled, and kept after him diligently to say words even though they were not connected to make a whole sentence. We just wanted him to use language; the rest might come. We were amazed that his first words came in phrases, and wondered how long he had known how to talk.

Kelton learned to operate the record player, the radio and the tape recorder, and kept himself occupied with music. He only listened to classical music, playing the same record over and over and over. I had always loved Madame Butterfly, but a few weeks of listening to it daily turned out to be a bit much. He hated any other kind of music, and he would turn it off or leave the room. He was attached to the tape recorder, and watched the tapes go around and around for hours on end.

Kelton's new therapist was Janet a recent college graduate. She was a tall and slender blonde, and would work with our son on play therapy. As she sat at her desk looking through Kelton's file, her shoulders squared, a concerned look on her face, she conveyed a certain confidence and eagerness to get started. I looked to her with hope. She appeared to be different from others who had attempted to help Kelton.

The clinic had a small room filled with toys and was equipped with a two-way mirror. Kelton was in the room playing, while Janet could observe his behavior at play.

Kelton was five years old then, had sandy-colored hair, a freckled nose, hazel-blue eyes, and was tall for his age. We arrived at the clinic for his session with Janet. I held him firmly by the hand. When I stopped to talk to the receptionist, Kelton waited for a chance to pull his hand away from mine and dart out the door. His eyes took in everything, although he never looked directly at an object. He looked mostly up in the air, but his peripheral vision took in everything. The moment I relaxed my grip, he was gone, fleeing the confines of the clinic. I dashed out after him and somehow I knew I would find him on the roof.

The clinic was housed in a long building surrounded by a parking lot with a small landscaped area in front of the door. A fence connected to the building and acted as a backdrop for the flowers and shrubs growing in patches along its sides.

In a flash he was over the fence and on the roof. There he sat, quietly surveying the world and waiting for what he must know was to come—excited adults searching, running to and fro, calling his name.

From the rooftop the world had a different perspective. He could see it all: the busy traffic with cars whizzing by and people hurrying this way and that. No one stared at him, no one confined him.

"Kelton, come down here," I yelled. But he just sat there, his eyes darting about swiftly. How had he climbed the fence so fast?

He moved around to the other side of the roof and disappeared from our sight.

"Someone get a ladder," a man's voice shouted behind me.

I ran around the building, dodging the parked cars, trying to see where Kelton was. "Kelton! Come down right now!" I yelled. My command was answered with silence.

Soon a ladder appeared from somewhere and two men went on to the roof attempting to corner him.

Kelton, agile, sure of foot, never slipping, continued to evade everyone as his would-be captors slipped and slid on the steep roof.

"Kelton is smart, picking a territory where he has the advantage," I thought, frustrated to no end, but astonished as always by the child's clever maneuvers.

"There is certainly nothing wrong with his large motor coordination," Janet said admiringly, as she came up beside me. "And there is something delightful about his great fight for freedom," she added. Later her words made me stop and think.

Three men closed in on Kelton and brought him down. I couldn't help but notice that the child stopped screaming and struggling just about the time his half-hour appointment was up.

I was glad to get in the car and drive home. I was embarrassed and angry with Kelton and at myself for letting him get away from me,

Some of my acquaintances decided that I must have offended God, the doctors felt autism was a parenting problem, others wanted to remove Kelton to an institution. Who was right, who was wrong? Part of me questioned the validity of their opinions, the other part of me rejected them strongly.

In spite of the fact there never was enough time to get things done, we managed to be active in church work, went on bike rides and took time out for the beach. I continued my ironing business to help meet some of our mounting medical bills and the rising expenses of our large household.

Jack had gotten out of the import business and now held down two jobs: managing a motorcycle shop during the day and repairing watches in his spare time. Even ten-year-old Vern had a paper route. Sharlene, Vern, and Lynell were growing into beautiful children. Vern was enjoying Little League baseball, Sharlene was in great demand as a babysitter and Lynell helped me around the house and spent hours playing with Kelton.

At times it seemed that Kelton was frightened from within. Unconcerned about life and events around him, he continued to live in his own world. He heard his own voices and went through his own daily rituals, wanting his toys in the same place, washing his hands at prescribed intervals, jumping up and down, and throwing the ball up and over the roof for hours. He made few demands and took care of himself.

Doctors and specialists questioned the autism diagnosis, they could find nothing wrong with him. "Give him time," they said.

I hated those words, as much as I hated the empty days of watching him rock back and forth on his horse, going into a trance, glassy-eyed and silent. Who was this strange little boy who raced around screaming and then grew silent and lost? How could I cross the threshold to determine his needs, interpret his silent call for help? Somewhere, someone must have the answers.

Our search for a solution left us no rest. Every failed attempt added to our frustration and emptiness. Each doctor gave us a different diagnosis. One said brain damage, another preferred retardation. Kelton's medical files continued to grow. We contacted every specialist we heard about, hoping to find one who could help.

Finally, I had to accept the fact that we were on our own. We prayed as a family, and I spent many hours alone on my knees. If there was to be help for our son, it was up to God and our family.

I was inspired to put aside all rules of conventional behavior and training as I worked with Kelton. We did things in a different way every day so that he did not get conditioned to one way of doing things. We tried every method of teaching that came to our attention.

I jumped with him, sat quietly with him. I communicated with him in silence, but never knew if he heard me. I watched him wash his hands over and over until the bar of soap had dissolved. I praised him where I could and searched to understand his needs. We lived for the moment, mute as darkness, seeking a new light. We ran the circles but we never won the race.

Our doctor believed certain drugs might improve Kelton's speech pattern. When the medication didn't work, he prescribed higher and higher doses. I had doubts in my heart about this treatment, yet was convinced doctors knew more than I. I still came from the old school, which had placed the medical profession high on a pedestal.

Our weekly visits to the psychologist didn't do anything for us. To the contrary, the sessions left us guilty as he badgered us with questions, and did his best to convince us Kelton's condition was our fault. Were we bad parents? All we knew was that our other three children were normal and happy individuals. Common sense told us we were not the destructive parents the experts made us out to be.

When Kelton turned six, we gave him his first birthday party with invited guests. He didn't like the other kids coming, and kept taking them by the hand and leading them outside. When I went out to get them and bring them back in, Kelton locked me out and wouldn't open the door. Nervously he constantly twisted his shirt. He liked the cake and was fascinated with the candles and wanted them lit again and again. Out of all the gifts he picked out a dart gun as acceptable but hated his new clothes. Just the same, this birthday party was a vast improvement over the previous ones.

Kelton loved tools, and behind our backs took apart light fixtures and cupboard doors. We made him put everything back together, and as soon as he was sure we'd seen his work, he would reassemble them. Next he took the telephone apart. When the clothes dryer quit working, he took it apart.

Jack had a fit when Kelton took the lawn mower apart. But our homemade engineer had meticulously arranged each screw above the place where it should go so he would know where to put the pieces once he began rebuilding it. To our delight and surprise, the darn thing worked perfectly when he had reassembled it. Later on he would learn to start the machine and mow the lawn.

Surprises never ceased. One day I discovered all the neighborhood kids' bikes in our garage. "Where did all these bikes come from?" I asked. No one knew.

I found out who owned what bike, and sent Vern around the neighborhood to tell the kids to come and claim them. Jack and I sat down to talk with Kelton. We were really concerned. Stealing was something Kelton had never done before.

"Maybe he just wants a bike," Jack suggested.

"But he can't ride a two-wheel bike," I answered,

"Knowing him, he'll learn," Jack replied, remembering how Kelton taught himself everything he saw done by others.

We bought Kelton a bike. Without the slightest hesitation, he bounced on it and started riding. Once again, he just took off, doing something he had never done before with ease, as if he had always known how.

One of our neighbors had a cerebral palsy child, Johnny. I talked her into bringing the boy to the pre-school, and it turned out well—the boy loved it. Paralyzed from his waist down, Johnny crawled up the street by himself, lifted himself up, and banged on my door. Getting to school on his own was a freedom he had never known. He was so proud of his newly-discovered independence.

I got to know Carol, Johnny's mother, who was a lovely, quiet person. She, too, had a large family, and had kept Johnny in the house hidden from the world. We were good for each other. I helped her to be proud of Johnny, and she helped—as did all her children—with Kelton. She became a very good friend. The day came when Johnny became too ill to be taken care of at home, and had to be institutionalized. It was a sad day for us and we all cried.

Carol invited our family to use her swimming pool, to our delight. One afternoon, Kelton casually sauntered over to the diving board, quickly climbed up, and jumped into the deep end of the pool before I could stop him. I jumped after him to save him from drowning. But before I could get to him he was swimming to the other side of the pool, with the same natural ease he displayed in riding a bicycle or balancing himself on the edge of the roof.

We all cheered his accomplishment. He jumped off the diving board over and over again for the rest of the afternoon and swam like a fish—no big deal.

Kelton learned effortlessly, only his method was different—close to sheer genius I thought sometimes! He had a habit of standing at the sidelines seemingly uninterested in what was going on around him, and the next thing we knew, he was doing something he had observed. When his interest and curiosity were piqued, he learned fast. When something did not appeal to him, he made no attempt to learn.

The doctor who prescribed the drug therapy for Kelton was a specialist in the field of disturbed handicapped children. I told him how badly the drugs were affecting Kelton. Instead of listening to me, he increased the dosage. I was upset, to say the least. Again, my faith in doctors—ill-placed as it was—rose from the depth of my inbred respect for the medical profession and I meekly followed his instructions. We felt frustrated. We knew so little about drugs at that time.

One night we were awakened by short, loud screams, and we rushed in to Kelton's room. He sat on his bed, shrinking into the corner hugging his knees, the blankets were off the bed, the sheets rumpled, exposing the mattress. He pressed against the wall as if to get away from whatever he was seeing. I came close to him. He screamed and hit me. I backed up yelling, "Kelton it's me, mother, it's ok, Kelton!"

His lips were cracked and he held his head, covering his eyes with his hands. His screams continued.

Jack pulled me from the room and said, "You're making him worse, let me try!"

We had taught Kelton to say a simple prayer. He kept yelling parts of it over and over. "Help me be good, help me!"

I fled to my bedroom. The night was frightening, moonless, and dark. I turned on my bedside lamp. "What is it all for?" I cried. "I can't stand to see him like this! Help us God," I prayed. I ran to the bathroom, sick to my stomach as his cries echoed across the hall and burrowed into my very soul.

Jack stayed near Kelton, watching him for the rest of the night. If he got too close, Kelton got worse. Toward dawn, Kelton finally fell asleep, still hugging his knees.

I didn't sleep much that night, but when I did doze off, I had nightmares. I was frightened for Kelton, terrified at what he must be experiencing, and my heart was filled with my own brand of fear.

Kelton slept off and on all the next day, only drinking water every now and then. While I was working on my ironing, I prayed that Kelton would be all right.

"If we just knew what to do to help him," I cried to Jack. "If we could just find someone who could give us some answers!"

The nights were interrupted by his screams. Jack always got up and watched over him. He was very gentle with Kelton and considerate of me. But my sweet husband was at a loss to help his son just like the rest of us. He was there for him and relieved me from watching over our child.

For a while, the days were as disturbing as the nights. Kelton took off and would run down the road, like a soul haunted by dragons and ghouls. I would get into the car and follow him. Exhausted, he would fall to the ground and I'd pick him up and take him home, praying he could go to sleep. When sleep took over for awhile, he would rest uneasily and soon wake up screaming, still chased by the same ghosts and phantoms that had sent him racing down the street.

My world was crazier than ever. I lived a lifetime each day and had little peace and less hope for the path I had to follow.

The pages of life turned one by one; days and nights blended and passed; a million and one dreams shattered on the reality of the moment. The call to battle was real, but where was the battleground? Which weapons should I choose? My strength floated by on tears. Kelton was a beautiful spirit, and I prayed he would not close the doors behind him.

My lamp gives back a feeble light
Lack of knowledge looms so large
Time has lost its meaning.
I'm weary,
Tired,
Afraid.

Stumbling down this path
I taste the tears that roll
Past my cheeks.

Please turn up your lamp—
No, don't run away,
I fear this path alone.
You have no trouble seeing,
I am the one who is blind,
Confused by your rituals,
Not understanding.
Had I not loved beyond this darkness,
Searching for your light,
Perhaps I would have listened to the world,
Given up,
Never to try again.

A lifetime begins each morning
Strangely new
And of itself.

We never know where our courage
Comes from,
But it's there in the morning
As if sent with the rays of the sun.
Courage for another day

*Another hour.*

*Any day now, I may be admitted*
*Into the garden*
*Be allowed to till and plant*
*In the soil,*
*Clear away the underbrush*
*Understand the stirring in the trees*
*End the endless search.*

*Any day now, I may love without shadows*
*Find the sky splashed with color,*
*Discover a deeper meaning from*
*An ordinary experience.*

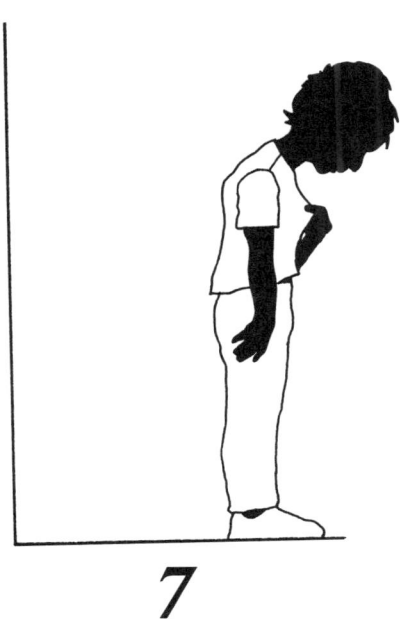

# 7

$T$horazine, Mellaril, Stelazine, Dexadrine and Ritalin made up Kelton's daily diet of drugs for one solid year and created more harm than good. The doctors neglected to tell us that little was known about most of these five drugs, never mentioned their side effects to us, and showed a total disregard for our grave concerns. Ritalin had a very bad effect on him. It caused extremely aggressive behavior. He ran wildly through the house like a crazed dog, washed his hands in a frenzy, hurt the cat and destroyed things at random. From the way he ran—tipping things over, holding his head in his hands—we knew he suffered severe headaches and was beside himself with pain.

Though Dexadrine and Ritalin are generally given to adults as stimulants, they are used to control hyperactivity in children. In autistic children the drugs are often ineffective, and in Kelton's case, they made him more hyperactive and aggressive.

At the beginning of the therapy, Mellaril controlled his rocking and jumping. He was calmer and less apt to rock. We took advantage of the situation and gave away the rocking horse. He displayed no signs that he missed his wooden pet, but began again to jump up and down,waving his hands.

At times Kelton withdrew into his world, as if to gain the strength he needed for living in a place he found frightening. In spite of our talks with the doctor, telling him the disturbing and devastating effects his prescribed treatment had on Kelton, he continued the drugs for the rest of the year. It was a year of sheer terror and hell for us all.

Trouble was on the way, as predictable as rain in spring.

I had gone to the grocery store with mother and left Sharlene and Vern in charge of the smaller children. Kelton had been sleeping in his room when we left.

When we got home, I climbed the stairs and quietly opened the door to his room to look in on him. His room was a shambles; the bed was torn apart and moved out from the wall. The drawers had been yanked out from the dresser, clothes were dumped and tossed everywhere. There were small piles of newspaper, torn in tiny bits, stacked here and there. Kelton lay among the rubble asleep, his face flushed, his lips cracked, one arm flung carelessly over a pile of toys. He had accomplished this destruction very quietly, unnoticed by the children in the house.

"It's just the drugs," I kept reminding myself "I wish the doctor had to live with him, maybe he would do something," I sobbed, as I went about restoring a semblance of order in my son's room.

The arrogance of the medical profession to never listen to the people who take care of the afflicted, the people who are around their patient for 24-hours a day, year in and year out, equaled the level of ignorance of their so-called scientific knowledge. I was no longer impressed with physicians and the questionable advances of medical technology. Most doctors could save millions of dollars spent on tests, countless hours of pain and suffering, if they just listened, looked, and heard what they are being told. I had placed the medical profession in the same category with an auto mechanic, some are better than others, and a good one is hard to find.

Along with the screaming, Kelton had developed an obsession to smell cleaning fluid, the car's exhaust, or anything with a strong odor. Tearing up paper became one of his rituals. Every piece of paper he could get hold of, he tore into tiny pieces, including cracker boxes and cereal containers. He continually twisted the front of his shirt, no matter what his mood would be.

Later, we discovered Kelton's drug therapy had been an experiment. (And here I thought the doctors knew what they were doing). However, in Kelton's case there was no adequate monitoring during the treatment, and the dosages were increased until the side effects were so visible a blind man would have noticed. I threw all the drugs away, unaware that it would be a long time before the effects would wear off.

Two long years went by before we felt certain that the effects of the chemically-induced behavior had disappeared. What a sad waste of time and energy, not to mention the emotional and physical suffering we experienced.

With the horrors of the drug therapy behind us, we started giving Kelton vitamin supplements. Research in the area of vitamins and nutrition may have been considered inconclusive, yet we found great improvement in his behavior when he took B complex, biotin, folic acid, ascorbic acid, and calcium with magnesium. He was calmer and his talking increased.

Many parents of autistic children with whom I have spoken agreed that vitamin and food supplements are helpful for their children.

I read everything I could on the various treatments and training for autistics and repeatedly came across the information that *educational methods to behavior modification* is not only a safer alternative to drugs, but in most cases highly effective. After a drug or mode of therapy has been sufficiently tested, it may be proven inadequate. Even though some positive effects might be found, the negative effects in the long run often outweigh the positive ones in a patient. Furthermore, a therapeutic method may work for some children, but not for others.

In my opinion, drugs should only be used if adequate medical monitoring is available, and then only if the situation or the child's symptoms merit their use. Drugs can interfere with learning and further insulate the child from his inner feelings and the outer world. Even tranquilizers affect learning ability.

*Time and days passing*
*Then more time and more days passing,*
*That your mind will learn to*
*Knit smoothly, deftly,*
*Finding a balance within.*

*I love you—that love suffers*
*It comes back again and again*
*To plead, to coax,*
*"Please try."*

*Disaster has not fully prepared me*
*Into what you feel.*
*The heartbreak I feel needs acts,*
*Not words of patietice and faith.*

*I need to see your perseverance,*
*Your daily courage.*
*I cry when you hit yourself*
*Knowing it is because you want so much*
*To be different than you are.*
*If only you could know of*
*Your inner spirit and*
*How beautiful you are to me.*

*We speak to each other without words*
*As we learn to care.*
*You look into my eyes now and*
*I see so much growing awareness,*
*If I am to help you,*
*I must look within myself*
*A red win the war that has torn all*
*My hopes and dreams for you.*

*Time will pass—an hour, a day*
*At a time.*
*I will not dwell on out, tomorrow*
*But will labor today*
*For the insight—the deeper—love,*
*And God willing*
*We both will find inner peace.*

## 8

To the delight of the children, Jack brought home a fluffy white rabbit. While he built a hutch in the backyard for our furry friend, the children held and cuddled their new pet. The rabbit hopped all over the yard, with Kelton following at a distance. Finally, he consented to hold a carrot in his hand and let the bunny nibble at it.

When the cage was ready, bunny moved in. Kelton couldn't stand seeing the rabbit locked up and constantly let it out. We gave up trying to keep the animal confined and Jack and Vern plugged up all the holes in the back fence. Now the bunny had the run of the yard as it hopped about entertaining us. The children named it Snow White and loved to hold it and feed it carrots. As the bunny grew, so did Kelton's attachment to it.

I sat on the back porch watching Kelton playing with Snow White when a large dog wandered into the back yard and took after the rabbit, barking his head off. I jumped up, grabbed a broom and chased after the unwanted intruder. I did not get to him in time. The dog had already snatched up the rabbit and gave it a thorough shaking. Kelton began screaming. I whacked at the dog with the broom with all my might until he let go of the poor bunny and fled. Kelton ran to the injured animal, picked it up and tried to make it stand on its hind legs. I attempted to get the rabbit away from him, explaining the bunny was hurt. He would not let me have it. Over and over, he tried to make it stand up. Sadly but firmly, I pried the rabbit loose from his clutching hands and put it in the garage. It was a sad experience for the children.

Snow White died, and we had her funeral in the back yard with the family attending. The children mourned the loss of their pet, and Kelton went through one of his worst withdrawal periods ever. Days went by before we could get him out of his silent, glassy-eyed stare. Unresponsive to our efforts, he would sit for hours and watch the tapes in the recorder go around and around.

It wasn't long after that, when we discovered that Kelton's cat was going to have babies, and we hoped that a litter of new kitten—new life—would bring him out of his far away withdrawal. But suddenly, the cat disappeared. We searched the neighborhood, calling her name, but there was no sign of her.

A week later, while moving some things in the garage, I came across a hassock with the lid closed. I heard a noise and a movement coming from it. When I opened the lid, and our cat leaped out, wild-eyed and skinny. She disappeared in a flash, leaving one little kitten behind. She must have eaten the rest her litter in order to survive, I thought with horror.

How did that cat get in there? I wondered. Kelton must have placed her in what he considered to be a safe place. He had learned a sad lesson from Snow White's death, and wanted to protect his cat from a similar fate.

True to the heart of a mother, the cat returned to take care of her baby, and Kelton came back to us as well, leaving his silent place behind. He took over the kitty, packed it around and played with it.

Because he spent most of the nights wandering around in the dark, both inside the house and outside, he never got enough sleep. We used every trick in the book to keep him in bed and help him to go to sleep. Perhaps, I pondered, he wanted this time at night to really be alone, to heal the wounds of the day with no one around watching him.

I had been awakened by footsteps crunching on the gravel outside our bedroom window. Kelton again, I thought. I put on a robe, quietly slipped out of our bedroom, went downstairs and looked outside. I could see him standing in the yard, a shadow among shadows. Familiar with the sounds of the night, at home with the stillness, he was as unreadable as the dark night.

As I watched him, I saw a new version of my son—something I had never considered before. *He was too sensitive for this world.* Somehow, I felt he knew and understood secrets of life and God's creation that most of us had not yet discovered. He was unaware of me as I stood in matching silence and reflected on our two worlds—his and mine.

There was a light rustling in the branches and a wide-awake owl hooted softly in to the still night. In delight Kelton mimicked the sounds of the bird's call, and boy and bird talked back and forth for quite a while. A great love for him flooded my soul. I asked God to help me avoid comparing him with other boys who seemed normal. "Help me to understand and accept him as he is. Help me savor the love that has filled my heart at this moment," I prayed.

But it seemed that each sweet and gentle moment with our son was followed by months of mischief and turmoil.

With concern and curiosity, I watched Kelton collect plastic bags. What now? He hoarded bread wrappers and plastic bags of all shapes and sizes. I opened the freezer to find eight loaves of bread dumped out, their protective plastic bags gone. Reprimands and punishment did not reach this child. I just had to wait patiently what he had in store for the bags, I didn't have long to wait.

There were three bathrooms in our house, two downstairs and one upstairs. Behind our backs, while we were busy, he stuffed his plastic horde into the toilet bowls, plugged them up and delighted in the waterfall that cascaded from the overflowing porcelain bowls onto the floor. To our dismay, there would be water dripping from the ceilings all of a sudden. Kelton had flooded the bathrooms. Again. And again.

I don't believe he understood that it was wrong. In his mind, in his world there must have been a different set of laws, and all we could do was to outguess him, to stay one step ahead—if that was possible? We stopped buying bread in bulk, and kept plastic bags out of his reach.

It was one obsession after another with Kelton. He went from taking the lawn mower apart to opening all the cans of food or removing the labels from the containers. Opening a can for dinner was like betting on the horses—we never knew who was going to win.

Jack was frustrated with Kelton's obsessions and their unpredictable results. We tried everything. Nothing we did brought about a change in his patterns. Some days the messes he created were more than I could take. I was grateful for my mother's presence and her helping hand.

Soon, his behavior pattern shifted again. This time I was quite disturbed and even more frightened, when I saw Kelton hitting himself. With his fist he would hit himself on the face and chest. At times he scratched his arms and face until they bled. The only thing that calmed him down was to remind him of all the things he did well. We let him know how much we loved him, that he was all right and we accepted him as he was. Sometimes our ways worked. At other times, only running fast or riding his bike helped to relieve the apparently unbearable tension and stress he felt.

We realized it was better not to react when he got upset, and to ignore what he was doing. I would talk positively to him without looking up or acknowledging the fact that he was hurting himself. (He rarely hurt others, only himself). When someone cornered him or hurt him, he did fight back and then run to escape further confrontations.

We worked tirelessly with Kelton through positive reinforcements, rewarding him when he did something right. We used the reward system—behavior modification—when he had done well, i.e., he could eat after taking a bath or he could ride his bike after his bed was made.

Before these tactics would work, we had to discover what was really important to him. We knew he treasured his shoes. To get him up and out of bed, I would take his shoes, leave his room and yell, "Get up Kelton, I have your shoes." That got him out of bed at once. I kept his shoes hidden until he dressed, brushed his teeth and was ready for the day.

But he was so smart! He started sleeping with his shoes on or hid them under his pillow. We were not always on target in our search for ways to teach our son, but most of the time we found a method that worked. We had one rule—use anything that gets results.

The biggest lesson we learned was not to show emotions around him. Even praise had to be soft-spoken, unaccompanied by a loving hug. For some one like me, who loves to hug and express love, not touching Kelton was hard. Our family went about touching and hugging each other, demonstrating how nice it was to express feelings for one another. But that was not for him—he remained aloof.

*You, are in another world*
*Wearing yesterday's mask.*
*We've been through this too many times*
*For me not to notice!*

*You are nature's*
*Winter child,*
*Going through a dormant time*
*When nothing outward*
*Grows.*
*It must be necessary*
*For balance.*

*I have learned to accept*
*Your seasons,*
*The lost moments*
*Of your winter.*

*After your cocooning*
*Comes the lifting of*
*Yesterday's mask,*
*Then the time*
*For transcending.*

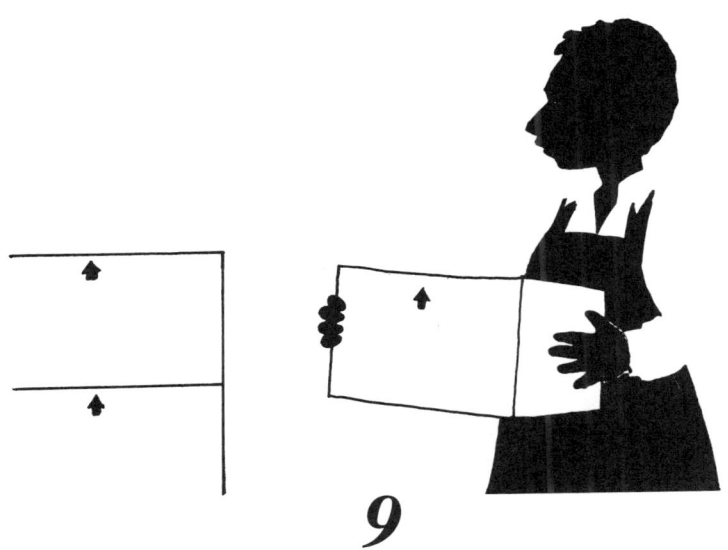

# 9

In my sleepless nights I listened to Kelton's nocturnal roamings around the house, wondering if there were any answers for my son, and if so, where could I find them? Prayer helped me the most, as I turned to God for strength and courage.

"It's your problem, Ranae," I screamed out loud one night, waking Jack. He just held me in his arms while I cried. I felt so alone and defeated.

Steady, quiet Jack worked two jobs and was as supportive of me as he knew how. Dealing with Kelton was beyond Jack's ability—he was at a loss about what to do. The strain began to show on his face and in his eyes. Things were left up to me. I felt old and weighted down with the responsibility of being in charge.

"God will just have to help me, I can't do it alone!" I demanded. Help would have to come from Him, it certainly didn't come from the people around me.

The two school teachers next door were an example of general ignorance and a total lack of caring. Instead of learning to understand our situation, they judged and condemned. They let us know in no uncertain terms what they thought of us and our incompetent ways. They insisted Kelton should be in an institution where he would be trained and watched over constantly.

Kelton sensed their dislike, and in his strange and mysterious way got even with them. It took us a while to realize what he was doing, and the discovery of his prank left us dumfounded, confused and exasperated.

We were awakened by a loud banging on the front door one morning. I jumped out of bed, ran downstairs and opened the door to find myself nose to nose with our next door neighbor.

"Just come and look what your son has done," the irate man greeted me without as much as a good morning.

I walked out in the yard with him. Without saying another word he pointed to his roof. To my utter amazement I saw a row of bricks arranged in a precise straight line on the edge of the roof, along with his morning paper. Just the day before, as they had for several years, these very same bricks had sedately edged the man's cement walks. Now, a gaping narrow trench yawned from where the bricks had been removed.

How in the world could this man have imagined that Kelton, a little boy, could have transferred the bricks form the yard to his roof. Bricks don't fly!

*But how did they get there?*

Before I gave the problem another thought, I yelled for Jack. He saw the dilemma, and without a comment, he quickly got the ladder out of the garage, leaned it against the house climbed up, took down all the bricks and piled them on the cement walk. He made Kelton return the offending hunks of baked clay to their appointed places, where once again, they formed the decorative border between lawn and cement.

Our furious neighbor warned us that this just better never happen again. We nodded our heads in mute agreement and went back into the house.

Our day had started. Kelton? How did he do it? Jack and I refused to speculate how the darn things had gotten on the roof.

We tossed a few hundred ideas and possibilities around like confetti on a parade, discarded all of them and came with a thought or two we didn't want to consider. It must have been a fluke. Surely it wouldn't happen again. Kelton remained uninterested in our talks with him about the flying bricks and went his way, shutting us out. I thought I saw a hint of amusement in his eyes. Kelton?

The next morning the bricks were back on the roof. We don't know how Kelton got them up there, but there they were in a neat row just like the day before. Whatever was going on apparently was not for us to know. Kelton knew. Just like he knew how to get on any roof, how to disappear and return; how to swim and ride a bike without a lesson; how to zip over eight-foot fences; how to take care of himself; how to unlock combination locks without the combination; how to take a lawn mower apart and put it back together—how—how—?

I almost slept on top of Kelton at night in order to keep him within reach. I set the alarm clock so I could get up at pre-dawn to catch my junior Merlin in his act. I never did. Every morning, for weeks, we were greeted by a straight line of bricks sitting on the edge of the neighbor's roof with the morning paper nestling cozily along side.

He never bothered anyone else on the street, but he had it in for the two teachers and their unaccepting attitudes.

For weeks, it became a regular morning chore to get the newspaper and bricks down from the neighbor's roof and return them to the ground before they woke up. We did not know what to do, and sometimes, in spite of my healthy curiosity, I did not want to know how Kelton did it. Jack tried to hold on to his sanity and I restrained my wildest imaginings.

Oh, the wondering that went on in my head along with worry and fear, and the acrobatics of my far reaching speculations. With no one to understand Kelton, the loneliness and frustration in my heart was unbearable at times. This heartache, this wonder, was my child, my winter's flower.

I suppose it would make into a Disney movie—like Chitty Chitty, Bang-Bang or Flubber, except that we were ordinary people and we did ordinary things and we had no magic up our sleeves— unless of course Kelton had something up his sleeve? Well, maybe?

My thoughts returned to the dreaded unknowns, the tomorrows and what they would be like? What would come next? When? How bad would it be? How...?

We never had to wait long.

One hot summer day, Kelton decided to wash the same neighbor's car. He used their hose to do the job. He stuck the garden hose through the car's open window and turned on the water. Before we discovered our busy little helper at his best, the water had reached the car's door handle. What an incredible mess. We had quite a time drying and cleaning the car, not to mention our song and dance to keep the owners of the car from tearing us apart.

Regardless of our efforts to keep the neighbor's wrath at bay, they were so angry that they prepared another petition to have Kelton put away. Fortunately, no one else on the street would sign it.

I felt sorrow and guilt when Kelton did these things yet at the same time I possessed a boundless sense of curiosity to find out the actual mechanics of his pranks or accomplishments— whichever they may be.

How to stop him? We were helpless. Again and again, I considered the workings of Kelton's world and recognized his unawareness of the right and wrong that dictated the acceptable behavior of our society.

Thanks to the efforts of the school psychologist and a lot of begging on my part, Kelton received special permission to attend kindergarten on a trial basis. If I thought I had won a round, I was proved wrong the day I took him to school. Kelton fought me all the way, and I left him crying among a bunch of happy Kindergartners in a bright and cheery classroom.

The tall chainlink fence surrounding the school yard was no hindrance to Kelton when he decided to escape; he got out of the school yard and walked away. No one noticed him—he was gone!

The police were out looking for him, and so were we. I should have known better. Just like Little Bo Peep who'd lost her sheep:..."leave'm alone and they'll come home..."

Kelton managed to elude all of us and found his own way home before we dragged in, worried and exhausted. That was the end of his 'formal' schooling. It was back to plan A, and pre-school at home.

I was disappointed that he wasn't able to attend a regular school—and again I picked myself up and started all over again. I dedicated my energies to helping Kelton get an education.

I looked for new and different sources of support and help that we had not tapped as yet, and discovered that the University of California at Los Angeles offered special training for special children. Six months later, I took Kelton out of the program which had done nothing but harm. UCLA's methodology was based on the reward system and—true to his nature—our son became conditioned immediately. It took several months to undo the results of that special training and convince him he would not receive a reward for the tasks he performed.

Although I had conveyed to the instructors at UCLA the methods that best worked for Kelton, it was apparent no one paid any attention to it. What indeed does a mother know?

Very much the same thing happened when he attended the speech clinic in Orange County. Well meaning as the program may have been, its method had set up such a structured environment for Kelton that he refused to grow. He became used to the limited routines which the 'professionals' performed the same way each day. The conditioning at the clinic presented new problems at home. Kelton had always resisted change and preferred the safe, structured ways which eliminated challenges and did not require effort or pain.

It became increasingly harder to teach him at home. I was at a loss whether to continue with therapy, or to teach him at home. My respect for trained, titled and seasoned professionals overshadowed my untrained and untitled efforts—even if they worked.

At the clinic he was given graham crackers and milk at therapy, and he developed an obsession for them. That was all he would eat for months. *Nobody would listen to me. No one would believe me.*

My frustration reached heights I did not know existed. "It's unfair. I'm always undoing someone else's mistakes," I told Jack discouragedly. "Why won't they try something new—give it a chance. Just because it isn't in their text books, doesn't mean it wouldn't work." I had had it with all the learned, single-minded hard heads. I would keep him at home in our little school. My system worked. I had learned it the hard way. I had on-the-job training.

Kelton and the two autistic boys at our pre-school became experts at putting puzzles together, and learned to interact. Kelton took part in some group activities, and as a result of the pre-school training, he improved markedly. Being around other autistics was good for Kelton. When the other boys would scream, Kelton would stop. When they would hit him, he'd back off. They became his mirror.

Kelton was a healthy little individual, but when he did get sick, he took care of himself. If he was sick to his stomach and made a mess on his sheets, without waking us, he would change sheets and put the soiled ones in the laundry room and go back to sleep.

He was amazing in many ways, and I had to remind myself that the right and wrong of our world did not compare to his—

whatever that was. All I had to do was stick to my guns, and as they say: *Be Prepared!*

I wasn't quite prepared for the next happening.

Kelton must have decided he wanted to cook. At six in the morning, when I got up to prepare breakfast, Kelton had taken over the kitchen. He mixed oatmeal, brown sugar, flour and water and distributed the sticky mixture not only in the kitchen but throughout the house. The kitchen was a wreck, and the rest of the house wasn't much better.

I was stunned.

"What's wrong, mother?" Sharlene asked when she came into the living room and found me sitting in a chair, crying. She hadn't been to the kitchen yet. I showed her Kelton's latest antic. I was fully aware it could happen again. After all, Kelton lived on routine and repetition.

Sharlene hugged me and patted me on the back trying to ease my heart.

"Look at it this way, Mom," Sharlene said wisely, "first we clean the counter, then the table, then the chairs, and then the floor and so on. We start with the table and make-believe it's the only thing that's messy. Don't look at the whole picture. It isn't so overwhelming that way."

*Since that time I have remembered to look at all trials I encounter in small parts—one thing at a time—one day at a time.*

*There's a silent child*
*Isolated,*
*Held in bondage.*

*He wants to be free:*
*That need keeps*
*Calling to me.*

*There's a clamorous child*
*Forcing my growth,*
*Creating pressure,*
*Stretching my limits,*
*But he wants to be free and*
*That need keeps calling to me.*

# *10*

People kept telling us that autism was a mental disease. I felt in my heart that it was physical disorder. After all, no one really knew much about the condition, my guess was as good as theirs.

A lot of time might go by before it would be discovered whose theory was right. In the meantime I had to do the best I could raising this child and learning how to deal with him from one experience to the next.

When Kelton was about six years old, I bought him two pair of blue boxer pants and matching shirts. He loved his tennis shoes and wore them most of the time.

Because he wore the blue outfits more than any other clothes, he became conditioned to them, and wouldn't wear anything else. I tried to get them away from him when he was asleep, but he screamed so long and loud that I finally gave them back to him. After he was asleep we'd remove his clothes to wash them. Once he woke up during this procedure and went into such hysterics that we had to put his clothes back on. He would have nothing to do with the clean outfit even though it was identical to the one he had been wearing. We had to get the wet ones out of the dryer and put them on him.

When we recuperated a bit from that ordeal, Jack held on to a kicking and screaming Kelton while I took off that darn blue outfit, and then threw both sets in the garbage. The garbage man hauled them away in his truck. As soon as the truck was out of sight, Kelton stopped crying, dressed himself in something different and acted as if nothing had happened. Try and figure him out!

I made arrangements with the clerk in a shoe store to bring Kelton in to buy a pair of new shoes. I explained to him that we would be buying leather shoes, and that Kelton preferred to wear his tennis shoes. I explained Kelton's condition, his obsession with his tennis shoes and his stubborn resistance to change. I also warned the clerk that Kelton would make a scene. The young man kindly agreed to help.

"Come on Kelton, we're going shopping!" I said. "You can help mom."

"Get in the car." He hopped in and off we went. I never mentioned that we would go shoe shopping.

"Hello, Kelton!" the shoe clerk greeted him cheerfully when we arrived at the shoe store. "You're getting new shoes!" Kelton started screaming on cue and tried to run away. Several people looked at me critically and began talking about us. It took both the clerk and me to get Kelton's shoes off and the new leather shoes on. As planned, the clerk held out a waste basket in front of Kelton, dropped the old tennis shoes ceremoniously into the basket and walked out the back of the store.

As soon as the salesman was out of sight, Kelton stopped crying, took my hand and led me to the car.

This child has to be forced to change in order to learn, I thought. But what an exhausting method. Did I have the energy to be that consistent? "I'll never get into a rut," I mused. Living with Kelton helped me to develop self-esteem and a total disregard for what other people thought about me. I was aware of their critical thoughts and their severe judgements. But that was their business. I had to live with this difficult child. I had to work with him. It was my responsibility coupled with my love to help this child grow and develop. The ones who talked did not have to raise him.

There were times it was necessary for me to be assertive, and demand that doctors and educators listen to me. I had to fight failure and guilt, and finally realized that the answers and the strength were within me, nowhere else. It was hard to understand and cope with daily life, but I did it. Tears and prayer were my best release. I learned quickly the fact that what one feeds thrives—be it negative or positive.

Thoughtless people would say cruel words. Once someone asked me, what I had done to deserve this? Another one assured me that all I needed was faith! This may have been the case, but I was looking for answers. I am certain these good folks meant well, but did not have the poise to offer their concern in a gracious manner.

After I got over the "Why me, God?" stage, I discovered I had learned some valuable things—things I would perhaps never have learned without the experience of raising Kelton.

I learned to love unconditionally. I loved Kelton when he was screaming, or when he withdrew. I loved him in the quiet moments when we communicated. I would fight for him as long as I lived. I had courage. I felt my own pain and saw his. I learned compassion, the ability to cry with those who hurt and to leave my own pain behind and move on.

I learned unselfishness, and respect for the space Kelton needed. I prayed for peace to heal my spirit. I fought bitterness, fear, and rejection. I had periods of being wounded, depressed, discouraged and angry. I learned that these feelings were born of guilt feelings I had picked up from others and given them reality. I was a good mother. I did the best I could and then some.

I learned to be patient with myself, and with the doctors who were just as much at loss as I was. I had periods when I would withdraw from the world, and stay away, caught in a web of false safety. It was a cruel world and I had too much to face.

My feelings of failure would pass eventually, and I would remember that the world is as we perceive it, reflecting the reality we bestow upon it. I changed my attitude, and the world became a place of love. I found people reflected what I felt about myself. Sometimes, I thought I had more to learn than Kelton.

"What am I doing here?" I'd ask myself. "What is all this for?" I had asked myself a million times. Then the quiet peace of God would embrace me, and I would know my purpose was to learn unconditional love. That's what this life is for…that's what it's all about.

Often, when I cried, Kelton would laugh. He would laugh out loud at occasions where laughter was out of place. Our children were angry with him when he laughed when they hurt or were sad. Like many autistic children, he laughed when he was embarrassed, nervous or afraid.

"Kelton has learned more than we have," I'd tell them. "He is the only one who can laugh at his troubles."

Before Allen was born, we had taken great pains to prepare Kelton for the new baby, but he gave no indication that he understood what was about to happen. Jack took Kelton along to the hospital to pick us up, when it was time for Allen and me to come home. In the car Kelton leaned over the seat and pulled the blanket back to see the baby. At the sight of his new little brother, Kelton threw himself back against the seat and started to cry. Large tears rolled down his cheeks. It was evident that he felt Allen had replaced his standing in the family.

"We love you too, Kelton," I said again and again. "Now *you* can be a big brother just like Vern. Would you like to hold the baby?"

Kelton shrank back in the corner of the car and continued to cry. Jack gently tried to console him, but the child would not be comforted. Finally Jack stopped at an ice cream parlor, and bought Kelton his favorite cone. Our troubled youngster stopped crying for the moment.

For the first six months of Allen's life, Kelton refused to be in the same room with him. We tried everything to draw him into our circle, but he stayed clear of his new brother, and basically withdrew from the family and the world at large. He roamed the neighborhood and explored a five-acre area that was at the end of our street. He preferred his own company to that of ours, and most of all, of his new brother.

When Allen was four months old, we took him swimming for the first time in the neighbor's swimming pool, a privilege we all enjoyed so much. In a short time, Allen was swimming under water from my arms to Sharlene, who stood about four feet away. Soon the baby was surfacing for air and swimming well. Kelton was fascinated with Allen's swimming, but still kept his distance.

We applauded and praised when Kelton jumped off the diving board and swam to the side of the pool. He liked jumping into the pool better than swimming, and bounced in and out of the pool.

One summer day I went to answer the phone in the kitchen. Allen was crawling around on the floor near me. Kelton was out in the backyard. Part of the yard was being prepared for a garden, and Kelton had been working for several days digging a large hole. Filling the hole with water had kept him entertained for days. I'd been talking on the phone for a few minutes when Kelton appeared in the kitchen; his face was white and he pulled on my hand. Sensing his urgency, I went with him at once as he led the way to the family room. Our sliding glass door was open.

"Where's Allen?" I asked, trying to be calm.

Kelton turned and fled out the front door. I ran out the

sliding glass door into the yard looking for Allen. Kelton had left the doors open, and Allen had crawled out and over to Kelton's big water hole. The baby had fallen in. My heart stood still as I saw Allen going under and coming back up again. I grabbed him, pulled him out of the mud hole with the speed of light, turned him face down, slapped him soundly on the back. His mud-covered body shook as he vomited up a stream of muddy water.

When I knew he was all right, I took him into the house and bathed him, grateful he was unharmed and equally glad he had been taught to dive and resurface.

With Allen taken care of, I looked for Kelton and couldn't find him. I quickly put Allen in the car and set out looking for his big brother. I came upon him about ten blocks from home—running down the street, as he always did when he was upset. I paced along side of him, pleading with him to get in the car, telling him everything was fine. He did not hear me and kept running.

I stayed by his side keeping him in sight, and let him run until he was too tired to take another step. When he dropped to the ground in exhaustion, I picked him up and drove home. He did not protest and seemed glad to see Allen.

When we got home, I had a long talk with Kelton. I praised him and told him how proud I was that he came to me when he saw his little brother was in trouble. I told him he had saved Allen's life. I also talked about the rabbit dying, and explained to him that Allen could have died, just like the  rabbit, if it hadn't been for him. From that moment on, he accepted Allen. I had won another round.

Strangely enough, Kelton filled up his hole with dirt, and never dug again. I was amazed how he had understood my words. So many other times he seemed not to comprehend at all. I always believed he was intelligent. I just had received confirmation of my belief. He was so much smarter than any of us gave him credit.

Never a day went by that I didn't look for signs of autism in Allen. There were none. He was a lively, loving, normal baby. Our gratitude was boundless.

When Allen began crawling, Kelton crawled around with his little brother everywhere he went. They crawled from room to room, with Kelton following behind. When Allen stopped to explore something, Kelton waited patiently, watching him. Allen loved Kelton, laughing and waving his arms when Kelton came into the room.

When Allen was older, he had only to reach for something and Kelton would hand it to him. It became quite a problem to keep things away from Allen. If my mother and the older children hadn't watched Allen and Kelton in their act, I may not have survived. It was just like having two toddlers around.

One afternoon I walked into the family room, and found Kelton near the blackboard pointing at the large red letter alphabet pinned above the board.

He was singing the sounds as we had done so many times in nursery school. I listened until he had finished reciting the alphabet, and ran up to him. I was so excited, I forget his dislike for affection for a split second, gave him a big hug and told him how proud I was of him. Wrong! He screamed and pushed me away. It was months before he would sing the alphabet again. In my excitement I had broken our rule of not expressing emotion around him. For some unknown reason it made him withdraw.

It was no wonder what with all my attention, energy and time going to Kelton, I was surprised when the time came when Sharlene and Vern had reached the age to take driving lessons. How come the years had flown by so quickly? Where had I been that I almost missed my two oldest grow into young adults?

Jack purchased an older car so our teenagers could practice driving without tying up the family transportation. Kelton jumped up and down excitedly as he watched his big brother and sister behind the wheel of the car as if he was applauding their latest achievements.

During the next few months, Kelton displayed a noticeable spurt of growth. He started coloring a picture, keeping within the lines, instead of scribbling all over the page. He still used only one color, but now it looked neat and orderly.

We were having success with his response to listening to recorded dialogue with questions and answers. When someone would ask him a question that was on the tape, he would answer them many times. He never gave a complete sentence in reply, but spoke in phrases, avoiding the pronoun "I", and using "you" in place of it—as if the person Kelton didn't exist.

It didn't matter, he learned. He was intelligent. He also showed a remarkable improvement in his living skills.

On a warm, lazy summer day, we were running in and out of the house with our things to load the car for a trip to the beach. By now, Allen was walking and was all over the place. We didn't notice when he left the driveway and walked down the street. I looked up and out of the corner of my eye, saw him toddle off, and started after him. Just then a car backed out of a driveway a few houses down the block. I screamed for Allen to watch out.

Kelton was further down the street, riding his bike. Suddenly he saw the danger, jumped off of his bike and shouted, "Allen get out of the way!" as he ran toward the moving car.

The driver saw Kelton running toward her, and stopped the car just short of hitting Allen. Kelton gently picked up his brother and carried him to safety.

We were amazed and shocked that Kelton had spoken a complete sentence, and reacted so swiftly to danger in a normal and adult fashion. For the second time, he had saved his younger brother's life.

I would always get my hopes up when something like this happened. But after each peak, each high Kelton reached, we were plunged back into the depth of disappointment when Kelton once again would withdraw into his own world of silence, and return to his rituals and his jumping.

We were still fighting the withdrawal affects from his drug therapy. It was a battle to keep him from taking gas caps off of the neighbor's cars and smelling the gas—anything to get the high the drugs had provided him. Nightmares were a common occurrence. Complaints from the neighbors were as frequent as was his running away episodes.

We were awakened one night by a pounding on the front door. Jack answered the door, and faced a policeman holding Kelton by the hand.

"Is this your son?" he asked.

"Yes," replied Jack.

"He's kind of young to be out at this hour." he said sarcastically.

"We thought he was in bed." Jack replied.

"We got a complaint from a man about two blocks from here. He found him fooling around with his gas cap."

"How did you know where to bring him?" Jack questioned.

"I just asked him to show me where he lived. He took my hand and brought me to this house," he replied.

Jack explained our unorthodox son to the officer, while I put Kelton back to bed. To say we were getting used to Kelton's shenanigans would not be true, but it certainly wasn't as horrifying as the first time it happened. We coped. We lived one day at a time—waiting and believing that this too would pass.

In the meantime my mother, my two sisters and brother had moved back to Utah. It had been a long time since we had been by ourselves as a family. It was great. I loved my mother and my little sisters and brother, they had been helpful and supportive, but it had been a strain to have that many people in the same house.

I wondered if Kelton missed his grandmother. He went about his life just as before not showing any signs of concern about her absence.

He was still enthralled with the turning and tumbling action of the clothes dryer. Unfortunately, he placed pieces of wood, shoes, toys, books and other items in the machine to watch them do their dance. Whenever I went to use the dryer, I never knew what I was going to find in its dark recess.

Once, I saw a dark object going around and around in the dryer. More than curious, I opened the door of the machine, and our cat jumped out. She was not pleased and streaked like oiled lightning through the house, not to be seen for days. Poor cat. It had not been a good week for her. She had been through a lot, including being thrown in the toilet. Kelton had popped her in the john, put the lid down and flushed the toilet over and over. He laughed for days about his deed and repeated over and over again, "Get the cat wet!"

I knew these acts were not an expression of cruelty. Kelton simply did not understand he might hurt and frighten the animal. The rights and the wrongs of our world just did not apply to his.

The cat would run away and hide for a while after one of its misadventures, but it always returned. There were many times when Kelton packed the cat around and was very good to it. The cat in turn, seemed to accept the bad with the good.

Kelton's "creativity" and his "research" projects never ceased to surprise us. However, it was unfair that he had become the scapegoat for our family as well as for the neighborhood. Whatever happened, whatever disappeared, whatever was broken— Kelton had done it. One day a man from the post office appeared at our door.

"The people next door have filed a complaint against your son, Kelton Steele, for tampering with their mail. Their letters had been torn into little pieces and stuffed back into the mailbox," the man said. He was referring to the neighbors who owned the 'flying' bricks and who had tried to have our son put away. The postal official went on to explain what a serious offense this was, "I don't know if Kelton did it or not," I answered. "He has never bothered mail before, but I'll watch him." I thanked the man for telling us and he went on his way.

The neighbors continued to find their mail torn up, but, no matter how watchful we were, we never caught Kelton in the act. We were visited again by the man from the post office, and received several threatening phone calls from the neighbors.

A few days later, a little girl who attended my nursery school, told me that her older sister had torn up the neighbor's mail. I talked to Wendy, who admitted she was the culprit. I informed the neighbor the real perpetrator had confessed, but it was hard to convince them. They preferred to believe that it was Kelton. However, their mail was never touched again.

Jack had gone to Spokane, Washington, to investigate a job with a brokerage house. We had come to love California and I hoped we would not move away from all the things we had come to like so much. But fate would have it otherwise.

Jack took the job. He felt it was a fine opportunity to earn a good living. After all, he did have quite a family to support. When he called, he sounded excited about the new project. He told me to put the house on the market, and he would come back to move us. This time everyone was quite upset about moving and the mood in the house was at a real low. I was fortunate to sell the house quickly and had most of our things packed and ready to go when Jack returned from Spokane.

I had a lot of faith in Jack's abilities as a salesman. He had proven that when he sold books to pay his way through college. But it would mean for him to go back to school which would give him less time with his family—for a while at least. But in the long run it would mean a better income, security and funds for the children's education. We did what we had to do, said good-bye to California and all the people we had come to love, and went on to the next chapter in our lives.

## 11

Okay, we're rolling," Jack shouted, as he put the huge moving truck into gear, eased the van down the driveway, and our little caravan was on its way east. He and Vern would take turns driving on the long trip to Spokane; Sharlene and I followed in the family car, towing our black Ford. Kelton rode with his father and brother in the truck, which pleased him to no end.

I had been tired and sick a great deal during this move. Sharlene shared the driving, with me, while Lynell took care of Allen in the back seat. I was just a little sad, knowing I would miss California and all its gifts. But I also knew I would adjust and enjoy whatever the future held. I have been practicing adjusting for a long time. The trip was uneventful and we were glad when we arrived in Washington and the long ride was over.

Mother and her family had been in Spokane for a while and were settled in a small, comfortable house. We stayed with her for a few days until we could move into our own place.

My sister Elma and her little girl were living with mother while Elma's husband served in Viet Nam. Having helped with the raising of my brothers and sisters, they have always been more like my own children. It was a happy reunion.

We were thrilled to see grandmother again, even Kelton showed his delight. His reaction to this move was better than the last one, but unfortunately he brought his problems with him. He remained quiet, yet enjoyed the special treats his Grandma fixed for him. I believe he had really missed her, even though he had shown no emotions at the time she left California.

We decided we would not live in the city, where we would have to explain ourselves to everyone around us. We were tired of petty neighbors, their critical eyes, their quick—to—judge minds and their lack of compassion and understanding. We rented a pleasant house in the country and kept looking to buy our own place as soon as we found one that would fit our needs.

Jack and I bought the boys a black and white puppy, which they named Candy. I had high hopes Kelton would take to this dog as he had to Ginger, but he ignored the puppy.

Candy became Allen's pet and followed him everywhere. Kelton's cat had disappeared before we left California, and when we presented him with a pretty calico cat, he fell in love with kitty at once. Calico-kitty took no nonsense from Kelton, and scratched him when he got too rough. Boy and cat seemed to have had a clear understanding.

Allen was destined to be the next explorer in our family, and he very cleverly convinced Kelton to open doors to the outside for him, Kelton followed his younger brother around, sometimes imitating him and laughing at him. The two adventurers would wander off and disappear. Candy displayed a great deal of smarts when she'd grab Allen by the seat of his pants trying to keep him in the yard. The dog was a great help in keeping track of the two boys. When Allen wandered into someone's backyard and was hidden by tall grass, Candy would lead me to his hiding place in true Lassie style.

The mystery to my feeling ill for several weeks was solved, when I discovered that I was pregnant again. Allen was a healthy and normal infant and would be two years old when the new baby arrived. I looked forward to having another child and worried less during this pregnancy about my baby being autistic. Not feeling well during most of the nine months, I rested as much as I could and had less strength to watch after the little boys.

One day I heard the front door open. I looked out the window and saw Kelton walking toward the front gate. When I checked on Allen napping in his room—I thought— I found his bed empty.

"Allen!" I called. No answer.

Kelton must have let him out the front door. Hurrying to the front of the house, I looked up and down the block calling for Allen, Kelton and the dog. I discovered Candy in the backyard— the boys had left without her.

Kelton appeared shortly from down the street, but Allen was not with him. I kept on looking, calling and searching, getting more worried by the minute. I had good reason to worry.

Allen had crossed the street and wandered into a pasture among several grazing horses. Unconcerned, he toddled around under the big beast's bellies. I ran toward boy and horses, keeping still for fear of spooking the animals. A double-wired electric fence kept the horses from leaving the pasture and at the same time kept me from getting in. I had to lie on my back and wiggled under the fence. I was seven months pregnant and must have been quite a sight as I snaked my way under the fence, trying unsuccessfully to be no bigger than string bean. I didn't clear the fence and received a few good jolts of electricity when my watermelon belly touched  the wire.

Scared silly but in one piece, I grabbed my baby from in between the horses' legs, and headed back for the hot fence, pushing and rolling Allen ahead of me. Needless to say, I hadn't gotten any thinner in the last few minutes and endured another set of shocks to my body, wondering what my poor baby must also feel. We made it back to the house and no one was worse from the wear and tear.

Wonders, miracles and turmoil never ceased in our lives.

We enrolled Kelton in a Catholic school which admitted children with special needs. The drive to school took about 40 minutes through heavy traffic, and I would have to turn around three hours later to pick him up again. It wasn't a pleasant drive in the heat of summer, and a lot worse on the treacherous winter roads. It was too early to tell how effective the school was. I knew Kelton did not like it there, but at least he did not run away.

Our first winter in Spokane was one of the most severe the city had experienced in years with a record snowfall and stubborn low temperatures. How I missed warm and sunny California as I bundled up kids in layers of thick clothing, boots and mittens and wished away the snow.

None of us liked Spokane at first. It was a very conservative town where people disapproved of change and were happy to keep things the way they were—quite a contrast to the ever moving-ahead-pace of progressive California. Sharlene and Vern had the hardest time adjusting to their new world, and we began to have trouble with our two teenagers.

After several months of diligent searching for our dream house, we found a place in the country and moved our family once again. The red Cape Cod sat in the middle of a beautifully landscaped garden. Trees and bushes concealed the yard from the road. Among the flower beds, shrubbery and trees sat a greenhouse and small green benches offered rest and repose. From our upstairs bedroom the garden looked like the picture of an English country scene straight out of *Better Homes and Gardens*.

"I may not like Spokane people as well as Californians," I thought, "but I like all the greenery, the trees, the shrubs and all the flowers."

A sturdy fence with secured gates offered us privacy and safety. I hoped we might be able to keep Allen and Kelton within the boundaries of our domain.

The house was a quality-built older home with lovely wood paneling, built-in book cases, fireplaces, shiny hardwood floors in the living room and dining room. A stairway flowed gracefully into the entry hall and climbed to three bedrooms and baths upstairs. Stairs led to the unfinished basement from off the kitchen. The basement could also be reached from an outside staircase in the breezeway which connected house and garage.

I loved my big kitchen with its roomy pantry, generous counters and cupboards, even though there were a lot of wasted steps between stove, refrigerator and sink. I needed roller skates to prepare a meal. When I voiced my concerns to Jack, he promised to make some changes, since the house required remodeling anyway. On top of being a fine businessman, he was also handy with tools and able to build anything he'd set his mind to.

Jack set to work immediately. He started in the basement, building bedrooms for Vern and Lynell. Since we had been married, Jack either had been going to school, starting businesses or holding down two jobs. This left me with most of the tasks and responsibilities for raising our family. Now, he would have more time for his family. Jack needed to know his children better, and the children needed to know what a kind and good man they had for a father.

Next, Jack put up a swing set and built a large sandbox for the little children. He bought a few rabbits. True to his nature, Kelton let the bunnies run free, prey to attacks from stray dogs.

There was a fish pond in the back yard to the delight of Calico Kitty who went fishing without a license when not hunting birds with equal gusto. The place was a little paradise for all of us—a gracious setting for people and creatures alike.

Jack and Kelton had a project of raising a rare breed of chickens who laid colored eggs. When Kelton gathered the small fragile eggs, he never broke any, but he constantly let the chickens out of their coop. One hen remained at liberty when she took up residence in a tall tree, while others became victims of hunting stray dogs.

We were always herding chickens trying to get them back to the safety of their coop. Kelton was amused by the frantic chasings and laughed and jumped up and down at our attempts to corner the runaways. Most of the time we ended up with a bunch of feathers in our hands and a bunch of balding chickens still on the loose.

While Jack built a new coop, Kelton spent hours watching his dad saw and hammer, Jack tried to get him to participate but Kelton wouldn't try anything until he first watched.

Eagerly, I watched for changes in Kelton's development, chiding, guiding, insisting in the never ending effort to draw this strange child into our world and into the reality of our lives. I kept up the battle, got a little tired but never gave up hope. It wasn't easy when I realized that little had changed except that he grew bigger and taller.

For long periods of time Kelton was content to just swing—back and forth, back and forth, lost in the hypnotic motion of gliding through the air. He still sniffed gasoline at times, acted strangely and seemed afraid of us, at other times, he withdrew behind the silent walls of his private world.

He did not enjoy school. I had to drag him and coax daily to make the trip to school. He would hide from me or run away when it was time to get into the car. It was very hard to know what was troubling Kelton when he wouldn't talk. His teacher encouraged us not to visit the school until he had better adapted to the new environment. Dutifully we stayed away, listening to the experts, doing what was best for our child. It took a long time to find out why he was upset with school.

Kelton was growing tall, broad-shouldered, very good-looking except that his teeth were protruding. We took him to an orthodontist for braces. Although he seemed all right during the procedure of fitting the braces, the next day he had pried them loose. Sharp edges were sticking out all over his bleeding mouth. I rushed him back to the dentist.

The agitated dentist couldn't understand how Kelton had pried the braces loose without hurting his teeth and removed the offending metal wires.

Next, we had his eyes tested and the doctor prescribed glasses. It was difficult to be certain if the tests were correct, because Kelton refused to talk and respond to questions. We told him how nice he looked in his new glasses. He seemed fascinated by the world he was seeing through them. When we walked into his school, one Sister took one look at him and said, "Oh you poor child." Great child specialists they were!

Kelton wouldn't wear his glasses after that. He broke one pair after another. After he had demolished the sixth pair, we never replaced them.

In our California home pre-school, Kelton had learned to print his name, write, recite the alphabet and name objects in pictures. In school, the Sisters made him write pages of K's in their attempt to help him improve his penmanship. From that time on, his writing consisted of nothing but K's. It would be several years before he wrote his full name again.

I encountered the same problem over and over again. *No one listened to me.* Professionals—from teachers to physicians to psychologists—refused to accept or even consider new methods of teaching that worked and had brought Kelton this far. I was beating my head against the wall of their 'educated' ignorant resistance. The method wasn't written up in a book, it hadn't appeared in a doctoral paper, it wasn't published in Reader's Digest. *It just wasn't—anywhere.*

Kelton related to photographs of objects better than drawings, and was creative and inventive in many ways. He could take things apart and put them together again since he was little. We encouraged his efforts and gave him things to break down and rebuild.

Once, Jack let Kelton paint the rabbit hutch blue. Left alone to do the job, Kelton—just like writing pages of the letter K—our son got carried away with the task and painted most of the garage blue. We also had a blue rabbit for a long time. If he kept at doing one specific chore for too long, it became an obsession with him. We knew that. After all, it did not take a degree to come to these conclusions, but every professional in the teaching and medical world had a real problem with the simplistic measure.

When a ventriloquist performed for the children at school, Kelton was fascinated by the talking doll. That Christmas, we gave him Pat, a ventriloquist's dummy. Kelton lugged Pat around with him everywhere, watching the mouth open and shut as he pulled the string, making him say words.

I let Pat talk to Kelton and tell him stories. Kelton talked with Pat and laughed with genuine pleasure. Unlike avoiding eye contact with people as was his custom, he looked straight into Pat's painted blue eyes.

I would send Kelton regularly on errands, but he rarely carried them out unless I forced. That meant taking his hand, going with him, and insisting he carry out my request. Sometimes, I just didn't have the time or energy to follow through, and Kelton got away with a lot. He never had to do his share of the chores, because he had learned to manipulate us into thinking he couldn't do them.

But with Pat around, he improved remarkably. "Kelton, go tell the kids to come and eat," I told him, "and hurry, before dinner gets cold."

Kelton left the kitchen with Pat in his arms, appeared in the living room where the children were watching TV. Pat's mouth moved to Kelton's words, "Come and eat."

Everyone clapped and laughed with excitement. He was so pleased with his performance that he continued to let Pat talk for him.

But he still used brief, clipped expressions. He could repeat any word spoken to him, clear beautiful words, but only a few got put together to make a complete sentences. He used just enough words to get by.

Mark, weighing in at nearly 12 pounds, was born after long, hard labor. My pelvic bone separated again as it had at Kelton's birth. I was weak and sick and stayed in the hospital longer than usual.

Our new son was a beautiful baby and a delight to all of us. Even Kelton loved this chubby brother, and spent lots of time just standing by his crib and watching him when we were out of the room. As if embarrassed by his affection for the baby, he ran away when we appeared.

I nursed Mark for a short time, and when I put him on the bottle, Allen, although he never had a bottle, would stretch out beside Mark, wanting to be a baby and have a bottle, too. Kelton didn't like Allen to be around Mark so much, I think he missed the company of his little playmate. I let Kelton feed his baby brother and I know he felt grown up and useful.

As soon as I was back on my feet, I visited Kelton's school. I was quite concerned about the fact that he was regressing. He refused to be taught at home. Each time I tried to get him to color or play, he ran away. I was sick at heart when I observed him sitting quietly in the school room, ignored by the busy Sisters, whose attention was directed at the noisy and rowdy troublemakers and the task of keeping a semblance of order. Kelton stared at the ceiling, crawled under the table, and behaved like a mentally retarded child. I cried all the way home.

He had regressed to his four-year-old level. He had been ignored at home as well. With Allen and Mark to care for, I had been too busy to notice that he rarely spoke. He had all of us well trained to give him what he wanted without making him ask for it. He was quiet, content in his own space, while I tried to manage my upside-down world of teenagers and the constant demands of two babies.

I immediately took Kelton out of school. There were no other schools available for Kelton. I let it be known at our church that I was opening a pre-school in my home. I still had all the equipment from the one I ran in California. I had enjoyed good luck with my previous enterprise and I prayed I would be successful again.

Ten children enrolled on the first day—more than I had expected and even wanted. School hours were from eight in the morning till noon, five days a week. During the four hours pre-school was in session, Kelton disappeared. As soon as the mothers had picked up their children and driven away, he showed up for lunch.

"Kelton, are you going to stay and help me with pre-school today?" I asked him one morning during breakfast.

"No!" he yelled and ran for the door. I was ready for him and blocked the way. He hit at me and tried to get past. I took hold of him, controlling my voice.

"It will be fun Kelton," I said, as we wrestled in the kitchen doorway. I held on firmly to my squirming and screaming child.

The pre-schoolers started arriving. Mothers looked a little worried as they watched Kelton kick and scream. For the first hour he continued to fight me. Finally I let him go and he streaked out of the room. I was exhausted and some of the children were beginning to cry. I settled the class down and proceeded without Kelton.

The next day Jack stayed home and made him stay in the classroom. Kelton was seven now, twice as big as the other children, and needed different training than pre-school.

In lack of something more suitable, I kept Kelton at our little school, but he would not participate. I did not have the success with him I had experienced before. He drew pages of the letter K, and colored whole pages using one color only.

I was downhearted, frustrated and slightly terrified of the future. What would life be like for this child—this child on his way to being a teenager, an adult? A man?

Once again the search for a school began. We were told of a college in nearby Cheney, where we might find help. We took Kelton to the special department at the college where he repeated all the tests and evaluations he had gone through so many times before. According to the teachers, Kelton was manipulating the tests. In spite of their evaluation, Kelton was accepted at the program.

Once a week I drove him to Cheney for speech therapy. It didn't help. Pat, the talking doll, did more than the trained specialists to help Kelton talk. There was nothing wrong with Kelton's ability to speak. His vocal chords worked well. He just did not find it necessary to communicate for whatever the reason, and that was the door that had to be unlocked. Was that possible? I didn't know.

Vern had gotten in with a tough bunch of boys at school and started lying to me, skipping school and smoking cigarettes. Jack had his hands full working with our oldest son to get him turned around. He found a job for him. Now Vern was able to save money for a car. The day finally came when he had enough in the bank to buy the original clunker that needed work.

Father and son spent Saturdays working on the engine and managed to get the car in good running order. I liked to watch the men working together. Vern was taller than his father now—both were slim and well-built and of a quiet and gentle nature. Despite the similarities, father and son were quite different. To add to our problem with Vern and Kelton, Sharlene skipped school and ran around with a rough bunch of kids.

It was not a good time for us. I worried about Vern and Sharlene and didn't like what they were doing. Instilling values and responsibilities had always been a top priority in raising our children. We were a close family. We did things together. We were there for each other. I couldn't understand this rebellion and their unbecoming and destructive behavior. I knew that children had to grow up and find their own space, but I thought they would chose a better friends and a healthy environment. All of a sudden I couldn't communicate with them any better than I could with Kelton.

We did the best we could. We worked with them and prayed that this too would pass.

We each had a motorcycle and spent many weekends riding up and down the mountains. Kelton loved the bikes. He jumped up and down and waved his hands waiting for a ride. It wasn't long before he learned to ride by himself.

The year Kelton turned eight, we enrolled him in the Garfield School for the Mentally Retarded. It had been a difficult decision to make. I felt so strongly that it was not the right place for him. What alternative did I have? Apparently, I was not able to teach him myself in the environment I created for him. It had worked three years ago, but it wasn't helping him now.

I had met with the teachers at Garfield and I was impressed with their commitment to the children and the quality of the programs the school offered. I enrolled Kelton and became active in the Garfield Parent-Teachers Association, and later served one year as PTA president.

Our PTA group worked diligently to get legislation passed which would help the disabled, and in 1975, President Ford signed a bill giving all handicapped children the right to an education. It was a step in the right direction, one battle won. I was glad I had been part of it.

Reflecting on the past two years, I couldn't help but count the heartaches. There was the nightmare of Kelton's drug therapy and the consequent horrors of withdrawal; the disheartening lack of progress he made, and the great void of understanding that waited for me like a dark cloud in the well-appointed consulting rooms of doctors and psychologists.

I had the feeling that we had taken one step forward and slid back three. The extra burden and worry of Vern's problems made my load almost heavier than I could carry. Almost! But carry it I did. What else could I do? Give up? No. There was too much good, whole and wonderful on this planet. I had to step out of my small world—troubled and painful as it may be at times—look at the big picture and see the wonder and the magic of it all, and live one day at a time.

I enrolled in several psychology classes at the college and became involved with training people in group therapy. I worked with Dr. Nelson and other physicians at the crisis clinic, and was trained in facilitating groups. I continued this work for the next five and a half years. It was a time of learning and personal growth for me which laid a solid foundation for expanding my own world and presented opportunities to help others.

Mark was walking. He was a cute, happy baby. He and Allen were great playmates and their big brother Kelton, a willing cohort in their adventures. The little boys would grab Kelton's hand and point to what they wanted and he would happily oblige them. Nothing was safe, and I had to get up early in the morning to keep up with their juvenile creativity. We enjoyed the boys so much.

Autumn came, and the trees on our land shed their golden, red and brown leaves. We raked them into huge piles to the delight of the boys who found a new playground in the fragrant, rustling hills of fall foliage.

This year we decided to burn the leaves instead of hauling them away. The fire fascinated Kelton, who danced up and down around it, waving his hands until the last ember died. He quickly found some sticks to toss on the embers to keep the fire burning. When at last all the leaves were ashes, Kelton still wanted a fire.

One morning something woke me earlier than usual and I felt uneasy. I got dressed quickly and hurried downstairs. I checked Kelton was not in his room. Something was wrong, yet everything looked right. I walked into the kitchen which was as neat as I had left it the night before. Then I saw smoke coming up from under the door that led to the basement.

*Vern was asleep in his bedroom in the basement.*

My loud yells of "fire, fire" got Jack out of bed and like a streak of lightning sent him running out into the breezeway to open the secondary basement door, so the fire wouldn't spread from the burst of oxygen created by the opening of the inside door.

I dashed out the back door, hooked up the hose and turned on the water. Smoke poured out the back door from the breeze-way.

"Jack," I screamed, "What's going on? Are you all right? Can you get to Vern?"

"Bring the water," he yelled back. Pulling the garden hose behind me, I ran through the smoke, down the stairs.

One entire wall looked like it was on fire. I turned the hose on it. Coughing and gasping for air, Jack rushed by me, guiding Vern upstairs. We were able to put out the fire without the fire department. We opened all the windows and cleaned up the mess. It was more mess than damage—one scorched wall, lots of ashes on the cement floor, and a heck of a scare.

We discovered that Kelton had gathered newspapers and built a fire that had spread to the wall. We were very fortunate that we caught it in time; it could have been a disaster. Our fear was real and well-founded considering that fire could develop into a new obsession with Kelton and he could set fires at random—everywhere.

We found him down the street and brought him home to show him what his fire had done. Jack and I talked to him at great length, explaining the danger of fire, how it could burn everything, everybody, even the animals, wondering how much of our explanations and reprimands would sink in.

We had spanked Kelton before, but never hard. Jack took off his belt and hit him once across the back of the legs, telling him if he ever built another fire he would receive an even harsher punishment. Kelton screamed and ran away, avoiding us the rest of the day.

The next day we found Jack's belt cut up in little pieces. Every time Kelton was hit with a spoon or fly swatter, we found the offending object broken to bits, If we bought replacements, he destroyed them promptly.

We were all on fire watch in the days to come. Finally, we relaxed our vigil a bit thinking we had made an impression on Kelton. But several months later, I woke up and thought I smelled smoke.

At that same moment Jack yelled, "Wake up Ranae, quick! I smell smoke!"

We rushed down the stairs to the kitchen. A cereal box on the counter was burning, and in horror we watched flames leap to the cupboard above. Smoke was pouring out of the toaster. We grabbed towels and beat the fire out. The cereal box fell off the counter onto the floor. The house was filling with smoke. Coughing, we opened the windows and doors, and went in search of Kelton.

We called everyone to the kitchen and tried to find out what had happened. It was simple. Kelton had evidently tried to make toast. The bread probably got lodged in the toaster and finally burst into flames. The nearby cereal box caught fire, and the flames spread to the cupboard.

At that point, Kelton ran away, afraid of the consequences. We talked to him, explaining he needs to come to us when there was trouble. Kelton looked at us fearfully, wondering if we were going to spank him. He kept yelling "No! No! No!" over and over.

I told him we didn't punish for accidents, but I was disappointed he didn't come and get me when there was trouble. We talked about fire again and how it could hurt us. I also made him clean up the mess.

He learned his lesson well, which was a great breakthrough. Fortunately for all of us, fire did not become one of his obsessions. We were more than grateful, we could all have been killed. We kept a watch on him for years, always afraid he might forget and start another fire, but it never happened again.

# 11

My sister Karla came to live with us for a while—something she had done off and on all her life. Vern, Sharlene and Karla were close in age and shared many interests. Lynell was eleven and a great help with Kelton and the boys. The older children accepted Kelton and included him in some of their activities. They took him to the movies, they went roller skating or bowling together, and he was happy to be with them.

When Vern would tease Lynell and the two would start yelling and fussing at each other, Kelton became agitated and hit himself. The children would stop their squabbling immediately and tried to calm him down. His space was one of peace; loud noises and the sounds of his brothers and sisters fighting among themselves disturbed him deeply.

He still needed a lot of quiet time. He wouldn't take part in family talks or watch TV with us. He joined us for our meals and would retreat to his room as soon as he had finished eating. He was shy, and avoided people. Nevertheless, we continued to involve him in our activities. We took him roller skating, which he enjoyed and learned to do quite well. He swam in the river, which was only a few blocks from our house, jumping off the bridge like the older kids did. But he always kept apart, alone, and silent. He never spoke, only echoed words spoken to him.

When he was ten years old, he started riding the city bus to town. We made arrangements for him to go to the Spokane Mental Health Care Center after school, and return home on the city bus. We met with the bus driver, acquainted him with our son and told him where he had to get off the bus. The driver would stop on the corner nearest to our home, and Kelton jumped off without ever being told. He knew exactly where he lived. After all, no matter how far he had wandered, he always found his way home.

One night, the regular bus driver was ill and a substitute drove the bus. The man did not know that he had to stop at a certain corner and kept driving with a silent boy sitting quietly in the bus, staring out the window. Kelton got off at a stop across town. He had never been there before and it was getting dark.

When he didn't come home we got worried. I called the clinic and they called the bus service. The driver remembered the silent passenger getting off across town—far from our home.

Jack and I jumped in the car and went searching for Kelton, but we couldn't find him, Tired and worried, we returned home only to find him safe and sound in the living room. One of Sharlene's girlfriends recognized him walking down the street and brought him home.

"He was headed in the right direction anyway," the young lady informed us.

Our commuter continued riding the city bus. He never talked to anyone on the bus, and knew exactly when to get up from his seat and walk to the front as the bus neared his stop. It was very important for him to experience a sense of freedom and get release from stress and tension, which he accomplished by riding his bike with the wind in his face following his roaming spirit. He took longer and longer rides, sometimes as far as to the busy highway. Worse than that, he would get onto the highway and race cars. Usually, he was picked up by a policeman and either taken to the police station or brought home. We had to take his bike from him for a while, until we felt certain he understood that there were places he could not go. The highway was one of them.

Kelton would discover new and different things just like any curious child would, only in his case his behavior was termed unorthodox, as were his actions. Trouble followed his explorations like the proverbial thunder followed lightning.

Whenever I felt down and depressed, I only had to think of how many hurdles and boundaries our child, our winter's flower, had to overcome. There were times kids threw rocks at him, spat on him and called him a "retard." He learned to avoid them by riding on little-used trails in the woods—finding safety and solace in loneliness.

Kelton's brothers and sisters may have teased him or shifted the blame for their deeds to him, but let a stranger attack their brother, and they would form a solid front of defense. Quite a few battles were fought over Kelton, which usually ended with beat-up neighborhood kid swearing he'd never do it again.

Our problems with Vern were not over by a long shot. He was more involved than ever with the wrong kids on the block. He lied to us, he smoked cigarettes and was using drugs.

I had so many band-aids on my breaking heart, I didn't know there was room for even one more. I fell apart. I really didn't know if I could survive another child on drugs. For most of Vern's life our attention had been upon Kelton and the countless problems that kept us occupied—looking for answers, dealing with Kelton's pranks, and spending long hours to teach him something new, or to help him unlearn whatever was destructive or unproductive.

There had been the long battle with drug therapy and withdrawal from it; the emotional struggle to understand and cope with autism; the years of trying to get him to talk; fighting one obsession after another. The years where our energy was directed to Kelton had taken their toll on the other children. Now I was losing another son to a world I didn't understand. Heavy with guilt, I blamed myself for losing touch with Vern.

Jack made every effort to reach Vern, but our oldest son shut us out. For the next two years, Vern got himself from one trouble spot into another—we fought drugs, alcohol and the law. Vern's unexplained absences from home were as long as two weeks at times. I spent hours on my knees, pleading with the Heavenly Father to show me the way to reach my son. Vern had become a stranger to me, as remote and uncommunicative as Kelton.

I thought of all the goals Vern once had. Baseball was his life. He had been a star in Little League; he wanted to be a pro. I thought about how hard he worked his paper route to help out with the family budget when money was tight. How had we lost him? Kelton was still our great concern, but Vern had become our priority.

With Dr. Nelson's counseling, we tried to support Vern and accept his problems. Jack spent more time with his oldest son, and we made it a family project to let Vern know we loved him.

Feeling the strain and lack of harmony in the family circle, Kelton reacted in his way. To our great dismay he would beat himself and scratched his arms and face.

One day, Kelton came into the kitchen and caught me crying while getting supper on the table. Vern had not come home from school. When I called the school I was told he hadn't been there for three days.

"Don't cry, mother!" Kelton yelled.

Startled by giving voice to my display of sadness, I stopped crying, looked up at Kelton and said, "I'm okay, Kelton; I really am."

"Don't cry, mother!" he yelled again, hitting himself in the face.

Alarmed, I quickly dried my eyes and talked calmly to him, telling him he was good and that lots of people loved him. He hit himself over and over, and then began to dig his fingernails into his arms. I walked toward him, and he ran outside, screaming, "Don't cry! Don't cry, mother!"

I didn't run after him. Experience had taught me to leave him alone in his struggles. He usually worked things out best when he was off by himself.

Kelton's upset was the final straw. I wondered if I could cry any more tears. I had studied psychology, attitudes and behavior over the last few years, looking within myself, trying to find me. Somewhere I had gotten lost. I didn't have an identity anymore. Who was I? Why was I standing in the kitchen, numb, hating my children, hating myself, wanting to run down the road screaming like Kelton?

But I didn't run down the street screaming. Maybe I should have let it all out as Kelton did. But I just stood there, letting the feelings pass through me, like water flowing through a sieve. Negative feelings rose to the surface first, like so much flotsam from a shipwreck. I would have to send them over the horizon of my self-imposed limitations and make room for positive thoughts.

I became still and let it all flow through and out, and then went on to find the many me's hiding inside. I chose to feel the moment, then consciously choose to which feeling I was going to respond.

When I first practiced this quiet, private time a few years ago, I felt trapped by feelings of frustration, feelings of fear, feelings of love and of hate; resentment of never being me, with no time to be my own person, to write poetry, to be creative, or to just dream.

I thought I would never overcome these feelings. But eventually, I realized they were based on two emotions: love and fear. When I faced my feelings, they became more positive.

After admitting I sometimes hated my children, felt trapped in my house, and was resentful of my husband being gone so much, I usually felt better and became more positive. "Accept reality as it is now," I told myself. Anxiety had become my reality; anxiety over Vern, over Kelton, and Sharlene.

"Don't fight it, Ranae, deal with it," I told myself. "I'm not a bad person for hating my children—or rather hating what they are doing to themselves," I thought. "I feel badly; I hurt inside. I am fleeing from something I don't want to look at—something I want to run from."

"Don't let the fear control you Ranae," I spoke out loud. Some days I literally had talk to myself to remain in control. "Act out of love and respect for yourself, live from the inside out, not from the events on the outside. The way to help your children is for you to help yourself right now."

Sometimes the only way for me to find out how best to handle a situation was to be patient and wait. I would get busy cooking, cleaning or writing. Sometimes it seemed that sewing was best thing to do. The moment I started to give my actions direction, my feelings became clear.

I was upset with Vern and Kelton because there is something in me I had misunderstood, I had to learn to accept whatever it is. I could not judge Vern, Sharlene or Kelton. A judgment of them left out that which is unique about each one. It is my interpretation of what they did that produced the pain. They were not communicating or sharing their feelings, so I could understand them better.

"I know that we all are ever-changing—no one remains the same. I am going to see this through. I am in a state of learning and always will be," I counseled myself.

"The reason for feeling insecure about my children stems from my lack of self-knowledge. I don't know how to handle situations when they don't agree with my preconceived ideas. I must show more respect for the way I am. I'm not perfect. I am so uninformed about what is going on inside my children that I believe them to be wrong. I don't understand. I'm not seeing the world as they see it. My fear comes from only seeing part of the picture."

I kept up this dialogue with myself, and discovered I was good company, and I would learn more about the many me's the more I talked to them.

Life went on.

From the upstairs window, Kelton liked to watch the cars and people going by. We never found him on the roof of this house. To look out of the window was all he wanted.

One day he was upstairs, Allen and Mark were in their bedroom taking a nap, and I was downstairs sewing. The little boys had been watching us paint Sharlene's room the day before.

The paint and brushes were on the closet shelf waiting for to apply the second coat of paint. Allen told Kelton to get the paint down, get the brushes from the shelves and open the can. He followed Allen's instructions and the boys painted the bed covers, the suitcases, the floor and themselves.

"What is that all over you?" I asked Kelton when he came down the stairs.

"Boys!" he answered. That was enough of a cue for me and I ran upstairs to find Allen and Mark busy at their task. Paint was everywhere.

"What a mess!" I cried. "Sharlene is going to die when she sees this!" I was right.

Angry and upset, she chose this incident as another excuse to further estrange herself from us.

Our family was not holding together, and I didn't know what else I could do, but keep on loving and caring and praying.

# 13

Sharlene was 17 years old and dating a fellow who had not earned our approval. She began skipping school to be with him. She lent a deaf ear to our efforts to talk her out of seeing this boy, and against our wishes, quit school and announced she was getting married.

I cried on the day of her wedding. I had wanted so much more for her, as I did for all my children. I wanted to make the wedding a memorable occasion for my oldest daughter, and I was glad when all the preparations turned out well. Everything looked festive and pretty. Kelton, Allen and Mark looked so cute dressed up in their suits. They were excited about participating in the ceremony.

As I watched the young married couple, my thoughts were heavy and I prayed my dark thoughts would not take on reality. Perhaps this marriage would work.

I wished I had forgotten my dreams and enjoyed my kids more. Time goes so fast—one day they were children and the next day they were getting married and leaving home. I felt I had been left behind somewhere in time and lost touch with who these young adults were. I learned a lesson that day. Dreams do not exist in the future, nor did I. I had to deal with today, enjoy the now, be of some value and be happy for Sharlene. "I must listen to you, Sharlene, not to myself. It is important what you want, not what I want for you." She would have to learn about life, about herself her way, on her time. I couldn't do it for her or any of my children.

Kelton missed having his big sister around. She had taken care of him all his life, and he looked to her for love and encouragement. He never stopped telling us to "Go get Sharlene."

To keep up with the swift passing of time, my youngest brother, Leon, got married also. Here was another "child" growing up and growing away to be on his own.

My mother's health had not been good for years, and I worried about her a lot. Between Karla and mother there was such an age difference that it had created a noticeable generation gap, and Karla spent a lot of time with us or with our brother, Mont. She had lived with us so much she was like my own daughter.

Mark was two when I went into the hospital for a hysterectomy. Kelton and Allen went to stay with grandma. Kelton reacted to change better than he used to, but a different routine and strange surroundings still affected him. He hit himself a lot while I was away.

We knew Kelton was not attending the kind of school that was right for him, but Garfield School was the best we had been able to find. Discouraged, I felt Kelton was just putting in time. He would advance in some areas, both at home and at school, and then regress. The pattern of one step ahead and two steps back still haunted his progress, and dashed our hopes for a more lasting development of his living skills.

It was Kelton's task to mow the grass, a job he liked. He put gas in the mower and took care of the job all by himself. Then one day, he quit mowing the lawn in the proper manner and ran over pine cones and sticks to watch them fly out from under the machine. We looked at his refusal to keep on with a job he had performed so willingly for a long time as a sign of boredom.

But what job could we give him to take its place?

The same pattern emerged at school. He would do a task for a while, sometimes only once, then became bored. He acted as if he didn't comprehend the task. Not understanding Kelton, the teacher would keep him doing the same thing to get it right. Consequently, he regressed. Without challenges, Kelton did not learn. Why wouldn't the teachers understand that?

"He is a very complex boy!" one teacher remarked. "He is hard to figure out. One day you are convinced he is really retarded, then he will do something that tells you he is probably smarter than you are in some areas. He's a puzzle."

No kidding!

Kelton spent a great deal of time wandering around in the woods, day and night. He preferred to be out at night, as if the darkness and stillness gave him the peace he needed.

In answer to our prayers, Vern settled down and decided he wanted to graduate from high school. He went back to school, kept his nose to the grindstone, and graduated. We were very proud of him.

Unfortunately, we didn't see much of Sharlene in those days. We all missed her presence in our home. Kelton was especially lost without her; she had always taken him so many places.

Lynell turned thirteen and was quite a beautiful young lady. She did a lot of things with Kelton. He wanted to belong and be part of her activities. Not everything suited his nature, and when he felt uncomfortable in a situation, he retreated.

The children tried to find games he could play. In the summer they would play in a hay field next door. They made a circle by stomping down the hay and built connecting tunnels going out from the free zone. The person who was "it" had to catch the others. Kelton loved the game. He was never caught, but he refused to be "it."

He responded similarly to other games and wanted to play by his own rules. Kelton's version of baseball was to bat the ball high and wide then refuse to run the bases.

He continued to learn, but his progress was slow. It was a blessing that I kept a diary. On the days when I was discouraged, I would read my entries from the beginning. Only then could I see just how far he had come. The days of screaming and obsessive actions were nearly gone, and so was his complete withdrawal. Now, he would retreat to his room or go outside; his eyes were not glassy as often, and he would answer us when we spoke to him.

Minute as these changes may have been, they were steps forward and revealed a definite pattern of growth. I was grateful for every little bit.

Through our church I did some counseling, working with troubled families and single parents. Regardless of the fact that I was volunteering my services, working with people in need and my continued studies were fulfilling experiences. At the same time, I was learning a lot about myself I only wished I could help Kelton the way I was able to reach other people.

Maybe that time would come, too; I just needed to be patient—something I had practiced a lot.

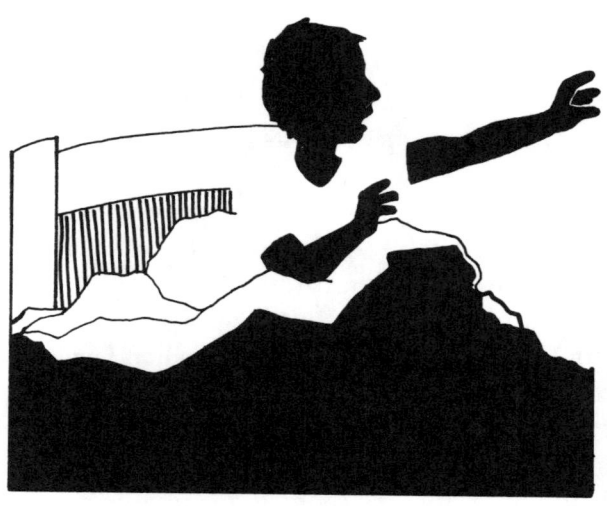

## 14

It was true, of course, that Kelton was a complex person. On one hand he hated change, on the other he loved travel and exploring. He was a hard one to figure out. Over the years we learned to do things with him in different ways, at different times. It was a good program because it allowed him to become more flexible. So when we made travel plans one summer, I was not concerned with Kelton's reaction to going places.

Each year we took at least one trip to visit Jack's parents in Paradox, Colorado—a small town in the western part of the state, near the Utah border. The children enjoyed the visit with their grandparents, and Jack's folks always looked forward to seeing our family. I was glad Kelton took the announcement of the upcoming journey as good news. But the events of the trip turned out to be a hardship for all of us.

One June morning, shortly before we were to leave for Colorado, the telephone rang. It was bad news. Jack's good friend, Fred, and two of his children had been killed in a plane crash on their way to Fred's father's funeral in Paradox.

The news of the tragedy was devastating for Jack. We packed our things, piled in the car and immediately left for Paradox. Jack and Fred had grown up together and their families still lived in the sleepy, small western town.

In the hot, dry desert outside Moab, Utah, our car overheated. Jack pulled off the road, opened the hood and was wrestling carefully with the radiator cap, when the force of the steam blew the cap into the air. The built up steam shot out from the radiator and burned Jack's arms and hands. Kelton began to laugh hysterically, yelling, "Burn Dad!" We knew that laughter was sometimes his reaction to being frightened.

I soaked several small towels in the ice water from our cooler and put them over the burns on his arms, then filled the radiator with water. When the car cooled down, we continued on our way.

Jack was in a lot of pain. As soon as we pulled into Moab, we went to see a doctor. Jack had second degree bums on both his arms and on one hand. He was hurting. Our car acted up the rest of the way. We had to slow down several times. We made it to Paradox barely in time for the funeral. It was a terribly sad day, and as I stood by the four new graves, I counted my blessings having my husband and children by my side.

It was a rare occasion that Jack and I had an opportunity to spend time alone together. During our brief stay in Colorado, we took off one day by ourselves and visited the old places of his childhood. He shared his early memories with me as he talked about growing up. I had never seen this side of him before. I ventured with him through his dreams, watching the unfolding of his life. It was a rare and golden day where all cares were put aside and the moment held us in its warmth as we read from the pages of the past and opened wide the door of understanding to each other. Jack and I savored the time we spent together.

I loved Jack's family. They were easy to be with and accepted Kelton just as he was. They respected his fight to his own space and the time he required to be alone. He hid from people during most of our visit at their house. It was almost as if he used the hours of solitude to heal his emotional turmoil. This world was a foreign place he didn't understand. Some days, his mind seemed to race from one thought to another, his frustrations deepened, and he would withdraw to get in touch with the now of feelings inside.

At times when my own frustrations reached a dangerous high, I followed his example. I could feel a force from within quietly directing my steps. It was not always necessary for me to go over my past experiences, it was enough to just listen and be open. I could then be more spontaneous, more courageous and able to function in the present.

We left Paradox saddened by the events and strengthened by the moments we had together.

We arrived back in Spokane hot, and tired, but in one piece. We had hired a neighbor boy to water the grass during our absence, and everything in the yard looked well kept. What we didn't know was that hornets had built a nest right smack over the front door of our house. The neighbor boy told us later that every day he had turned the hose on the nest, hoping to break it down or dislodge it, so the hornets would go away.

We pulled up in the driveway, the children got out of the car and went around the house to the backyard to sit in the shade. Vem and Jack unloaded the car and joined the children, using the back door. I made some sandwiches and opened the front door to bring our lunch in the yard. Opening the front door must have created enough of a vibration to dislodge the nest and knock it to the ground. In a split second, wild hornets swarmed over me before I realized what had happened. I dropped the tray and screamed as they crawled into my clothing and hair, biting and buzzing furiously.

Kelton was nearby, and watched as the winged stingers swarmed around me. A wasp separated from the swarm, landed on Kelton and stung him. He screamed over and over, "Kill the bees!" and ran to the far end of the yard.

In a flash, Jack got the garden hose and turned the water full blast on me. Frantic, screaming in pain and terror, I ripped off my wet clothes which were crawling with hornets, while trying at the same time to ward off the deadly stings of the relentlessly attacking angry hornets. I felt like I was choking to death. Within minutes my face puffed up like a balloon. Jack threw a blanket over me and rushed me to the nearest hospital—not a moment too soon. I was given an antidote for the deadly effects of bee stings, and a bit of friendly advice to go home and rest.

Late that night, lying quietly beside my sleeping husband, pain and terror were slowly fading away. I reflected on the week which had brought us one calamity after another. I wasn't going to get trapped in the folly of looking for answers, instead I managed to be grateful about where we were *now, here—at the moment.* I finally settled down to sleep. But all night long I would wake up to hear Kelton talking in his sleep, yelling, "Kill the bees, kill the bees."

He was afraid of bees from that time on. If a bee came around, he wouldn't rest until he had killed it. I understood, we both had had a bad experience.

The next day I was sick. I rested a great deal during the day, but I could not sleep. The antidote to the bee stings kept me wide awake. I wandered around the house most of the night, alone with my thoughts.

The years had flown by. Sharlene, Vem and Karla were grown up. I wished I could stop worrying about them. I wished they would learn from the experiences of others. I also wished I could accept the choices they had made for their own lives. I so wanted them to be happy and productive.

Lynell was the middle child, feeling cut off from her older brother and sister, and left out by the younger children. We talked a lot about life, and she tried so hard to avoid making mistakes. She was devoted to her father. In the evenings, when he repaired watches, she almost always visited with him while he worked.

My thoughts turned to Allen and Mark, two delightful children, who had brought laughter and sunshine into our lives..The brothers had formed a loving friendship and played together constantly. They loved and accepted Kelton as a compatriot, a tall brother who could reach goodies in high places and open doors.

Jack, who had been so busy all these years, was able to spend more time at home and was getting to know his children a lot better. I realized with a start that because of our busy lives, I didn't know Jack as well as I wanted to either. I was thankful for the hours we had shared in Paradox, and the fact that he had come into my life. I had never known a man of such complete goodness.

I was filled with love and thanksgiving for the many blessings that had come my way. We now had the time to really get to know each other, and Jack could spend more time with his kids.

When we got Kelton into Garland School, I closed my nursery school and I had more time to myself. Karla was getting married to a man she had met in Arizona, and I was working on a quilt for her as a wedding gift. It was as a perfect time for me to do nothing but sew.

Lynell had taken over the responsibility for running the house and children while I was busily sewing. Jack had returned from work, headed for his favorite chair and promptly fell asleep; it had been a hectic week.

We were preparing dinner when Gene, a friend of Jack's called. We had bought a new canoe, and Gene suggested he and Jack take it out on the river near our house. Before I could say anything, Jack was loading the canoe on the top of the car.

"I want to go, too!" pleaded Allen.

"No one can go this time," replied Jack, "the river is too high from the spring runoff. It's too dangerous."

"Then you shouldn't be going either," I remarked, alarmed.

"We will be okay. I'll be careful. You know I'm a good swimmer," he assured me. He kissed us all, and I watched as they drove off—two grown men as excited as two young boys trying out a new toy.

During the long evening I continued sewing. Lynell put the boys to bed, then came downstairs to talk to me.

"It's been a crazy week!" exclaimed Lynell. "I hope life settles down now."

"Don't count on it," I replied. "But it would be nice."

"When is dad supposed to be coming home? It's almost ten o'clock," Lynell sounded alarmed.

"I don't know, I've been worried for the last two hours. I hope they're all right," I said.

"I hope they didn't go up above the rapids. They're really bad this time of year," Lynell added.

About a quarter to eleven I tried to call Gene's wife, Sherrie, to ask if she had heard from the men. There was no answer. Just as I put the phone back on its cradle, there was a knock on the door. Lynell went to answer the door. Two policemen stood in the doorway.

"There's been an accident," one of them said. "Is your mother here?"

I walked up behind Lynell. "What kind of accident?" I asked. Terror filled my chest. I was having trouble breathing.

"Is your husband's name Jack Steele?" the policeman asked in a businesslike tone.

"Yes!" I almost screamed. "What's wrong?"

"Apparently your husband's canoe tipped over in some rapids several miles from here. One of the men swam to shore.

Your husband stayed to try and save the canoe. We haven't found him yet."

I tried to speak, but no words came. Lynell put her arm around me saying, "You go with him, mother, I'll stay with the kids."

I slipped into a jacket and followed the officer to his car. We drove in silence to the river. Several cars were there with their lights on while people searched up and down the shore.

Someone hugged me; I recognized her.

"We heard about Jack on the news!" she said. "My husband is helping in the search."

Gene came over to me. He took my hand. "I'm sorry, Ranae. I couldn't get him to leave the boat. The water was so cold—maybe he made it to shore downstream."

I was numb as others tried to comfort me. Soon my brothers, Mont and Leon, came and joined the search.

For the next ten days countless people searched the river without any success. Every hour that went by, I prayed that Jack would be on the river bank somewhere—safe. I could not imagine Jack, alive hours before, now quiet, not breathing, dead.

I wanted to scream, "No, not Jack, please not Jack. He's so young—we had so many plans—he has to help me raise these children—surely he'll be found."

People came to offer hope. "Maybe he is just hurt somewhere, anytime now we could hear good news.

Numb with pain, my heart broken, I finally faced the fact that Jack had drowned. He was gone.

I guess I had known it from the beginning, but something kept me from accepting it. Someone remarked that it wasn't fair for him to die. I felt the injustice of life—death seemed the justice.

Jack was 35 years old. We were the same age. I could not face life alone.

Nights and days passed as relatives from all over arrived. Members of our church brought food, and men volunteered to watch the river day and night. So many people were kind and helpful.

I gathered my children around me and tried to give them a reason—which I didn't have—why their father had died.

Each child took the death in a different way. Kelton withdrew, puzzled by the presence of the people who filled the house day after day. I didn't think he understood that his father had drowned until we went near the river with him. He drew back. The river he had played in so many times had become a monster that had taken his father from him. It would be years before he would swim in a river again.

My wonderful mother came from Arizona to be with us. I had a great need to have all my children around me, as if something might happen to them, too.

I was amazed at the strength we found—a strength to endure, to face another day. Perhaps the ordeal of raising Kelton had toughened and strengthened us in preparation for this unbearable sorrow. Jack was gone, but we had been given another day to talk, touch, smell, and love—the love we would need in order to stay in rhythm with ourselves and with the flow of life.

I decided to hold a memorial service for Jack, even though his body had not been found. Ten days had passed since the accident, and I felt people needed to get back to their own lives. In answer to our prayers, Jack's body was found the day before the memorial service. We never saw him again. Someone else had identified the body and the casket was closed for the funeral service. May be it was just as well, we could remember him alive.

At the funeral I wanted to scream, to howl like a wounded animal in a winter storm. I wanted to tear open the casket to see if the corpse was really my Jack. Death had cut me off from him, and had cut me off from myself as well. I went through the stages of grieving. Anger, bitterness, sorrow, loneliness, self-pity and fear raged through my heart like a stampeding herd of wild horses, until, finally, the strength to go on was bom again from the rubble of my life.

I thought of all the things we didn't do—always waiting for the pot of gold at the end of the rainbow. The pot was not of gold, and I had not taken time to enjoy the rainbow.

I always believed I had a reason for living, a definite direction, a prescribed road to travel. Where was my direction now? The events of one day had changed the course of my life, eliminated my future as I had perceived it. The path in front of me was obscured by thick clouds of hopelessness, pain. I sat and held my little boys as they fell asleep in my arms. What more was there?

*Jack,*
*Long after the pain has faded*
*I'll remember*
*Your acceptance of me*
*Your gentleness, your devotion*
*Your love, your warmth.*

*I'll remember the distance*
*We traveled, the growth*
*I'll walk not in shadows*
*But look for the sunlight*
*But you*
*I'll remember—I'll remember.*

# 15

I forced myself into my new role—that of the single mother. Part of me had died. What I once was, I could never be again. I had to rebuild me. For now, I lived in the moment.

We timed mother's return to Arizona to closely coincide with the date of Karla's wedding, and I went along. I wanted to see my little sister on her wedding day. It also would delay taking the reins of my new life into my empty hands for just a bit longer. Reality lurked dark and sinister around the corner, certain to greet me and grab me the minute I arrived back in Spokane. The trip was indeed good for me. The two weeks away gave me a new perspective and restored conviction to get on with life.

In the past, I had been discouraged with Kelton's constant cycle of learning and regressing—going ahead two steps, falling back three. Now, I saw myself spinning in the same cycle. My sense of progress was based on the illusion that things would remain the same. But no one dances through life with a controlled, trouble-free existence. Life is a journey of solving problems, a tapestry of victories and defeats. You win a little, you lose a little.

I shall never finish adding to the tapestry of my life.

The children were glad to see me. While I was gone, Kelton had retreated into his own safe world. This time I had no strength to go after him. I could only pray for him and for all of us.

Mother came back with me to be by my side through the painful days to come. Jack had provided for us with an insurance policy, so I didn't have to go to work immediately. My brother Mont took over my affairs as the executor of Jack's estate.

It was hard to live in the house without Jack, who had been in the process of remodeling it. Everywhere I looked there was evidence of his handiwork, everywhere I turned I felt his presence, but he wasn't there any longer.

I threw myself into church and community affairs, running from the emptiness trying to fill the dark loneliness with activities. It hurt to remember, to see him everywhere in the house. I kept busy and stayed away from home a lot.

However, I did things with the children. I loved them so much, and we all grew very close during that time. We went places together, we played and had long talks.

Vern stayed away, busy with his work and comfortable with his friends. Lynell and the younger boys were my companions. It didn't come as a surprise when I discovered that Sharlene was having trouble in her marriage. I worried about her, but was wise enough to know she would have to find the answers by herself.

I had married at 15. Sharlene was born when I was 17. The years I spent studying, learning about new businesses, and raising Kelton along with the other children, had hardly left me time to prepare myself for a career. At least I had continued with my psychology classes.

I went back to school part-time, took some correspondence courses, and eventually I got my degree in interior design and decorating. I was grateful that mother would stay with me a while longer. Our paths had been parallel: we had given birth together, lived together, and now we were widows together.

Together, we had faced the death of several of her children, my siblings, and the passing of my father. Her unwavering faith was a constant example for me. Faith came through to me now and was ever present in my need. It came on the hush of an inner voice and lifted the mask of fear. I went out to work and began a new life as a single parent to finish raising my five children. Sharlene would be going through a divorce soon and would return home.

Kelton did not come near me. It was as if he blamed me that the people he loved had left him, He was better when Sharlene lived with us again—she had returned and brought the security of her love for him along.

A lonely year passed. Kelton continued shutting me out, leaving the room when I entered. He was eleven years old, five-feet seven-inches tall and had broad shoulders. Kelton's body had grown, and with it, his strength. He could bat the ball over the fence and lift things too heavy for me. He was going to be a big and strong man. He was shy, but looked normal in every way. It was only in the failed attempts of talking to him that his problems became evident.

I worried but I didn't know what to do about him.

Kelton went to classes at the mental health center every day after school, and I attended once a week. Each stage of his growth presented me with a kaleidoscope of new challenges and a shower of frustrating problems.

Then came the morning when Kelton did not want to get up. When I finally coaxed and threatened him out of bed, he refused to take a shower.

He hit at me and tried to run. He had displayed this behavior before, but now he was bigger and stronger, and knew he could get away with a lot more. I realized that if I did not establish my authority there and then, I would never again get the upper hand.

"Get in the shower Kelton, you have only 40 minutes until your bus comes," I insisted.

"No!" Kelton yelled, hitting at me.

"Don't make me hit you back, Kelton," I warned. "I love you and I'm trying to be nice, but you are making it hard. Get in the shower, then you can eat breakfast."

"No!" he yelled, this time trying to push me out of the way.

I held firm, not letting him pass.

Panic mirrored in his eyes, wild, like a cornered animal. He began hitting himself and hitting at me with all his strength. He screamed and grabbed me trying to remove me from his path.

"Get in the shower, before you get hurt," I said. I wrestled him to the floor and held him there with all my strength.

I am about five-feet eight-inches tall and strong for a woman. I had developed fighting skills growing up on a rough Wyoming ranch. With older brothers picking on me constantly, I learned to defend myself. Hard physical work had toughened me and although I hated these wrestling matches with my son, I held my own.

Kelton screamed and struggled. I was barely hanging on to contain him. "Now do as I say, and I'll let you up. Get in the shower!" My voice was firm and demanding. I let him up and he ran to the bathroom and locked the door.

I heard the shower go on. I waited a few minutes, then got the key and opened the door. Kelton was sitting on the toilet, letting the hot water run in the shower.

I turned the shower to warm. He tried to get out of the bathroom. I caught him and again, pinned him against the floor and the exhausting battle for control went on. Holding him back with one hand, I began to undress him with the other. He fought me, hanging on to his shoes and clothes.

"If you want to act like a baby, then I will treat you like one. I will give you a bath."

"No!" he screamed.

"Then you do it. I'm going to stand here until you get in." I said.

"No!" he yelled, trying to push me out. I stood my ground.

He finally got into the shower. He had missed his bus, and I was worn out. There were other morning wrestling matches, but Kelton knew I would not back down, and soon his respect for the rules returned.

He continued to keep to himself, joining us for meals only. I gave him his space, but insisted in his participation in family activities. I forced him to follow the rules we had set up, yet giving him freedom over his time. I told him I loved him; I touched him as often as he would let me. I gave him the respect and trust I had given the other children, but when he broke the rules, like the others, he jeopardized his privileges.

Mother stayed with us for most of that year, then returned home. My love and appreciation for her knew no boundaries. We shared much love and many hardship over the years, more than enough for several lifetimes.

I never fully appreciated the support and help Jack had given me until it wasn't there any more. My insecurities stemmed from the lack of self-knowledge. I couldn't rely on myself—I didn't know myself. Everyone told me I was strong and I felt I had to live up to their expectations. But inside, I was empty and afraid, not at all the superwoman people saw in me. Each day, I went forth because I had to, trusting time to heal my wounded spirit.

Vern, Lynell and Mark had a difficult time accepting Jack's death. Allen dealt with the loss of his father more readily, perhaps he believed that he would see him again some day.

Kelton surprised me one night with a startling remark. He still wandered around the house and the yard at night. One evening he was returning to his room from roaming in the garden, when I asked him where he had been.

"Talkng to Jack," he replied

"Do you mean dad?" I questioned.

With a curt "yes", he went into his room and closed the door behind him, leaving me a bit shaken with his revelation of conversing with his departed father. At the same time, I understood.

I, too, had felt Jack's presence many times, and the feeling eased my sorrow a little at a time.

It was a rough year for all of us. There was an emptiness in our lives that couldn't be filled with work and activities. Lynell started eighth grade that year, and to this day, she cannot remember anything about school, friends or most of the activities during that period.

The time had come for me to earn a living, and after tossing ideas around I started a wholesale carpet business with my brother Mont's help. Later, I opened a retail outlet, "Ranae's Home Decor." Mont remained the executor of my affairs. Following my brother's advice, I invested Jack's insurance money in his company. I knew I should be managing my own life, but first I had to get my emotional life in order and be in control of myself before I dealt with the world.

A year went by, and I still had not taken over my own affairs. Mont certainly knew more about stocks than I did, and I didn't take the time to learn. I would have some rude awakenings.

# *16*

Toward the end of that year, l started dating again. I went out with friends I had known casually. It felt a bit funny after all the years of marriage, raising kids and attending PTA meetings. Then I met someone I liked. I was still lost and lonely when I met Bob. I believed that a man was the answer to my plight.

Bob was handsome, six-feet four-inches tall, had broad shoulders and was five years older than I. He had recently retired from the Air Force, was divorced, and felt the same emptiness in his life as I did. He was very romantic and sang love songs to me. When we were together, the emptiness went away for a while. Our courtship was short, and we were married.

Our marriage was a class-A rebound act. I had not yet let go of Jack and put my love for him into perspective, while Bob was still feeling the hurt of his divorce. We were both holding on to the past. Loneliness was a poor reason for getting married, and the union would soon bear the bitter fruit of our separate disappointments.

Bob was very different from Jack. Jack had accepted me as I was and his love for me and the children was unconditional.

My new husband was critical of me and of the children as well. Jack had been very affectionate; Bob was not. He wanted to be alone a lot, while I needed to be with someone to share my hurts and my growth. He found reasons to avoid me. His needs were totally different from mine. I knew something was wrong from the beginning, but I closed my eyes to everything but the fact I was lonely and he was a good man. I had listened to the love songs, but I didn't hear the music.

I so wanted to be happy. I wanted to love and share again. I wanted to build a new life with someone who wanted the same things. Ever since Jack's death, I had become painfully aware of the importance of each precious moment. I wanted to make these moments count and not have them slip away into obscurity.

Bob tolerated Kelton in a kindly way, but never accepted him. The kids readily made room for Bob in their hearts. All except Lynell. She had been very close to her father and looked upon Bob as an intruder.

Bob had four children of his own who spent portions of the summer vacations with us. His son, Bruce, was Kelton's age.

The two boys took to each other immediately; they rode their bikes together, the explored and played together and got along well. For the first time in Kelton's life, he had a friend. Bob's other son, Ray, was Lynell's age, Christie was about as old as Allen, and Julie was near Mark's age. Our family had grown to ten children, and the blending of two families was an adjustment and a challenge for everyone. I spent my days counseling one child or another, making peace and sharing love.

It was time to make another change, time to leave the memory filled family house behind. It was time to leave the house where Jack and I had been so happy, and find a new setting for making new memories. We bought an attractive and spacious house on the other side of town. It was of a unique and different design—all the rooms faced a lovely indoor swimming pool. Kelton, along with the other children spent so much time in their swim-suits that I was convinced they would soon grow fins and gills.

I felt that the move was especially good for Lynell. She had to let go of the past and make a place for herself in the present. She seemed happier and her attitude improved. Kelton still did not like change, but was not as difficult during that time as I had anticipated.

Vern had married a young woman and was on his own. He was barely 20 years old, but bright and competent, and we hired him to manage our wholesale carpet business. He did a superb job in spite of his young years and lack of experience. I was so pleased with him.

Ray, Bob's oldest son, came to live with us year round, and worked with Vern in the business during the summer. Life had taken on a semblance of normality and there was a general ac-ceptance and comfort in our daily lives.

Kelton didn't get along in this new neighborhood. Although we lived in the country, there were neighbors around us, and we were having similar problems with them as we had in California. Kelton had grown tall and big by then, and the neighbors were afraid of him. People were so scared of what they didn't under-stand.

Our neighbors kept their children away from Kelton. The ugly acts from the past were repeated as some of the kids threw rocks at him and teased him mercilessly. My children handled the insults directed at their brother in their way and frequent fights erupted in his defense. Sweet—little but mighty—Lynell could punch the lights out of any boy on the block.

I finally took matters in my hand to educate my neighbors. I paid them a visit and told them about Kelton and autism. My visits made a difference with some of the adults, but they had little influence over their children who kept up their cruel games, and Kelton's life continued to be miserable.

The neighbor kids had taught him to yell foul language. When he used the street words, they laughed and mocked him. This was one of the worst experiences Kelton had in his life to which he responded with wildly aggressive behavior.

One day the door bell rang and when I opened the door, I faced a policeman.

"Do you have a son named Kelton?" he asked.

"Yes. Why?" I answered nervously.

"We have a complaint from a lady down the street that he is yelling bad language and threatening to hit her little girl," he stated. "This isn't the first complaint we've had about him," he added.

I went outside, but Kelton wasn't anywhere in sight.

"I'll find him and keep him home," I assured the policeman.

I went looking for my son and found him in the park, jumping up and down waving his hands, excitedly watching the children at play. I stood there with an ache in my heart as I heard grown people telling him to go away. "Get out of here!" they yelled, "get lost," they shouted, as they shooed him away with disgust in their eyes as if he personified obscenity.

I walked over to Kelton and told him gently that it was time to go home. He made no objections and ran ahead of me all the way home. We sat down in the kitchen and I tried to explain again that people didn't mean to be cruel to him, they just didn't understand.

"You can't go to the park any more or play down the street. You can go out in the woods in back." I told him. It was so sad. Kelton needed social interaction with children his age, but he didn't need cruelty and disrespect heaped upon him.

Bob and I were incompatible. The strain of all our problems took its toll on our relationship. Lynell tolerated his presence, but never accepted him.

We experienced some business reversals, and decided to make some changes. Maybe a new adventure would help us make life more—more of something! We put our house up for sale, closed our businesses and moved to Oregon.

I felt I had to get away from Spokane, where so many terrible things had happened. We chose to live in Corvallis—a pleasant university town—near Bob's children and family. Regardless of the change in our setting, our relationship went downhill rapidly, never to recover.

A fine vocalist, Bob wanted to pursue a singing career. He went back to school and immersed himself in theatre activities. He loved being an actor and was so like his friends from the stage, who lived their roles with reality, and lived their reality as a role.

Since I was familiar with construction-related work, and now went to work for a builder in Corvallis, coordinating designs and decorating the houses he built. I also took on consulting work for decorating restaurants and homes.

We purchased a lovely A-frame house in the country. But a lovely house does not make a home, and our problems exacerbated.

Just before leaving Washington, Sharlene had remarried and along with Vern, remained in Spokane.

We were able to get Kelton into a good program through the public school system. He responded well in the new teaching environment and improved remarkably. He was glad to live in the country again, and when we bought him a mini-bike, he had lots of fun riding around the hills. To his great delight, Bruce came to live with us about that time and the two boys carried on where they had left off a summer ago. I came to love Bob's children.

Lynell and Ray had a lot of trouble adjusting to the move. Ray found it difficult to make new friends, and Lynell had to leave a boyfriend behind. She cried for weeks. Eventually she made new friends, and was soon going steady with another boy. Allen was excited about the new school and liked all his new friends.

Mark was shy and had a harder time adjusting. He made his own decision to take first grade over again. After that, life was a bit easier for him. I always marvelled how different the children were and how that difference would direct the paths they traveled in their lives

Kelton's progress during the year that followed was exciting. For the first time teachers listened to me and grasped the importance of the methods I had used to teach Kelton as a small boy. His teachers kept after him and challenged him with new things constantly. He was put on behavior modification programs, teaching him to stop tearing up paper, to use good language and not hit at people. Now 15 years old, he even had sex education at school. His jumping and hand waving had stopped, except for times when he was extremely excited.

Despite all the growth and improved behavior, he still was extremely nervous and hyperactive. We refrained from giving him foods with sugar and kept him on doses of vitamin B-complex and vitamin C.

When Kelton was nervous and upset he developed a strong body odor. The only thing that helped during those times was an increased dosage of calcium and magnesium. I read up on everything I could lay my hands on, to find out more about vitamins and which would be most effective. I avoided all prescription drugs because of Kelton's terrible experience with them.

I also read everything I could find on the progress research was making in the field of autistic children. An update showed that in all those years there was little more knowledge about the condition.

That left me with Kelton just where we were the day he was born. Not much of a future for my son, I had to admit.

## 17

I was fascinated with Oregon. It filled me with a newness, and the comforting feeling that I had finally come home. Pressures of time and problems had blocked my ability to notice the beauty all around me. I had gotten into the habit of limiting my vision, and did not see what was right under my eyes.

Acres upon acres of majestic, tall, moss-wrapped firs reminded me of the picture of an enchanted forest. Lush emerald green meadows and brightly colored fields bursting with flowers heightened my senses to the wonders of the land, adding a new dimension to my life.

Rainy days gave me a feeling of security and coziness, so different from the dry, dusty lands of Wyoming where I was raised.

The stern beauty of the Oregon coast brought back memories of California's gentler beaches. As I watched the waves rush to shore, I was aware of nature unfolding a healing, peaceful force in my life gathering around me with such might that sent me on a journey beyond this moment in time.

For too long I had forced myself not to think and not to feel. I had kept myself busy with just plain surviving. As time passed it eased my pain. Unaware of how and why, I began to permit emotions and feelings to come back into my life. I was indeed healing.

I wondered if Kelton experienced these same feelings when he escaped to the woods or sat for hours watching the ocean. Children see and feel and question not, they know how to enjoy a spiritual alignment with nature.

I was always learning something from Kelton. The road he traveled was different from mine, yet sometimes our paths crossed and for an instant I understood him. We each have our own awakening in our own way and in our own time. Tomorrow was just ahead, I couldn't linger with my yesterdays, I would enjoy each moment of each day.

I longed for these peaceful feelings to last, but life always brought me back to its reality by presenting new challenges. Some of the challenges were connected to the happenings in the lives of my children.

After a short marriage, Vern divorced and moved to Oregon, and eventually joined the Army. I prayed he, too, would find his share of happiness in this world.

My work took me away from home for at least ten hours a day. It was an interesting job and I was learning a lot, but for the small amount of money I earned, I questioned its value. The days were too long; I was exhausted when I came home late in the evening.

Bob was willing to take over the chores of running the household, which proved to be a great help. But he didn't get along too well with the children, especially his own, which made for little harmony on the home front.

He went to school on his G.I. Bill to further his education. With his retirement pay from the Air Force, the Social Security check for the children, plus my earnings, we were able to get by. It was a good thing, because the nest egg Jack had left for me was gone, Bob and my brother had invested it all in a ranch in Washington, which turned out to be a poor investment, and we lost a lot of money. It was one more unwanted detail I had to deal with.

Bob's fine singing voice opened the door for him to a local musical theater group, and he became involved in musical productions. He took voice lessons and spent many evenings with practices and rehearsals.

Our marriage, already strained, continued to deteriorate. After a year struggling to keep our relationship afloat, Bob chose a different path and we went our separate ways.

His rejection of me was hard and painful. I knew in my heart that we were better off apart, but I looked at it as one more failure for me at the time.

*Pain, can I bear it?*
*How deep can I bleed?*
*What is the limit*
*Of the soul?*
*Deprivation is an excavation*
*Of the heart*
*Leaving a void,*
*Perhaps to fill with*
*Compassion.*
*Now past, the pain*
*Flickers...*
*Till I stir, and weep.*
*Not for the pain*
*But for the joy of its passing.*

Once again, mother came to my rescue and travelled from Spokane, where she was living with one of my brothers—to be with me. She took over the household and the care of my family. I knew I couldn't be gone ten hours a day any longer. I quit my job and worked for myself as a building contractor, designing and building homes. I had some difficulty getting started, and worked with another builder for a while until I had established my credit. When that was accomplished, I would be on my way. I looked forward to being my own boss and a contractor—a woman contractor at that!

After my divorce from Bob, I put our A-frame house on the market. It sold quickly, and I rented a house in the country.

About that time, Lynell broke up with her boyfriend. Now we both felt rejected. She took on two jobs to help out with our budget—one as a bookkeeper on work release from high school and one in the evenings at a fast food restaurant. She worked hard and still kept her grades up, but had little time for social activities.

She became very protective of me. Perhaps she felt that I had been through enough and it was her duty to shelter me from the world. I soon realized that our roles had suddenly reversed—my daughter turned into my mother. She wanted to know what I did, and when I would be home, where I was going and with whom. She even became critical of my friends.

When Bob moved out of our lives, Bruce of course went along with his father, and Kelton was at a loss as they had been good friends. One night I heard a strange sound coming from the room he shared with Allen. I found him sitting on his bed rocking back and forth, covering his eyes with his hands.

"What's wrong Kelton?" I asked.

"Go get Bruce," Kelton sobbed in a deep and strange voice. I sat down beside him and put my arm around him. He went stiff, but didn't turn away. He held his emotions inside so much that I hadn't realized the extent of his suffering. My heart went out to him.

"You will see Bruce again, Kelton. He is still your friend. People move away from each other, just like Vern and Sharlene did—and they always come back to see you. They still love you. Believe me, you'll see Bruce again." I explained.

He kept rocking, but stopped crying. "Go back to sleep now and tomorrow we will find some pictures of Bruce and you can put them in your book." He had a photo album full of pictures of all his favorite people, his pets and objects he cherished, and would look at it often.

Kelton reacted differently to the change brought on by Bruce's absence from our household, than he ever did before. He began going on long walks, mostly in the rain. Dressed in warm rain gear, he started out at daylight and walked all over the woods that stretched out behind our house. From his morning outings he always returned in time to go to school. The moment he came home from school in the afternoon, he was off to the silent woods again. He walked all winter long. It was different than his previous withdrawals. This time, his behavior seemed more like a search for solitude, a need to be undisturbed to sort things out.

There were other noticeable changes as well. He began to talk more and showed signs of wanting to be around kids his age. He enjoyed it when I took the boys swimming and roller skating. Whenever Kelton enjoyed something, he became very good at it. In this case, he became an excellent skater. He was well behaved when we went out as long as I was there. He used to cause the other children some embarrassment because of his running away and his practiced silence.

But now he was growing up. Mark and Allen couldn't control him in the skating rink since he could skate faster than the younger boys. He wouldn't follow the directions of "couple skate only" or "girls only." He just stayed out there and skated. I always had to go along to keep him under control. Sometimes he would mind Lynell, but not always.

Taking him swimming had its problems. He scared the small children with his splashing and yelling and I had to stay near him to keep him in line. As long as Kelton could see me he would behave, because he knew I would immediately take him home if he acted up.

Lynell and the three young boys enjoyed being together, and we all helped each other in the good times and in the not-so-good ones. I couldn't ask for better children. They were concerned for my welfare and showed me a great deal of love and respect. Sharlene and my sister, Elma came to visit and brought a bit of their lives to mingle with that of mine.

My mother must have felt the same way about me—I was her child, and I was hurting. She stayed with me for about three months after my divorce. I loved every moment she was with me and appreciated her deep love and unlimited understanding.

I asked her once, "Mom, how did you survive the loneliness since dad died? It's been eighteen years?"

"Well, you know better than anyone, Ranae. I've lived near you or with you most of that time. Of course, it is lonely. And we all do the same thing. We keep growing, keep busy, and build a new life."

"I'm tired of starting over," I declared. "There's been one adjustment after another in my life—so many unfulfilled dreams."

I told mother that I knew I could not permit thoughts like these to hang around too long. I didn't even think much about having a relationship with another man in the future. I wanted to build a wall to protect myself from being hurt again. I was not going to wallow in self pity, it was a luxury I certainly could not afford. I realized happiness was a *now* attitude and not a *future* condition.

"I am getting rid of the bitterness over my divorce. I'm ready to have a lot of fun...get lost in crowds, laugh and not have to hear about heartbreaks or problems. I married so young, I've never had any fun," I told mom.

"Then do it!" was my mother's simple reply.

"You know, I thought I would die when Bob and I broke up, even though I knew it was for the best," I continued. "For months I felt like a lost little girl holding a broken life in my hands, searching for an answer to the 'why me syndrome.' I wanted something in life and in our relationship Bob couldn't provide—and so I was unhappy. I discovered I had a great fear of making a mistake, but making a mistake is a reminder of the way I am, not what I intend to be. I want to learn from my mistakes so I will grow."

"I've seen a remarkable growth in you over the years," mother said. "Let me tell you how I feel about relationships," she continued. "At first you see only each others' virtues, then you begin to notice the faults. You have false expectations for one another. When you want something and don't get it, you are dissatisfied. When there is no flow of communication between two people, there can be no future. If you can make it through the fault finding stage, then you learn to really love each other," she said thoughtfully.

It was wonderful to have a mother. I wondered if my children feltlike that, too?

Mother,
My memories of you are
Prayers for your children
Praise on your lips and
Your tender hands.

Many besides your children
Have come to drink
From your cup
You gave them courage
Confidence and charity.

You have always directed
Your passions with reason
You set the example
So when the storms of life
Came to me, I was
Better prepared.

You taught me through
Your own pain
To accept my pain and to understand
Most pain is self chosen
You taught me to move
Quickly to tomorrow.

What I feel for you
Is love in the solitude
Of my heart
That can only be expressed
By a look, a touch.
Words are insufficient.

## 18

The next year, 1976, was a happy one for all of us. I was having a great deal of fun designing, building and decorating houses and doing things with the children. I made a decent living and my brother helped recover some of the money from the ranch property and I had no financial problems. I met a lot of wonderful people and made a few good friends.

It was a great feeling for me to be in my own business. I graduated rather quickly from the basic mother-housekeeper-cook position to becoming a business woman. I was still all those other things too—mothers never quit. And, there was always Kelton to spring something new and different on me that would send me flying for a my bag of tricks.

Kelton periodically tested his strength against mine. One day I tried to get Kelton to change his shirt.

"Please put on a clean shirt, Kelton," I asked calmly.

"No," he yelled, and ran into his room.

I followed him. "I mean it. You have worn that shirt for two days, you need a clean one."

"No!" he yelled and started to get around me. I blocked his way, and he pushed me.

Where before I could easily win a tug of war with my boy, this big strapping fellow delivered quite a push and shove befitting his size. I had to call on every ounce of my strength.

I was prepared for him. "I have a big stick," I threatened, "and I'm going to use it on you if you don't change your shirt."

He struggled against my body blockade, and I wrestled him to the floor. I tried to take the shirt off of him and it ripped. The struggle ended, and he changed his shirt. Later, I found the ripped shirt cut up into tiny pieces. From then on, he changed his shirt fairly willingly, I just bad to remind him that I'd remove it for him if he didn't.

Kelton started high school in a special education class. A buddy system existed in two of his classes, where a mainstream student worked directly with the special kids. A lot of pressure was put on Kelton to behave normally.

He learned quite a bit from the program that winter, but he also had a lot of negative reactions—he hit himself a great deal and preferred to be alone for long periods of time. It seemed forcing him to learn, never letting up the pressure with heightened challenges, was still the best way for him to advance. But few were willing to teach that method, and gave in to his way which limited the progress he could have made.

His autism was gradually ameliorated. After he turned 12, he stopped withdrawing into his own world. His jumping and waving became contained unless he became extremely excited or upset. He began bowling in a league and became very good at it. Bowling became one of his favorite activities.

The people of Corvallis were supportive of their handicapped citizens, and offered progressive programs in which Kelton was able to enroll.

He didn't speak a lot better, even though he had been in speech therapy since he was four. At home, we insisted he ask for things before we would hand them to him. Occasionally, we would slip up and gave him things without making him ask for them verbally. We knew him so well we could second guess almost anything he wanted.

For years Kelton stuck to his pattern of doing things the same old way, and eventually we fell into his pattern, too. I know now that we could have been more consistent in his training, but we did the best we could at the time.

Throughout Kelton's life I clung to the hope that he would come out of his autism and be like the rest of us. Kelton was emerging but he still was, by definition, functionally retarded—he was unable to perform self-sufficiently, and he was developmentally delayed according to the norm for his age. We had been handed so many learned opinions over the years, that finally we disregarded all of them, and were grateful for everything he learned to do. He grew out of his autism so gradually that we hardly knew it.

One day I realized that he did fewer things then he used to do, some of which were irritating and disturbing. I got my diary out and read the entries I had made years ago. I was grateful I kept a record which was my base for comparison, a measure by which to gauge his growth.

I was excited how far he had come. He had evolved from being a child—sometimes silent and withdrawn, sometimes hyperactive, with endless obsessions—to a youth who was exhibiting signs of wanting to become part of the world around him. He made attempts to remain in the presence of visitors, even though he left the room after a while—but not as abruptly as before.

One winter day, Kelton was up at daylight. I heard him in the kitchen fixing his breakfast. He has been preparing his own meals for quite some time, and enjoyed the independence of eating what he felt like. I hurried into the kitchen.

"Where are you off to this morning so early?" I asked him.

"Off to!" he said.

"Kelton, I asked you a question. Where are you off to this morning?"

"Hills," he replied.

"You like walking in the woods, don't you?"

"Don't you, yes," he answered. He started for the door.

"See you," I said.

"See you," he replied.

I watched him walk away. Where had the years gone? He had grown so tall—nearly six feet tall—and would have been very good-looking if he had left the braces on his teeth.

I prayed he would continue to make strides, take big steps forward, and catch up on life. I remembered the regressions, recalling the frightened, frantic feelings I had associated with them.

At four o'clock that afternoon, the sheriff's department called.

"We have your son Kelton here," the woman dispatcher told me. "He needs a ride home."

She explained that Kelton in his wanderings had joined high school kids out on a twenty-mile fund raising hike for a local charity. The walk was over and Kelton needed a ride home.

"Too bad he didn't have a sponsor," the dispatcher continued "he walked the full twenty miles."

I savored the impact of that report, allowing all its implications to sink in, to flood me, to drench me with joy. For the first time in his whole life, Kelton had, of his own desire and of his own accord, voluntarily integrated himself into a group. He had joined a crowd! I was exalted.

Lynell went to the sheriff's office to pick up her brother and drove him home. We praised him to high heavens for his efforts, and judging by his expression, he seemed pleased himself.

Kelton had been coming and going on his own for many years. As soon as we were sure he could take care of himself in traffic, we let him go. He always had a great compulsion to be free and to explore. He watched life from the rooftop or through a window, standing outside in the dark, looking in, never quite being a part of life. But today, Kelton had joined it!

He climbed the hills and watched the city from their summits, an outsider. Now, once in a while, he was coming down from the pinnacle to be a part of it. I had to turn him over to God. Kelton was fortunate in that he never got hurt unless some kids ganged up on him. Fortunately, most of them left him alone.

His adventures would continue to add excitement to my days whether I needed it or not.

The phone rang and brought me out of my reverie.

"Are you Kelton Steele's mother?" the voice on the other end asked.

"Yes," I answered. My heart always sank when I heard that question over the phone. "What now?" I thought.

"We own a laundromat in Corvallis," he stated. "Kelton comes down and watches the dryers tumbling around. He doesn't hurt anyone, but our customers are complaining. Please keep him away."

When Kelton came home that night, we had a talk. I told him about the phone call.

"You can't go back there, Kelton," I informed him.

"Go back, yes!" he cried.

"If you do, they will call the police and lock you up," I said.

"No!" he screamed, and shut himself in his room.

He didn't go near the laundry for several days until the following weekend when the phone rang. It was the police, again.

"We have your son Kelton here," the officer said. "A complaint was filed against him for loitering around the laundromat. Could you please come get him?"

"I'll be right there," I answered, and was on my way—rescue Kelton!

I picked him up and we had another little talk. This time I must have gotten through to him. He stopped going to the laundry after being arrested.

His next target of fascination was the electric eye doors at super markets. He walked in and out, in and out for hours. Finally a complaint was filed and I found myself in the police station, again.

"Kelton," I said, "You need a job. You have to have something to keep you busy, keep you out of trouble."

"Job," he answered.

I scoured Corvallis trying to find work for him, without luck. Finally I took him to our construction site and gave him a hammer and told him to take all the nails out of some refuse lumber I had piled in a comer of the lot. Kelton was delighted, and refused to leave until he had all the nails out of all the boards.

"Nails!" he said, as he handed me a large can full of them.

I took my wallet out of my purse and paid him.

"You did a great job!" I told him. "I'll hire you again."

The next day I put him to shovelling rock. He was great. Work was the answer and his tasks became very important to him. Even so, he did only the jobs he liked. When I gave him something to do he didn't like, he disappeared.

I didn't pay him that day and didn't allow him to go back to work for a while. I wasn't able to make him understand that we all had to do work at times we didn't like. There was a limit to his grasp of reality.

Kelton had long ago learned to prepare simple meals and do his own laundry. After years of fussing and feuding, he kept himself and his room clean. He mowed the grass, took out the garbage and went to school. But it wasn't enough. He was very restless. He had always done what his younger brothers wanted him to do, but now that he was older, they got on his nerves. One day he hit them, and Allen and Mark were brokenhearted.

"Just leave him alone. He's having a hard time growing up," I advised them. But my heart sank, and I was struck by a terrible fear. What if I can't handle him? What then?

The fear never left me as he continued to be restless and temperamental. Kelton was cranky and hard to live with.

His behavior carried over to school. First came a note from the school, "Please keep Kelton home today, he misbehaved." Then came phone calls, and finally a meeting with the teachers and the school principal.

We all worked together trying to help Kelton and looked for solutions. We came up empty-handed. Luckily the school year was about over, but then summers always brought new problems. Now that Kelton was venturing into the city, there were constant complaints about him.

"Why are you crying, mom?" Mark asked as he put his arms around me.

"I'm okay," I said. "I'm just so worried about Kelton. He needs a father to handle him. He is getting so big and strong, I'm really afraid one day he will realize it and I will lose control."

"I know what you mean. Allen and I just stay out of his way, we don't cross him at all," he said seriously. "He is really strong." Allen came into the room and we sat and talked, trying to decide what to do to help him. We had no answers.

"I guess it will have to be like it has always been: take one day at a time," Allen voiced the familiar motto.

For awhile I withdrew
From my heart and
Let it get overgrown with
Bitter weeds.

I waited on the weeding.
No flowers will grow
Rooted in soil choked with hurt.

Consider that all mistrust
Is driven away.
My soul recovers enough
To cry—hold on.
Will my heart ever
Leap at another rainbow?
Give up the night wanderings
And the frosty winds.

See the apple trees
Covered with blossoms
Bear fruit;
Build again its lodge
In high places—
Roam the solitary hills
Of life again
Holding someone's hand.

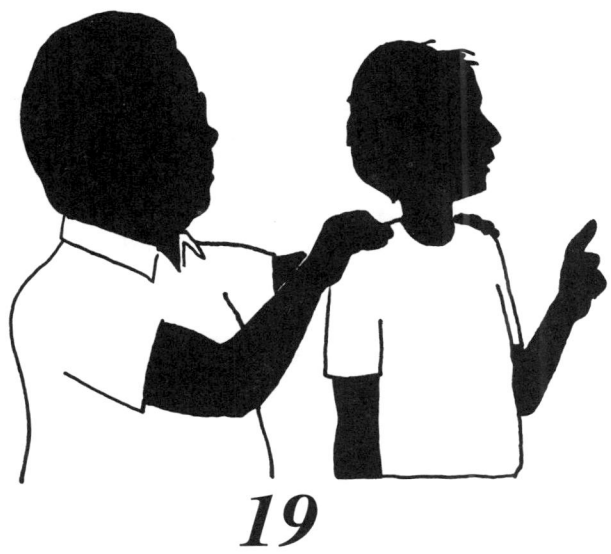

## *19*

Since I had been single I had made several good male friends and dated all of them. I also had a girlfriend whose company I enjoyed. We took our families on a camping trip and did a lot of other activities together. I had made up my mind to raise my children by myself. I told myself that I did not want any more hurt and disappointment. I had several casual friends so I wouldn't get attached to any of them.

Bernie had become a good friend and visited often in our home. He joined us in family activities and went skating and swimming with us. The children, except for Kelton and Lynell, liked him, He made us laugh and kept things light and on a humorous plane.

Joseph was another good friend and became a steady visitor too, and soon Bernie and Joseph were competing for our weekends. Lynell, still in her in motherly role, was protective of me and would have been happy if I had avoided all encounters with men. But I enjoyed my friends and we all had good times together.

Mark had been born on my birthday, so when Joseph wanted to take me out to celebrate, he had to take the whole family. It was a very enjoyable evening. Kelton liked Joseph, even though he stood by watching Joseph, not saying much.

When Joseph came to visit us at the house, Kelton smiled at him, jumped and waved his hands.

"Do you like Joseph, Kelton?" I had asked him.

"Joseph, yes," answered Kelton.

Joseph was wise enough to let Kelton have his space, and visited with him on the boy's terms.

Christmas was just around the corner and I went about preparing for the holiday a little less joyful than the season prescribed. However, Joseph spent Christmas with us, and made what could have been a very lonely time for me, a joyous occasion. The house looked festive, we baked and cooked up a storm, and the family was together. I had to keep my mind directed to all the goodness in my life, and look at each day as a special gift—never to come again.

In the meantime, Lynell was participating in a church project, called *Adopt A Grandmother.* She had been visiting Irene, an elderly lady from a nursing home, taking her shopping and running errands because the dear woman had a broken hip and was wheelchair bound. Irene had no family, and Lynell was a godsend for her.

Prescribed by her doctor, Irene—tongue in cheek—referred to her daily glass of wine as her 'medicine', and asked Lynell to go to the store and purchase a refill when her supply had run low.

Lynell left for the store thinking "I'm too young to be buying wine. How do I get myself into these situations?"

At the market, she picked up a gallon jug of wine Irene had requested, and stood in the check out line feeling particularly conspicuous. Who should wander into line behind her, but a staunch member of the our church? He looked at the under-age shopper toting a big jug of wine, greeted an embarrassed Lynell but was considerate enough not to comment on her purchase.

When Lynell returned to the nursing home a little shaken, she told Irene her story. Her adopted grandmother roared with laughter and said it was the funniest thing that had happened in ten years.

Lynell's adopted grandmother became a welcome guest in our home—especially on holidays and birthdays. During the course of her visits she had met Bernie and Joseph.

One day Irene got me off into a corner and said, "Ranae, you have two good men who think the world of you, and you just put them off. What are you going to do about it? You like having a man around and your children need a father."

I laughed at her observation and gave her a bug hug and a kiss. She had become a part of our family. Kelton sensed that the grandmotherly woman had accepted him, and he was comfortable with her.

My mother visited me often, and in our talks she expressed her feelings about Joseph and how well she thought of him. Soon, I was even getting hints from the boys about how much they liked Joseph.

I was afraid and confused. When I felt good about myself, I wasn't lonely and I tried hard to keep those feelings alive. The more I was able to take risks, the more I discovered it wasn't a risk at all—but a new experience. I had to examine how I felt about myself. I had told myself I did not want to marry again. More learning was in store for me, I wanted to be open to accept the lessons that came my way. How else could I grow?

I had always gone about living by risking everything, allowing myself to be vulnerable, and caring about people. I had pursued my personal quest, struggled not to be afraid and to welcome life even at its worst. I knew in order to be happy, I must become all I can be. I had to look at my experiences, explore my feelings and then come to my own conclusions: it was important never to cut myself off from that quest. Love is a most serious responsibility, the highest form of relating to someone. I wanted to have that experience again. I had days when I was terrified of loving. What if I didn't work? What if I would be hurt again? What if...?

I kept proceeding with this inward journey, this discovery of self. Loving others creates more loving, I knew, but I felt shy and scared to love again.

"Love me enough to love," Joseph said to me one day.

I had to think about that. I had suffered a lot. So many people I loved had died or left me. I had fought to be more alive myself. One thing I knew for certain, I could not run away. I could not withdraw. I had learned that lesson from Kelton.

If I did love again, it had to be someone who would allow my life to happen, and demand the best from me. It would have to be someone who gave me the freedom and room to grow—my way. I was beginning to realize Joseph would be the man who would let this happen.

When Bob and I separated, I felt utterly helpless for awhile. I had been furious because once again, I could not control the events in my life. The tears came in torrents, the loss was great, the pain terrible. I endured the anguish and tried desperately to grow from the experience of rejection.

I looked at my life with a new awareness and sharpened perception. I wondered what would lie ahead for me and my children in a life with Joseph.

We don't know what's in store for us. All we can do is to let it happen, allow it to happen, to live, holding back nothing and be brave .

It dawned on me finally that I had fallen in love with Joseph, but was too frightened to marry again. Up popped the question I had asked so often, "Why does my life have to be so complicated?" I wanted to have a simple life. It wasn't supposed to be this way. Joseph kept assuring me the fear and doubts would pass, and I decided to place my trust in him.

It was difficult for me to tell Bernie that I was serious about Joseph. He was hurt. I felt so indebted to him. He had been there to cheer us up during the bleak days after Bob and I separated. He had truly been a good friend and always would be.

Joseph and I decided to go Spokane to visit Sharlene who had a beautiful new baby girl named, Melanie I wanted to see.

"I had often wondered what it would be like to be a grandmother," I said to Joseph as we played with Melanie. "Now I know it's even more special than I imagined."

Sharlene wasn't happy in her marriage. Problems had finally surfaced that had always lurked in the shadows of her denial. I cried for her. She was such a gentle, loving person and deserved so much more. She was working diligently to make her marriage work, not throwing in the towel.

I introduced Joseph to all my family, and I was delighted with the warm reception he received. It seemed that their unspoken approval was the last thing I needed to make up my mind. On the way home, we stopped at Coeur D'Alene, Idaho, and got married.

Life had closed a door and opened wide another door. I welcomed life's gifts.

In Oregon we were transplanted.
Spring had warmed the earth,
blossoms were everywhere.

I question them not,
but it's good to have you near
to understand, to share responsibility and
        Love—
It's good to feel alive again.

I've listened to a tear,
learned to candle a
light for us.
Our love will race
the fleeting time,
move beyond the shadows
of yesterday,
appreciate the varied moments as
we sing our song of promise


Within me, you inspire
a crafting of me,
awaken the reflection
of my real self.
You expand my inner horizons,
make me tremble at the discovery of love.
My heart beats in time with yours:
I love how you love me.
Now you touch the center of my soul
with your kindness, your caring.
Togetherness is our beginning as we
learn to be one.

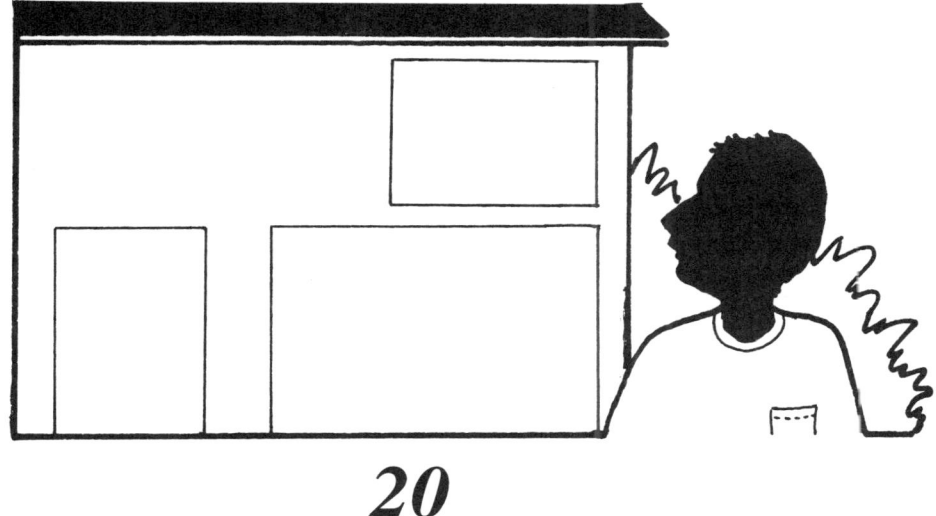

# 20

Our honeymoon consisted of our trip back to Oregon. Joseph had not felt well the last few days, and I was glad we were on our last leg home. We stopped briefly in Salem to pick up some of Joseph's clothes at his bachelor apartment, got back on the road and arrived in Corvallis late Sunday night. The kids were surprised that we had eloped, but I could read their genuine pleasure on their faces.

By now Joseph was very ill. Early on Monday morning I discovered he had been bleeding internally and had vomited enough blood to fill a large pan. My heart was in my throat as I fumbled with the telephone to call an ambulance. Joseph was unconscious when it arrived.

Within minutes we were speeding toward the hospital. The paramedics had started an I.V. in Joseph's arm and had given him oxygen. I sat staring at them all, thinking this could not be happening. My mind whirled like a dust devil on a barren field, kicking up old fears and unshed tears. If only it were a bad dream and I could wake up to sunlight chasing my nightmare back into the darkness where it lived.

But it was real, so real.

Joseph did not stop hemorrhaging. His condition was so serious that I called his family in Portland. Joseph's mother, stepfather and two sisters came to wait out the nightmare hours with me.

To complicate matters, Joseph had a rare blood type, and he was losing so much blood that the hospital had difficulty keeping up with the transfusions. My friend, Judy, contacted one of our local church leaders, and thirty or more people showed up at the Red Cross to give blood. Several people from the hospital donated their blood as well.

Joseph's doctor decided to perform an exploratory operation at once in order to discover the cause of the bleeding. Meanwhile, Joseph's condition had deteriorated further, and the doctors feared for his life.

"We don't like to operate under these conditions," the doctor told me gravely, "but we don't have a choice. He can't keep up this bleeding much longer, or we will lose him. How old is he?"

"He's 46 years old." Did I dream I heard myself speak? Was I going to lose another husband? When was this merry-go-round of mine going to stop? I had buried two husbands in their prime of life. Was death riding the grey horse again?

"Joseph has always been healthy," I heard Joseph's mother say, equally numbed by fear.

"We have to go ahead with the exploratory," the doctor said gently, and disappeared behind the swinging door that led to the operating room. The big door shut softly behind him, the red lettering of the stern "No Admittance" sign staring us in the face.

I watched as they wheeled Joseph into surgery, not knowing if he would come back alive. Joseph was a big, robust man with a dark complexion. Now, he looked so pale and helpless. I had to get away before I fell apart in front of everyone. I took the elevator down, fled to my car and drove into the country. I parked the car and threw myself on the grass under a stand of large trees.

"God," I pleaded, "I've never said 'enough'—through all my trials. I've never said I've had enough. Now I am saying it. God, I've had enough! I can't go through this again. Don't let Joseph die, please don't let him die," I sobbed.

I lost track of time as I lay stretched on the ground, my head buried in my arms, my heart aching. I walked back to the car slowly and drove back to the hospital to join Joseph's family in their vigil.

Joseph's robust nature came to his rescue and he survived the four-and-a-half hours of surgery without complications. The first ray of hope warmed my heart and eased my mind. My prayers had been answered, and my gratitude for God's gifts was boundless. It would be weeks before my husband would be his old self again, but I could handle that.

He stayed in bed for six weeks. The doctors had repaired the main artery in his stomach which had burst and nearly cost him his life. The damaged tissues had been removed, the vein patched—just in time. Joseph had been through quite an ordeal.

The nurses knew we had just been married, and, ready for a good laugh, put a "Do Not Disturb—Honeymooners" sign on the door of Joseph's room.

It was a day for celebration when I brought Joseph home from the hospital. We had moved his belongings into our house and began life as a married couple. Kelton who had liked Joseph as a visitor, made it quite clear he didn't like having him in the house. Joseph was recuperating nicely and was walking in the yard when he encountered Kelton. Joseph's friendly greeting elicited a strange response from Kelton, who ran toward him, promptly hit him, veered off and ran into the trees. Fortunately Joseph took no offense.

During the six weeks of Joseph's recuperation, we spent a lot of time together and got to know each other well. We talked about everything under the sun and planned our future. Since

Joseph worked in Salem, we decided to build a home there and proceeded with our plan at once, purchasing some land.

Eager to be closer to his place of work, we lived in a rented trailer in the backyard of our home site, while the house was being finished. It was a good decision since we did most of the work ourselves, and saved driving back and forth every day. Living in the trailer made the summer feel like one big fun camp-out adventure. The boys loved it, even Kelton didn't mind the temporary living quarters. To my surprise he seemed to like Salem and not to mind the change.

Each time Kelton adjusted to a new situation or environment with a measure of ease, I felt I had won another round. There were indeed subtle changes in his behavior and a noticeable improvement in his behavior. Every change for the better made the future brighter, and gave me a new lease on life.

Lynell was spending the remainder of her senior year with a friend in Corvallis and would live with us again after graduation before going to college, Whenever one of the children ended a period in their life and journeyed on, it seemed that the years had flown by without announcing their presence. As I watched Lynell's graduation ceremony, I asked myself the age-old question every mother has posed: "Where—but where—did the years go? And where was I during all that time? "

But I also looked at her with joy and a motherly pride. She had grown into a tall, slim, beautiful blonde young woman. I remembered the little girl, who had always been at my side, ready to help, eager to please, aiding me through thick and thin. She had worked hard during high school and had given up dating in order to hold down two jobs, and still kept up with her home work. She had earned enough money to pay a big share towards the purchase of a car.

She had saved enough money for a trip to Hawaii. Her good friend, Laurel, used to live there and still had old friends on the island who offered to host the two young women for the summer. Lynell was excited about the trip and about starting college in the fall. She had received a grant that would pay for most of her schooling. She was quite a girl.

Finding schooling for Kelton remained my primary concern, and I checked out the Salem schools before we moved there. Salem's public school system offered special education classes in the junior high as well as in high school. I was disappointed when I discovered that their programs were not nearly as advanced as those in Corvallis.

I was able to enroll Kelton in a summer program at Shangri-la, a school for the trainable mentally retarded. He adjusted to the move very well and settled down to the summer session.

Unlike previous years, we enjoyed a peaceful summer. I relaxed from the past trials and found great pleasure working on our new home alongside Joseph. Kelton helped every night after school, and he, too, enjoyed the labor. I fully believed that he understood that, unlike the other houses he had seen me build, this would be our own home.

When the boys started school in the fall, the downstairs and part of the upstairs of the house were finished. We were pleased our floor plan worked so well and liked finishing the details for the house—it really felt like our home.

At the same time our own house was going up, Joseph and I were building custom homes in Salem. Joseph was a good designer and knew a great deal about construction. He would design the houses and I supervised the building and completed the interior decorating.

The children adjusted to Joseph quickly and with ease. They learned to love him very much and made him an important part of the family. He was always fair, and they knew he really cared for us.

Finally, our house was finished and we settled in quickly. To keep our minds hopping, something quite unique happened. I had done my first load of clothes in my new laundry room, when the washer—perhaps not installed properly or unevenly loaded—moved from its spot and lodged itself against the closed door that lead to the hall.

There was no way we could open the door even a crack. The only way to get the machine back into its place was to cut a hole in the panel of the door, climb in and push the heavy machine back against the wall and see to it would stay there.

Kelton came home from school and wanted to do his laundry. When we told him what happened, he stood for a few moments quietly with his hand on the door knob. A few moments passed and he gently turned the knob. The door opened, the washer was back in its place, leaving a few dark marks on the linoleum—signs the machine had moved.

We realized then that Kelton had a unique talent for moving objects, which explained several episodes including the "flying bricks caper" on the neighbor's roof in California when Kelton was only four years old.

How do you tell that to your friends and neighbors? It didn't matter, we knew and understood—he could move things! In years to come we would still remember those moments.

Even though our children grew up and became independent, they remained a part of our lives, and we followed their progress as eagerly as when they took their first step and uttered their first word. Lynell was attending Brigham Young University in Provo, Utah. We missed her, but at least she came home for holidays and summers. She shared her adventures with us and we were transported back to the days of our campus life.

Vern's life was still not easing up. He was having a rough time in the Army. He didn't get into the school of his choice, but remained on the base and was kept in Texas on Red Alert. He was transferred to Germany, but stayed only a few months. He seldom wrote to us and we were in the dark about the events in his life. Typical mother, I worried a lot and was glad when he finally came home.

Sharlene's marriage continued to be rocky. She came to see us in Salem with our sweet granddaughter, Melanie. I secretly hoped she would move to Salem where I could keep an eye on her and watch Melanie grow up. Sharlene had been considering divorce. She discovered that she was pregnant and decided to stay with her husband. She tried harder than ever before to understand the problems that were destroying both their lives and, more than that, find a way to make her marriage work.

As much as I wanted to help my children ease the pain of their unhappy experiences, I also knew that we are on this earth not only to make our own way, but to learn the lessons life held in store for us. My own life has taken on new shape and form and I was grateful for the gifts each day brought from dawn to dusk to dawn.

## 21

One morning I woke up very early and watched the sunrise. I was marvelously alive, full of creative energy. I felt I had an appointment with the dawn and hurried out to greet it. It was a lovely rendezvous with nature. As the world came alive, I sat quietly gazing up at the tall trees and listening to the birds.

I heard a noise and looked around. Kelton was coming out from behind the trees walking toward the house. He enjoyed the early morning too. I watched him as he stopped to watch a squirrel climb a tree. My son stood still for a long time, lost in thoughts of his own. I returned quietly to the house, not wanting to disturb his morning solitude, the rhythm of his involvement with the moment.

I didn't want my spiritual high to end either. I reached for pen and paper and began to write about all the wonders of nature—about the blossom and the leaves and about the sunrise which had reached out to me. How fragrant the air, how glorious the day. I was so deeply tuned in to the magic of it all.

I've seen many sunrises
With crystals of color;
Felt one with the universe before,
But never have I felt
More appreciation for
God's creations and for you
Than this morning.

I've experienced in silence
The joy of being alive
To witness this miracle.
My feeling of love too.
I need your sensitivity,
Your time and our
Rhythmed partnership.

I need to hold fast
To our love;
To giving and creating
The lyrics in our lives,
The flowering melodies
Sung anew with a
Special warmth.

We hold today in the
Palm of our hands.
Wake up, Joseph,
Dance to the moment with me.

I knew this would all pass away in time. But I had this moment, this fragment of time. I had NOW. I forgot this world. I wanted to capture the feeling in words.

Our house was a large two-story, four bedroom home, nestled in two acres of trees. We had agreed when we planned the building site to leave as many trees standing as possible. We only made room for the house and kept the proud firs to frame our home with their graceful presence.

Allen and Mark shared a bedroom. It was impossible to keep them apart. Kelton had a room of his own, and Lynell's bedroom was waiting for her on holiday and summer visits.

The upstairs family room was large with walls of blue and buggy wood, an open-beam ceiling gave the room added space and height. We installed a pool table and a snack bar for the boys. Kelton preferred to play pool by himself—alone and by his own rules. If it took too long for the ball to make a the pockets, he just gave it a little extra push. His rules were the kind that never invited a quarrel.

That winter, my sister Elma, her husband John, and three children came to live with us until John found a job. They stayed for six months until they found work. Later, my sister Karla and her family also moved to Oregon. I always liked it when my family came together. We had always been a close-knit group, ready to support one another. That had not changed with the years.

We were all very happy the winter of 1977-78. Kelton adjusted to the new school and to Joseph's presence. Even our five house guests did not disturb him to any great degree.

Lynell was doing well in college and Vern returned after three years in the Army. We were glad to have him home again. When Sharlene had her baby, Christina, I went to Spokane for a visit. Christina was just as beautiful as Melanie. I loved my granddaughters.

It was difficult for me to leave Sharlene and her little girls in their unhappy situation, and I shared my concerns with her. She decided to come to Salem for a while. She packed some of their belonging, packed the car, and we drove back to Oregon. It was wonderful having her and the little girls with us. In no time we became attached to the girls. Kelton especially loved his nieces and was kind and gentle with them.

Sharlene had time to make a difficult but realistic decision, looking out for herself as well as the little girls. Unfortunately, she realized that she could only change her circumstances and not her husband's traits and attitudes. She filed for divorce. None of us had realized the strain Sharlene and her children had been under. Once again, Oregon became a sanctuary, and our home a safe place to be.

Kelton was excited that Sharlene had come home and he occupied himself with the girls. He held the bottle for Christina, with a big smile on his face. Many times I would catch him watching the baby sleep. He seemed to feel a great joy in having them around.

It was good to have moments like these when I could stop and look and listen to Kelton. I tried to understand his burdens, his inner hungers for something that was lacking, his inability to seek reassurance or express his discontent. Could I ever really understand the depth of his anguish? I was sure that he had come to the point in his life where he wanted to communicate, to reach out, but was unable.

It was great to have Vern home. We gave him a job with our construction company. He was, as always, a good worker. He was a competent person and had many good qualities; we loved him. He had made a few bad choices in his life, and did not think highly of himself. I prayed that he would find himself, and take responsibility for his life. If he could gain self-esteem and insight to his self worth, he would be fine.

It was spring again and we went on a family outing to the coast. Something happened on that trip that made us realize how Kelton had changed. It also offered us a peek at the next set of problems we would face as Kelton got older.

John, Vern and Joseph rented a boat and went fishing. As usual, Kelton was off by himself. When Kelton returned to where we were staying, he walked up to me, and asked, "Dad?"

"He went fishing with John and Vern," I replied.

"Go," Kelton said, as big tears rolled down his cheeks and he began pacing back and forth like a caged animal. "Go, too," he repeated, over and over.

We were dismayed that we had forgotten about Kelton. It dawned on me with alarm that we were still looking at him as a little boy, even though he was over six feet tall. He wanted desperately to be included in the activities of the men in the family. Kelton was 18 years old, and we were treating him like an eight-year-old.

Something new appeared on the horizon of awakening for this young man. We noticed that Kelton was beginning to like girls. At first he would just stand by them, and when they moved, he would follow. Then he became braver and found ways to touch them. Once Lynell took Kelton, Mark and Allen to the movies. As they were standing in line at the ticket office, Kelton kept touching the girl in front of them on the behind. She turned around and told Kelton and Lynell off. Her boyfriend threatened to beat Kelton up.

Lynell was upset and embarrassed, and we began a series of serious talks with Kelton about touching girls. Here we had gone out of our way to teach this boy how to hug and touch and be touched, and now we had to do a complete turnaround. I had to keep remembering that we lived in two different worlds and what made sense to us did not apply to Kelton.

"Remember when you didn't like to be touched Kelton?" I asked him.

"No!" he yelled.

I kept talking to him about the subject as long as I had his attention, but I had a strong feeling it wasn't going to be enough. This situation wouldn't go away with a heart-to-heart talk.

I was right. He continued to touch girls whenever he had the opportunity. He had the same feelings and urges every young man experiences, but he didn't know how to handle them, nor did he know how to act in social situations. I felt so sorry for him. How could I expect Kelton to understand the changes going on in his body when most normal teenagers can't even understand? Regular sex education wasn't going to work with him any more than any other social science education.

I dreaded what would happen every time Kelton was out of my sight. One lovely, sunny day we took our family to the Portland Zoo. We had to watch Kelton every minute because his only thoughts were of girls.

Joseph bought each of us an ice cream bar, and we were standing near the water fountain eating them and talking to one another. I looked up just in time to see Kelton reach out and grab a girl's behind as she bent over the water fountain to get a drink.

The girl jumped, yelled, turned around on her heels and slapped Kelton's face. Kelton reared back in surprise, holding his face with his hands.

"Creep!" the girl yelled, as she rushed away in disgust. The slap calmed Kelton down a bit, but it didn't stop him. Joseph and I talked it over and decided we would have to take some strict, if unorthodox, measures to put a stop to this or Kelton would end up in serious trouble. We told everyone in our family to slap him if he touched anyone inappropriately. We'd wait and see how far this would get us.

Joseph started wrestling with the boys in order to toughen them up a bit. Kelton interpreted the activity all wrong. He thought

Joseph was going to hurt him and he would run away. Then, cautiously he would come back to watch nervously as Mark and Allen tried to take Joseph down.

"No! Hurt yourself," Kelton yelled. He began running from Joseph again. When Joseph came into the room, Kelton would leave. Joseph did not give up and continued his attempts to play with him.

One day he said, "I'm going to tickle you." Kelton was cornered in the hall. He hit Joseph, pushed him aside and ran away. Joseph backed away from the frightened boy, realizing that 'ordinary' ways did not have the results they had with 'ordinary' people.

"I guess I've pushed him too far," he said, and for a long while did not go near him. If he did, Kelton would lash out at him and dash out of sight. Or, he would go up to Joseph take him by the hand and lead him out the front door, leave him out there, walk back into the house and lock the door on him. I remember when he resented the pre-school kids in our home years ago and how he would casually take them to the door and deposit them on the front step and lock them out. He hadn't changed.

Kindly Joseph appreciated the bit of humor in the silent rejection Kelton expressed, and simply carried the key to the house in his pocket at all times.

There was no end to the trouble with Kelton touching girls. It had become quite a problem. We decided to scare him into stopping. Everything else we had done to teach him not to touch had not worked.

One day Kelton touched a girl who had come to visit Lynell. Joseph grabbed him roughly, slammed him up against the wall, and said, "You stop touching girls or I'm going to beat the hell out of you!"

Kelton screamed, "No!" and fled from the house.

Harsh and tough as the action may have been, it worked. Kelton stopped touching girls, at least when we were around. However, if he did get close to a girl he very cleverly did sort of a casual brushing by, which went unnoticed. He soon replaced touching with looking. Even though it was an improvement, and perhaps more appropriate, Kelton's looks were extreme. He would stare directly at a girl's' breasts or at her thighs. The looks he gave them were lengthy and unnerving.

For a while we didn't take Kelton anywhere, and restricted him to the yard. He broke his bike when we wouldn't let him ride it, and regressed to a level of years ago. He rebelled at his limitations and our demands by tearing up paper and washing his hands. He did not understand. How could he?

I tried to make Kelton realize that if he would behave, he could go places with us, but each time we took him somewhere, he would disappear and soon would be in trouble. Some girls' boyfriends or fathers would be outraged, threatening to beat him up.

Kelton took out his frustrations on all of us, but especially on Joseph. He stole Joseph's underwear and hid it. Poor Joseph was constantly searching the house for his shorts and shirts. Kelton also took Joseph's razor and shaving cream to torment him. He used up all the soap in the house with his constant washing of his hands. He dumped shampoo and toothpaste out of their containers.

He would take things from Mark and Allen. He walked off with all their socks and put them in his own drawer. He picked up cassette tapes and other items and hid them in his closet. He was punishing the whole family in the way we had punished him as a child: by taking away things he liked and needed. He had learned that lesson well.

"This brings back the days when Kelton took our belongings and threw them down the chimney," I told Joseph despairingly.

Kelton continued to make our lives miserable. Joseph— who had not lived with Kelton as a child—became irate and agitated with the daily unpleasant surprises. I wondered how this new marriage would wear through all these trials?

I stood in the middle of the problems like a traffic cop, directing emotions and feelings—especially anger and frustration—like so many cars heading for each other on the road to collision.

Fascinated with motion, Kelton had loved to smash glass before, but used old bottles he found in the garbage. One day I caught him smashing a good dinner plate with the hammer. He always cleaned up the broken glass and put it neatly in the garbage. Our garbage consisted of tiny tom pieces of paper and broken glass. He even ripped aluminum pop cans with his bare hands into tiny pieces. We called him our trash compactor.

Years of experience with troublesome surprises and a heightened sense of humor were my armor and my defense. I just kept going and wouldn't give in to anything negative. There really was nothing else to do.

I was unhappy with Kelton's class in the public school. Every time I visited, I saw how Kelton was being ignored. He sat quietly by himself, looking into the air. The teachers could not reach him so they left him alone most of the time. He wasn't learning anything, just putting in his time. I had a meeting with the supervisor of special education in our school district. I complained long and hard. He told me a new teacher was being hired, and he would see to it that Kelton would receive more personal attention and consequently, a better education.

By the end of July, Kelton's new teacher called me and said he would like to take the month of August to get to know Kelton. I was delighted. A breakthrough was about to happen.

Mr. Stevens was fresh out of college. He had an open mind and a strong desire to help. He was newly married and had no children of his own. He invited Kelton on a camping trip, went bowling with him, and made a point of taking him along all over the place. Kelton loved him and begged to see "Stevens," as Kelton called him, on the days that marvelous man did not come around. That year Kelton learned more from Mr. Stevens than he had ever learned from anyone.

At school, Kelton was placed in behavior programs. Mr. Stevens consulted with us at length on how we had in the past worked with him—ideas and ways to reach him and teach him. Nobody before Mr. Stevens appeared in our life had ever asked us just what it was that worked with Kelton, and how we handled him. This was truly a first.

Soon a strategy for teaching our son was developed.

Vern had given his younger brother a pair of black army boots which Kelton never let out of his sight. He was proud of them and polished them to shiny, black perfection. Mr. Stevens kept a pair of Kelton's gym shoes at school. Every time Kelton touched a girl at school, his boots were taken away from him, and he had to wear his gym shoes, He would be given extra work of some sort in order to earn his boots back.

When Kelton arrived at his classroom late from lunch, he was deprived of something he wanted or liked. We did the same things at home. These were the methods we had used long ago and which had worked, but somehow we had lost control over him. We were so thankful for Mr. Stevens and the personal interest he took in our son. Kelton was aware that his teacher cared for him.

With things going well for him, Kelton stopped playing pranks on the family. However, he did not let up on Joseph and still plagued him. Finally, in desperation, we took him to a hypnotist in Portland once a week. Mr. Stevens came with us several times, interested to see if the treatment worked. Kelton cooperated with the hypnotherapist and the sessions calmed him down. It's hard to say if it helped him to learn, but his behavior did improve considerably.

Kelton blossomed under Mr. Stevens' tutelage. He learned to read. His skills in art work and writing improved. He stopped listening to nursery stories and songs, and wanted tapes popular with young people his own age. He still preferred soft and mellow music and refused to listen to rock and roll.

One day Mr. Stevens talked to us about exposing Kelton to other handicapped people so he could make some friends. Kelton was definitely lonely and needed to socialize more. Under advice and guidance from the mental health center, we investigated group homes.

In the meantime, Kelton went to Fairview, a training center for mentally retarded people, for evaluation. The therapist wanted to keep him at Fairview for observations, but our son kept running away. Finally, he was placed in a maximum security ward, where rows upon rows of beds were occupied by very sick people, who were yelling and crying all the time. It was like a scene from a madhouse.

This was no place for Kelton. He was not insane. What were they trying to do to him? It took all I had do to leave him there and I swore to myself I would get him out of there the next day.

I had nightmares all night.

I woke up feeling as if I had been thrashed. The phone rang. It was Fairview. Kelton had escaped their maximum security ward. He had gotten away from the institution and had successfully avoided the police all night.

Joseph and I got dressed in a hurry and were about to jump into the car when Kelton ran into the yard. He was exhausted and upset after escaping from the hospital and running the 11 miles home. He seemed terrified of going back to Fairview. He kept yelling, "Police get you!" I put him to bed, assuring him he wouldn't have to go back to Fairview and that the police would leave him alone. Joseph called Fairview to tell them that Kelton was home.

What terror he must have gone through! I never should have left him in that terrible place. I couldn't stop crying during the day. I had such mixed feelings about what was best for Kelton. Everyone was telling me that I had to let him go, that it was time for him to be on his own. These people didn't understand. In so many ways, Kelton was still a small child. Would *they* be able to turn Kelton out if they were in my position?

When he was a small child he certainly was a bundle of problems and caused us a lot of worry and concern. Now he was a big child and the problems exacerbated. We still did not know what to do, what was best for him and for us. Would there ever be an answer?

What would he be like at 30, at 40. What would happen to him when I died? The questions hadn't changed in all these years and the answers eluded me just as they had from the beginning.

Again, we turned our focus on investigating every pro and con, every angle of group home living. What were they like? Who operated them? What did they do for their 'guests'? We learned a few things, except of course, the unpredictables—and there were lots of those as it turned out.

In a group home, twelve to fifteen residents live together in a home environment. The trainer and the supervisor of the home develop programs that are supposed to fit the needs of the individual residents. We decided to put Kelton in a group home. He was 18 years old, and everyone I knew told me it was time he learned to be on his own. After all, I wouldn't be around to take care of him forever.

To say it was a difficult decision was an understatement. I knew Kelton was trainable, that he had some creative and artistic skills. I also recognized that before he could be on his own, he had to develop social skills, and he could do that better in an environment away from home.

Then we discovered, to our dismay, that we would lose our parental rights, our control over Kelton. In other words, the group home operator would obtain guardianship. I didn't like that a bit. That meant trusting a total stranger with major decision making concerning Kelton's welfare, when they didn't even know him, and perhaps never would understand him. I felt utterly helpless and frustrated, and prayed this trust would not be betrayed.

In conjunction with Marion County Health Center, we investigated several homes and found one we thought would serve him well. We had to wait a few months before he could be enrolled, but finally the day came when there was an opening. We talked to Kelton about it and prepared him as best we could for the change about to take place in his life . He took the news well and was excited about his new adventure. I told him he would meet new people and make new friends.

"Have a friend!" Kelton kept saying over and over again.

There were only two boys Kelton's age at the group home, the other residents were older men. I wasn't too excited about that, but we had to give it a try.

I took my son shopping for a new coat, shoes and a brand new suitcase. We marked his radio, electric razor and all his clothes with tags bearing his name.

"Go live in the cottage," Kelton exclaimed as we shopped.

"That's right," I said. "Are you excited about going?"

"Yes!" said Kelton.

Joseph and I loaded his things in the car, and as we rolled slowly down the driveway, Kelton looked back at the house to see the boys still waving good-bye to us. He looked at me, startled, as if he just now had realized that he was actually going to live someplace else.

"It will be fun, Kelton!" I said quickly. "You will make lots of new friends and you will come home to visit, just like the other kids. Remember, Vern and Sharlene moved away from home, so did Lynell, but they all come back to see us. We still love them and we will still love you. We aren't that far away." Kelton was quiet as I continued to reassure him.

The housemother was a grandmotherly type, whom Kelton seemed to like. She explained the rules of the home to Kelton, and to us. We wouldn't be able to visit him for one month, she said. They wanted Kelton to get used to living there before he started home visits. It seemed logical and we agreed.

I cried as Joseph drove away. I prayed that Kelton would find his way, hoping with all my heart he would find happiness. I kept telling myself not to worry. I kept telling myself a lot of things, but I didn't listen. I worried.

Mr. Stevens, who had done so much for Kelton, didn't renew his contract with the school because he had decided to go back to college to further his education for working with special children. We were terribly disappointed. Kelton, I knew, would be upset. The people from the school district assured me they had hired another good teacher.

"I hope so," I answered, doubtful that someone like Mr. Stevens could be found again. I knew Kelton didn't like change, and this was going to be the start of a rough year for him; a new home and a new teacher all at once.

The month passed swiftly and it was time for Kelton's first visit home. I was so glad to see him and was glad he looked so well. He had lost a little weight—that was good. As soon as he entered the house, he checked up on all his favorite places. He was glad to be back, even if he didn't talk much.

"Do you like your new home, Kelton?" I asked.

"Yes!" he answered as he walked away, restless. He hardly talked to us at all during the entire weekend. He stayed in his room or went on long walks.

His once-a-month visits home were not as comforting and satisfying for me as I had pictured them to be. Kelton was quiet and restless. He wasn't doing much at school, I heard, but I was less involved now with his education since the group home supervisor had become the intermediary at school.

Kelton came home for Thanksgiving, as did Sharlene and her new husband Jerry and their children. Lynell was home from school, and Vern was home too. Elma, Karla and their families were there, and mother came from Spokane to be with us. It was a wonderful occasion. Kelton still didn't care for the large gatherings, but he liked all the good food. It was wonderful to have most of my family together.

I enjoyed the holidays with all their colors and sounds, the gifts of love, the greens and candles, the big Christmas tree, the rich food and my family under one roof. We celebrated the coming of the New Year quietly, leaving the old one behind, grateful for its gifts.

In the first weeks of 1979, Kelton's group home changed hands. We had been impressed and pleased with the lady who had operated the place, and I had become more and more at ease having Kelton in her care. Unfortunately, she had hurt herself in a fall, and could no longer manage the place.

A young girl, her brother and his wife took over the management.

After the change over at the group home, we were uneasy and I did not feel good about the new managing trio. Each time we saw Kelton he had lost more weight. He seemed upset all the time, and when I called the school to see how he was doing, they told me they were concerned about him too. Kelton often hit himself; he was irritable and hard to get along with. His talk was fragmented and the subjects unrelated. I had not seen him like this before. I was disturbed and an inner feeling of doom did not let me rest. What was wrong? What could I do?

The answer was on its way.

Early one morning the front door opened, and Kelton walked in.

"Hi, Kelton," I said with surprise. "How did you get here?"

"Run away," Kelton said.

"Don't you like your group home?" I asked.

"No!" yelled Kelton.

I called the home and told the supervisor that Kelton had come home.

"He probably had a quarrel with one of the residents and was upset," the man in charge suggested. "You should bring him right back so he learns to work his problems out and not run away from them."

That sounded reasonable, and after Kelton ate and showered, we sat down to talk.

"You have to go back, Kelton," I said.

"No!" he yelled.

"What happened there?" I asked.

"No!" he yelled again with determination.

"If you would only tell me what's wrong, I could help you," I pleaded with him. There was no response from him.

When Joseph came home we discussed the situation, trying to fit together a puzzle with most of the pieces missing. We decided not to give in to Kelton, and to take him back to the home.

Kelton ran out the door and down the road. We got in the car and followed him.

"Get in the car, Kelton," I said when we caught up with him. We drove and coaxed, pleaded and cajoled. Finally, he jumped in the car and we drove off. As we drove into the group home's driveway, he became very upset.

"No!" he cried, as we went into the supervisor's office. I was very alarmed. I hadn't seen Kelton this upset for a long time.

We questioned Wayne, the supervisor, at length. I wanted answers to a lot of questions. He assured us that Kelton was doing just fine, he just needed to learn to get along with others.

"I'm very upset with how much weight Kelton has lost, and how nervous he is," I told him.

"We'll make sure he gets more to eat," he promised.

Kelton sat quietly in his chair until he realized that he would have to stay. Then he started crying, "I'm sorry, I'm sorry, Wayne," then ran to his room and buried his face in his pillow.

I left him with a heavy heart, ready to run away and hide my head in my pillow. Why was this so difficult for Kelton? He seemed fine with the previous manager. Was there something wrong with this new set of people? Terrible thoughts shot through my head, but I had to let them go. I had to let it rest.

I was filled with uneasy feelings and worried about Kelton's welfare as I waited for the next visit with him. The month went by, and our only contact with the home was through phone calls to the supervisor who assured us regularly that Kelton was okay.

"He's settled down, and we are seeing to it that he is eating more," he told us. I remembered the fear on Kelton's face when we had taken him back to the group home. My heart ached with anxiety. I have always trusted my inner messages and I just knew Kelton was not okay. He was not fine.

"I really would like to see him," I insisted.

"I don't think it's wise just yet," he answered.

I gave in to the man's assumed authority for the moment, but did not let it rest. I called the school, but couldn't get his teacher, but the teacher's aid called me back. The report I received over the phone shocked and angered me to the very core of my being. I was furious.

"Kelton came to school this morning beaten up," the teacher's aide said. "His lip was split and his eye was swollen and black. He has other bruises on him too, Mrs. Johnson. Do you know if Kelton is getting enough to eat? He comes to school so hungry that I buy him a malt so he can concentrate on his school work. I looked at his lunch, and most of the time it's only dry bread and cheese. No fruit or money for milk. Maybe I'm speaking out of turn, but I think you should see what is going on in that home. Kelton is upset all the time at school. Something must be very wrong."

"Did you ask who hit him?" I managed to ask between waves of anger.

"Yes," she said. "Kelton said Wayne hit him. And in my opinion, I believe Kelton is not being well taken care of. He isn't clean, and he has a bad body odor."

My heart sank clear to the bottom of my shoes, and a hot fear rose in my throat, dreading just what we would discover. I immediately called the home and asked for Wayne. The girl who answered the telephone told me he was out.

"This is his wife," she said. "Could I help you?"

I related what I had learned from the school. She was quiet.

"I'll have Wayne call you when he comes back," she said as she hung up. Didn't she know anything? She lived there, too.

Wayne called me back, and said Kelton had gotten into a fight with another resident. He was vague; he couldn't be sure which one. Well, it was his word against Kelton's. Who would the world believe? Certainly not Kelton.

"As far as the food goes," Wayne continued, "he fixes his own lunch. If that is what he takes, I guess that is what he wants. Breakfast is served, but I can't make him eat."

"Eating is one problem Kelton has never had!" I said angrily, and hung up. I would get to the bottom of this, Kelton does not lie. It may be difficult for him to reply to questioning, but when he does, it is the truth.

I then called the Mental Health Center and told them what I suspected was happening at that home. There was neglect and heaven knows what else.

"What are my rights as his parent?" I questioned.

"Well, he is his own legal guardian," she said. "Give me a day or two to look into it."

A day or two!

"I'm not going to leave him there," I declared. In a day or two, I thought to myself, he could get beaten again.

"I'll make an appointment today for us to meet with the group home tomorrow," she said. "I'm sure Kelton is all right for tonight."

I was helpless, scared and angry at the same time. This was my child. What was going on?

I cried all afternoon, frightened that I didn't have the right to take Kelton out of the group home, frightened that I had no right to decide what's best for my son, frightened of shadows and phantoms and the sinking feeling that there was more bad news to come.

Somehow, tomorrow Kelton is getting out of that place," I said to Joseph emphatically. He agreed with me readily.

What happened next was a nightmare, and we would have to piece together the story of Kelton's escape later.

We were not at home that night, when Kelton ran away and found the house locked and no one around. He had gotten off the bus after school and ran home. With no one at home, he started down the freeway toward Portland. A man apparently had stopped his car and picked him up. The man asked him where he was headed.

"Portland!" Kelton had answered.

"What happened to you?" The man asked, "did you get in a fight?"

"Hit you hard!" Kelton began to cry.

After driving a few miles, the man realized something was wrong with Kelton.

The man took him to a police station near Portland and left him in the care of a police officer. Kelton refused to tell them where he lived. When the officer realized that Kelton had some problems, as per routine, he called Fairview. We couldn't be reached, so the officer called the Mental Health Center. Our case worker was not available, but the center's records revealed that Kelton lived in a group home.

Still unable to reach us, the staff member of the center gave the police Sharlene's phone number, and she was contacted. Kelton could not be released into her custody, only a representative of the group home had that right.

When the police finally reached Wayne, he went to Portland and brought Kelton back to Salem. It was morning before we were able to get Kelton.

Since we had not seen our son since his last visit, we were shocked when we saw him. He was so thin that his clothes hung on him like empty bags. His face was swollen. Black and blue marks discolored his fair skin and silently accused the unknown abuser.

I was boiling with fury. I was so mad at Wayne that Joseph had to restrain me from hitting him. Joseph quickly gathered up Kelton's things, threw them in the car, and we took him home. Kelton kept repeating that Wayne had hit him. He had tried to tell us that the first time he showed signs of a beating. We didn't believe him.

He vomited all morning, and ran a fever.

"I'll call the doctor and make an appointment to take him in to be checked," Joseph said.

After the doctor examined him, he informed us that Kelton needed to be hospitalized at once. He said that Kelton was completely dehydrated and that the cause for his severe vomiting had yet to be discovered. There would be tests.

My heart hurt enough to break. Poor, innocent Kelton. From one disaster to the next. No one deserved that. No human being had the right to inflict suffering on another.

I sat in the waiting room and cried softly. Joseph held my hand and tried to comfort me.

"How could this have happened? I should have taken him out of that place when he ran away," I sobbed. "He was trying to tell me something, and I didn't listen."

"You did what you thought was best," Joseph said.

"I'm going to go after that man. I'm going to file charges. He's going to jail for this—for ten years!" I vowed.

The doctors discovered Kelton had an ulcer, and suggested he stay in the hospital until he could keep food in his stomach and was in better condition.

I walked into the hospital room where Kelton lay pale against the white sheets, hooked up to an I.V.

"Needle," Kelton pointed as I came near.

"It will help you get better, honey," I told him. I sat down by him and he let me hold his hand. What could I say? "I'm sorry that I let you down Kelton," I said. The first time I trusted someone else with his care, and this happened.

Years ago Kelton and I had learned to just sit, knowing each other's thoughts and feelings. I rested my head on his arm. In the quiet of the moment, the love for this child of mine welled up from the depth of my soul, reached out to him and a feeling that our two worlds had touched and merged began to soothe my anguish, and perhaps his as well. We understood each other with words unspoken in the flow of our feelings.

After a while, Kelton said, "Don't cry, mother."

"I love you Kelton. I'm so sorry this happened," I cried.

"Go home now," Kelton said.

"I wish you could, but you are going to have to stay here until you quit vomiting. When your stomach gets better, and you can hold food down, you will be able to come home." I told him. "You can have your old room back."

"Okay, yes," Kelton answered.

After a week Kelton was moved into the main hospital because he had pulled out the I.V. and started for home. The police picked him up and took him back to the hospital.

# 22

Once upon a time, I believed in fairy tales. Daydreams sketched out a pathway for me to follow, and more than often, the dreams gave way to reality. Even though there were detours, and occasional nightmares, I believed that eventually everyone lived happily ever after. This, unfortunately, was not the time, Another terror-laden nightmare had appeared in the night of our lives and stayed with us during our days.

I arrived at the hospital only moments after Sharlene and Karla. They were by his bed, trying to talk to him. He was slipping in and out of his inner world, not quite daring to come out and face his new prison—not trusting, When I saw him, I was numb with emotion and a feeling of helplessness.

The doctor hadn't even bothered to call me about his intent to isolate and lock up Kelton. He had taken it upon himself to put Kelton in the security ward. He probably never gave a thought to what reaction this would have on his patient.

After all, patients were there for the convenience of the doctors—not the other way around.

Through my mind passed the image of all the impersonal, uncaring doctors I encountered over the years. I was angry: "How dare he lock Kelton up without even a phone call to check with me?" I thought. Didn't he know Kelton was suffering from a recent emotional upset? Doesn't he care?

The answer was obvious. He didn't care.

"Hi, Kelton," I said, trying to control my outrage.

"Needle!" he said, "Take it out!"

"Does it hurt?" I asked.

"Hurt," he answered.

I had battled so many doctors, I would take on another one.

I left Kelton and the girls to go phone the doctor. I told him what Kelton was doing and why. I also expressed my anger at him for taking it upon himself to lock Kelton up.

"I'm taking Kelton home," I told him. "He's not getting better here. I want you to speak to the desk and leave your discharge orders with the nurse. My son is going home."

Reluctantly, the doctor called the nurse and gave permission to release Kelton. He was glad to be going home.

"Hate hospital," he yelled as we went to the car.

Life was a collection of ordeals for Kelton, and, in some ways for us too. We struggled from one difficult time to the next.

Kelton was ill all summer long. He spent most of his days in his room sleeping or venturing out to walk around the yard. A skinny Kelton seemed strange, compared to the young man who was always a bit overweight.

Kelton's life had been a kaleidoscope of shapes and colors, ever changing, never quite the same. Now, we saw his childhood pattern of withdrawal return as he retreated again. Now the 19-year-old withdrew to his bedroom.

We tried to restore some balance into his life by encouraging him to go places, ride his bike and take part in activities with the family, but all he wanted now was to stay in his room.

Eventually, the vomiting stopped, and he began slowly to gain weight. With the help of vitamins, wholesome and nutritious food, his health improved. We enrolled him in a limited summer school program for four hours a day.

We filed suit to prosecute the group home administrator. At the hearing, testimony was given which claimed Wayne's innocence because he had been out of town the night Kelton was beaten up. Nothing ever came of the hearings. We didn't have enough documented proof to proceed with legal actions. Not much later, Wayne sold the group home and moved away.

Our case was not unique. Mishandling and abuse happens in group homes daily. Since the residents are either older or mentally limited, they are rarely believed, in spite of the tell-tale black and blue bruises on their faces and bodies.

By summers end, our efforts to draw Kelton out had failed. We had made efforts to engage him in activities to give him more attention and love. I reminded Kelton that high school was starting soon.

"No!" he yelled at the top of his voice. "No more school."

"You have to go to school, Kelton," I said. "This year you are going to a brand new school right next door to Allen's school," making it as appealing as I could.

We went to a meeting with Kelton's prospective teacher. He had been Kelton's instructor before, and our son didn't relate to him at all. In the hopes of making some changes, I called the school district but was told that this particular class was the only one available. It was that or nothing—a poor choice to make.

"Kelton has to get out of his room," I told the bored person at the school to whom I was talking on the telephone, "what he really needs is a job."

Kelton had had a small job at the school previously and had enjoyed the challenge of work. He was getting paid a modest sum, and he enjoyed the freedom of buying things with his own money. I asked the high school administrators about Kelton's working in the cafeteria, telling them he did a good job of cleaning tables and sweeping. They agreed to give him a job.

He had regressed to the unpleasant, old habits of not taking a bath, not getting up, hitting himself, and hitting at people. Each morning it was a battle to get him up and ready before the school bus came.

"Time to get up, Kelton," I said as I opened his door. He jumped up and slammed the door shut, then held it shut until I went away. Then he went back to bed. We repeated this several times before I threatened to pull him out and throw him into the shower. Some mornings were worse than others, ending up in a wrestling match. I carried a big, threatening looking stick. I never hit him with it, but he jumped up when he saw it. He refused to use soap, but just stood motionless in the shower. I gave him a bath one morning, which he hated.

"No!" he screamed.

"Then you do it," I said. "You don't get anything to eat until you are clean."

When Kelton was under stress he emitted a strong body order; sometimes he needed to bathe more than once in a day. He resumed using calcium and magnesium, which seemed to help.

Our home turned into a battle ground in the morning and at night, when we tried to make Kelton do the simple things which he used to do. By the time we had accomplished some of the most ordinary tasks of daily living, I was exhausted.

He continued to tear up paper. One morning when I went into his room to tell him to get up and was greeted by piles of cut up little denim squares everywhere.

"Kelton, those were your good pants," I scolded. He had cut up his jeans to bits and pieces.

I searched his room for the scissors he had somehow acquired. He also had cut his own hair, leaving large shorn patches all over his head. What would he decide to cut up next?

Abruptly, Kelton jumped up and tried to push me from his room.

"You can't have scissors if you're going to cut up things. You know better than this, Kelton." I told him.

I found a box with two pairs of purloined scissors and removed them from his room. Kelton tried to retrieve them, following me everywhere, trying to see what I would do with them. Finally, I put them in a kitchen drawer, planning to hide them after he left.

Joseph came in the kitchen and told me our trash cans were full of tiny fragments of glass. "Most of your fruit jars are gone," Joseph sighed. "Kelton has also been in my things again. Several of my tools are missing. We just can't go on this way. We need to find work for him. We can't just keep him home, he needs something more."

This was not a new conversation. Joseph felt strongly that Kelton needed to be where he could receive proper training. I agreed, but where was such a place? I thought Joseph didn't realize the years and years I had searched; years in which I tried many things but found them sadly ineffective. We always had to come back to our own resources. Now every time Joseph brought up the subject, I immediately bristled.

"Can't you understand that I don't know what to do, or where to go anymore?" I told Joseph in frustration.

Joseph would nod his head in silent agreement, and the subject would be dropped momentarily, only to come up a few days later, when we were faced with Kelton's actions: stealing, tearing up paper, smashing glass, dumping out shampoo and throwing away food.

We lived a day at a time, realizing that Kelton hated school and that a lot of his frustration arose from it.

When I met with his teacher, I found Kelton still hadn't started on the projects we had discussed earlier. He had made no progress, he simply took up space and existed. He hated school, he hit the teacher and seemed frantic and disturbed. All my endless consultations with his teachers and school district officials were peppered with promises, but led to nowhere

It was clear that he was not being challenged to learn. The teachers taught him the same alphabet he had learned when he was five.

I was as frustrated as Kelton. My attempts to teach him at home were futile. He ran away or escaped on his bike and left our world behind in his flight down the road. How I yearned to join him some times,

In the meantime, my mother had moved to Utah. She had heard of a doctor who might be able to help her with the nasty problem of recurring blood clots in her legs. However, she was never really too well anymore. In the summer of 1980, she called her family to Utah. She told us calmly that she didn't have long to live, and she wanted to see her family before she died. Mother had always known about things that would happen before they did, so when the call came, we dropped everything and went to see her.

When I arrived in Utah, we got to visit with aunts, uncles and cousins I hadn't seen in twenty years. It was a grand reunion. But best of all were the two weeks I had to spend with mother. Elma, Karla, Sharlene, and Lynell spent a lot of time with her too. She explained to us in simple terms that all her children were now grown up and knew how to take care of themselves. She wanted us to let her go.

"I'm in a lot of pain," mother confessed," I have been for a long time. I want to be with your father and our seven children who have gone before me. I don't want you to pray that I'll live. It's time for me to go."

As frost lays its shawl
Across the slopes,
And spins its design in the valley,
I have no loom
To weave this tapestry.
Why must my forgetting mind
Yield up the image,
Pale with time the hue,
Or lose beyond recall
The way Aspens drop their golden leaves.

Far too soon the seasons go.
The master weaver knows
I will never pass this way again
Except in memory.

Even now the sun is setting—
Its majestic tones so purple and blue—
Its lights fade as does my pain.
I must embrace the memory
Before the dark can decree
That all must part.

Oh time, memories of my children
In various stages,
I must engrave your images
Into my heart.
It seems so short,
Such brief pages.

The words of my mother's poem lingered in my mind She had given all of us so much. She had always been there when we needed her. She had set such a good example for all of us in every way. It would be hard to let her go, we loved her so much. My mother's world had a large circumference because God was its center. She would always remain in my world.

Sharlene and Lynell had remained in Utah to care for her, and we returned home to Oregon.

During that summer, the kids and I traveled on to Colorado to visit Jack's parents. Since Jack's death, we hadn't seen much of them, and it was time to get back in touch. We enjoyed the trip and renewed all the love we felt for the Steeles.

Just before school started, we received word that mother had died. It was a painful loss for all of us; we would miss her greatly.

With both my parents gone, there now was no barrier between myself and my own mortality. With death comes an awareness of life so intense that for awhile life and the world are radiant and beautiful. Time is precious, down to the moment.

I tried to explain to Kelton that his grandmother had gone to live with Jack and with Heavenly Father. He didn't respond right away. A few days later when he was peeling potatoes in the kitchen, he threw down the knife, dropped the potato and said, "Go see Grandma and Jack," and disappeared for several hours.

Many times after that, he wanted to go see Grandma and once he even cried rare tears over the loss of his grandmother.

Mother,
I meant to call you that morning
But put it off awhile.
Death got their first.
I meant to tell you one more time
How much I loved you
And what you mean to me.
My procrastination will always
Haunt my memory and me.
I still go to the phone
To share something with you,
Then remember you've gone.
I wish for you when I write a new poem
I wish for you when I need a friend
I wish for you when Spring comes
Remembering how
You loved
When a bird looks
In my window
I see you painting
Preserving the beauty.
When a leaf drops,
And the harvest is in,
I see you canning

And giving of your fruits.
I see you in myself
And in my children,
You so touched our lives.
I wish for you again
Each day something of you
Rings in my mind.
I find myself
Trying to answer.

Life is for the living, and as much as I wanted my mother back, it wasn't possible and I went about my business of living.

Our contracting jobs kept us busy. On weekends I tried to get Kelton to work for us at our houses, but he would wander off the second I looked away.

I have always believed love stimulates growth, and we continued to show love and understanding towards Kelton. We balanced love with discipline, making him understand that he must follow the rules of the family.

He stood in silence, waiting for me to read the thoughts within him. My soul pushed me relentlessly in my search for answers, but none were there. We tried to see the roses in our lives instead of the thorns, but it was difficult. At times, I found escape in my work, putting in many hours of overtime to release the great worry building inside me. What would happen to Kelton?

Some moments seemed too heavy to bear—like the day Joseph left our home to ponder if he could live with all of the turmoil in our household. It was a dark day for me. I loved Joseph, I knew he had put up with a lot. He was so good to us, but I couldn't have Kelton in a place where he would be abused again. Once was too many. But I knew it could happen again. Joseph came back into my life and I promised again to consider a place where Kelton had a future. In the meantime, we endured Kelton's battles and pranks for the rest of the school year.

# 21

$S$ummers became a nightmare. It was hard to keep Kelton occupied and out of trouble. He forever unlocked combination locks on neighbor's sheds, or irritated the neighbors in some way or another, I wasn't very happy when I discovered Kelton rode his bike on the freeway.

Once, Allen came up to my room, "Mom, a man is here to see you." I went to the door and came face to face with a big, burly fellow who voiced a new complaint about Kelton in a rough and threatening voice:

"I live up on the hill. Your boy, Kelton, keeps riding his bike up there. It is private property and I want you to keep him off. "

"Did he bother something?" I asked.

"No, he just rides up and down the road, but I don't want him there. Next time I'll call the police," he threatened.

I wanted to tell the man a lot of things, but instead I assured him I would try to get my son to stay away from his darn road. I closed the door in his face, angered at the man's unreasonable request. Kelton wasn't hurting anything or anyone. Wasn't there any place he could be accepted?

I enrolled Kelton in Shangri-la. The school was located not too far away from our home. The bus would come right to the door and pick him up every day. He went somewhat willingly to classes, but would participate mostly in the arts and crafts. The teachers worked with him on his conditioning and social skills, and he learned new things from the variety of activities the program offered. School was out at half past three, which made for long afternoons and left him with a lot of time on his hands.

Near our home there was a steep, hilly street which merged with a main road at its bottom. Kelton loved to race up and down the road on his bike. The dogs in the neighborhood delighted in barking and chasing him and the other kids as they flew by at high speed.

It scared me to see Kelton swooshing to the bottom of the hill with the speed of a downhill skier. I had warned him he would get hurt if he ever got in a wreck.

A few days later he raced down the hill at breakneck speed when a dog wandered out in front of him. Kelton swerved to miss the dog and lost control of his bike. He hit the ground with his head, shoulder and one arm, and skidded down the paved street.

Mark ran to the spot where Kelton had fallen, while Allen hurried to get me. Fortunately I was at home. We picked up our bruised son and carried him into the house. His head was bleeding profusely; there was a hunk of skin missing from his shoulder, arm and hand, and his legs were skinned in several spots. Joseph treated Kelton for shock. I called the doctor who told me to keep him quiet and watch for signs of a concussion.

Kelton had to spend the next seven days indoors, which was no mean feat. Like the rest of the world, he didn't like to hurt and he kept showing me all the places where new skin was growing. Surprisingly enough even the most serious wound healed well and quickly. He was ready to resume his outdoor activities, but he would never ride his bike that fast again. That was comforting, but sure as rain, something else popped up that needed attention.

A neighbor came to see me. Kelton had tossed his kid's bike up a tree, the irate father complained.

"We have a problem," he said. "Kelton threw my son's bike up in a tree. I really don't want anyone with that kind of strength around my son."

"I know what happened," I replied. "Did your son also tell you that he and a gang of kids were racing toward Kelton on their bikes, teasing him, threatening to run him down? Did your son happen to tell you Kelton came home with spit all over him?

"If you don't want your son's bike in a tree, then tell him to leave Kelton alone. Kelton never bothers anyone first, but he does have the right to defend himself!" The man turned on his heels and walked away without saying another word.

The next day I called the Mental Health Center to see if the organization could recommend a place where Kelton might receive some training. We resumed our task of investigating group homes.

"There are some good group homes around, we just have to look," the case worker assured me. "Kelton will be a lot happier with friends, and he will get involved in a good training program."

I had a lot of trepidation as we checked on homes and the people who managed them. I wanted to look straight into their consciousness instead of their faces. I wanted to look inside them and see if they had a heart.

After painful and careful consideration, we settled on a place that passed our scrutiny. The house was at capacity and we had to wait for an opening that was supposed to come up. Kelton visited the home several times and liked it. The house manager took him on a camping trip just before school started. By the end of the summer, Kelton had regained his weight and was in good health.

I was as nervous as the proverbial cat on a hot tin roof when we deposited Kelton at his new home. They had the same rules we encountered before: no visits for one month. Why do they always insist on this? I gave the manager $200 extra for Kelton's school clothes, because the man wanted Kelton to buy his own clothes. The fellow running the home seemed dedicated to his work, the trainer appeared to be qualified, and Kelton knew some of the younger residents from school.

Kelton still had the same school teacher. Nothing had changed at school and the experience proved to be a total waste of time for him. The teachers did not know how to reach him. Our hands were tied from getting him a job, because he had to wait until he was 21 years old before he would be accepted at a sheltered work shop.

"That's not the right place for him either," Joseph said. I agreed. But our attempts to get him a job were fruitless. I asked the school to include me in the meetings and planning programs for Kelton—I would know what was going on and would be able to learn what opportunities were available for Kelton. However, the school did hire him for janitorial work, which gave him some purpose.

Kelton came home once or twice a month. I was worried. He was losing weight again. When I called the group home manager, I was assured he'd see to it that Kelton ate better and promised to give him a snack after school. Although Kelton was always a big eater, he was shy around people—even his family—and did most of his eating when no one was around. We never had to worry about leftovers—Kelton took care of them.

There was little privacy for the individual in a group home setting, and Kelton, especially, had a difficult time with that. He was nervous and fidgety, and he didn't want to participate in the Christmas festivities. Although he did come home for Christmas, he didn't open his presents until late afternoon on Christmas Day. But then, we had learned a long time ago that Kelton did things his way.

However, we noticed that he was talking with more ease and wasn't staying in his room so much. He joined us in the family room watching television and went bowling with the boys. He even played a game of pool with Joseph. There was a noticeable difference in his behavior which pleased us very much.

Kelton was always glad to be home visiting, but kept talking about Berl hitting him, Berl was his roommate and was quite talkative. He was quite the opposite of our son who preferred silence and needed his privacy.

"Hit Berl back!" he would suddenly yell voicing a problem in his typical delayed reaction way.

Apparently the two young men have had their quarrels, and I was not overly concerned that Kelton was at a disadvantage. Robyn, his case worker from the Mental Health Center, worked closely with me and with the home's staff trainer. She put in a lot of effort to help Kelton adjust and to keep peace among the residents.

It was late December when I realized that Kelton still had not yet bought his new school clothes. I called and complained to the home's administrators. During that week he finally went shopping for clothes. Why did I always have to be on somebody's case to do no more than their job? Sometimes I felt like a witch riding my broom rounding up nightmares!

Kelton definitely was not happy at school. The instructors did not relate to him. The programs were structured for the mentally retarded and Kelton was bored going over the same material every day. And, as he had always done in the past, he would act as if he didn't understand things, and refuse to participate.

As a result, the teacher assumed he didn't know the task at hand and would insist he'd stay with it until he was numb with boredom. Kelton's willingness to learn was rooted in his need for variety, because he was a quick study.

I explained over and over that if he performed a routine once, he knew it, and it was time to move on to something else. But I faced my age old problem of deaf ears and closed minds. I didn't have any credibility; after all I was just a mother and not a card carrying educator.

As it turned out, this would be the last year of Kelton's formal education. It had become more than clear to me that the school system was not set up to train and educate (formally) autistic children. I couldn't change the system overnight, or even over the years. I hoped he would receive on-the-job training in the future.

Time went so fast and I always looked toward the future, hoping that something new and good was on its way for Kelton— my winter's flower.

# 24

January 1979 was a rough month for Kelton. He was driven by restless emotions that none of us understood. His nerves were so on edge he couldn't stand for anyone to even talk to him. He hit himself for no apparent reason. Usually, when he acted distraught something was wrong in his life. I had questions about the school and the group home. I found out he did not receive his dosage of vitamin B-complex and complained. He was still losing weight. It was evident that he had problems somewhere.

To be at a loss most of the time, to be forever on the short end of the stick, was not a morale builder, nor did it ease the pain in my heart I experienced, every time I looked at my son. We had traveled together for a lot of years, and we had gone a few miles, but we were far from getting to our destination: to a solution, a way of life for Kelton that would give him dignity, a degree of satisfaction and comfort. Challenges may be the spice of life, but we were a bit overwhelmed as one difficult event chased the next—right into our laps.

During the past few years, our business had done well, when suddenly interest rates soared, and the house market dropped. We lost money on the last three houses we built. Joseph and I decided to close the business and invest in a manufacturing company. We worked hard and under pressure to get our new venture on its feet. We had had the company for about six months, when Joseph became ill again.

I was awakened in the night by a gurgling noise. I sat up and noticed the bathroom light was on, the door open. I got up to see what was wrong.

As I walked into the bathroom, panic rose in my throat. "Oh God, no," I whispered, "please, not again." Blood was everywhere. Joseph was unconscious. As he lay on the floor, blood gushed from his nose and mouth every time his heart beat. I was afraid he would drown in his own blood if I left him.

I sat him up. "Joseph," I screamed.

He revived a little, and we struggled to raise him up further. His head kept slumping down and he was floating in and out of consciousness.

"Allen! Mark!" I sat there screaming. "Someone help me."

The boys slept downstairs in a far bedroom and could not hear me. I propped Joseph's head up, ran to the phone and dialed the emergency number. I didn't know if they would get to our home in the country in time. I had to do something else.

I called my brother Leon who lived about two miles away, then ran downstairs to wake the boys. My legs could not take me fast enough and I fell down most of the stairs. I picked myself up at the bottom of the staircase and ran to the boys' room. I flipped on the light, yelling for help and pulled them both out of bed. They woke instantly, very frightened. Allen jumped up and ran to a neighbor's house for help.

I raced back upstairs to Joseph. Fear pounded in my heart as I saw him sitting there, surrounded by what looked like gallons of blood, He looked dead.

"Joseph, Joseph," I screamed as I shook him. "Don't die, hang on, please, you can't die."

I ran to the closet and got Joseph's robe. Hurriedly, I slipped on a pair of jeans and a sweater. Blood was pouring from Joseph's mouth again, streaming down his chest. I grabbed a wet towel and tried to clean the blood off of his body. I knew if I didn't get him to the hospital he would die. Blood kept pouring out of his mouth, Was there any left, I thought panic stricken?

Somehow I got him to his feet, as I experience a surge of strength far beyond any I thought I possessed. Each step down the stairs was agonizing. I was afraid we would both fall. It was a miracle that we made it without a mishap. Mark opened the front door for us and was headed for the car when Leon drove up.

"Get more towels," I screamed to Mark.

We got Joseph in the front seat of Leon's car.

The bleeding had mostly stopped, but both Joseph and I were covered with blood.

"Oh no, what's going on?" Leon yelled.

"It must be the vein in Joseph's stomach, it must have torn again. Please hurry, I can't find a pulse." I heard myself reply.

Allen had not returned from the neighbors. Mark ran out of the house with towels, "How did you get down the stairs with dad?" Mark exclaimed.

"I don't know. I'll call you," I yelled as the car squealed away.

Halfway to town we met a policeman and the ambulance on its way to our house. Leon stopped them, explaining we had Joseph, and directed them to follow us.

The police cleared the way ahead of us. It seemed forever before we got to the hospital. Joseph looked dead. His body was beginning to cool and I couldn't find any signs of life.

We pulled in the emergency entrance, where attendants were waiting. Quickly they transferred Joseph to a stretcher. They gave him oxygen and rushed him into the emergency room.

I had to stay behind to comply with the demands of hospital paperwork. Maybe Kelton knew something I didn't when he tore up paper into tiny bits.

"I want to be with my husband," I felt like shouting. Nervously I gave the receptionist the answers to her questions.

"Can't you hurry?" I said, "I need to be with Joseph."

Leon made some telephone calls, and before long the waiting room was filled with my children and my sisters.

When they finally let me see Joseph, he had an I.V. solution running in his arm, and wires monitored his vital signs. He was pale, his lips were blue.

"I want to talk to the doctor as soon as he comes," I pleaded with the nurse. "He has had this before and I know what is wrong."

Before the doctor could get there, Joseph was again vomiting blood. A fountain of blood gushed from his throat, robbing him of his life.

"A lot of this is the water," the nurse assured me. "Maybe you had better wait outside," she suggested kindly.

"I'm not leaving," I insisted.

Nine months ago, Joseph had been hospitalized for kidney stones. The stones had lodged in a dangerous place and he had to have surgery. It worried me that this was happening so soon after the previous operation.

Dr. Roberts got there, and as soon as he could get away from Joseph, he came to talk to me.

"You have to operate immediately," I told him. "The bleeding is not going to stop." I continued to tell him Joseph's experience in Corvallis several years ago.

"I don't want to operate so soon after his kidney surgery," he informed me. "It's just too dangerous."

"He'll die if you don't," I demanded. "Damn it, listen to me! Call the doctor in Corvallis who operated and talk to him. I mean it, call him!"

He stood up slowly. He started to protest, but I interrupted, "Do it now!" He told the girl at the desk to contact the doctor in Corvallis and I walked out of the room.

Joseph had another bleeding spell. The hospital personnel wanted to make me leave, I refused, and held my ground.

Morning came and they still had not operated, but kept giving him one blood transfusions after the other, and again the call for his rare type of blood went out.

Joseph's family arrived from out of town and I went out to talk to them. We were all scared for Joseph's life, and remembered only too well our shared anguish and fear when we waited for him to be all right the last time.

My battle with the doctors continued. "He is pretty weak," the doctor stated.

"He's getting weaker," I responded, "let's call in some other doctors for their opinions."

"I already have," he replied, "we'll probably operate this afternoon."

What in the world were they waiting for? For him to get stronger and walk out of here?

I stood by Joseph's bed holding his hand. His grip was strong; when I moved my hand the least bit his grip would tighten. Tubes and machines were hooked up to what seemed every inch of his body.

"Hang on Joseph!" I pleaded. "We love you and need you. Don't leave us. You can make it through this one."

Just then blood came up the tube from his stomach. It was red, fresh blood, not water. I called the nurse. She pushed a button and two other nurses joined her. They worked with him as he hemorrhaged again. The doctor came in, took one look at Joseph and said, "We will operate now."

"Thank you," I said simply.

It felt like being in another world as I looked around at other beds, most of them were filled with elderly people, all fighting for their lives. They took Joseph away, and I stood in the empty corridor feeling more lonely than I ever had in my life. Arms went around me as Sharlene held me.

"We love you," she said.

Soon Vern, Allen and Mark came up with Karla and Elma. We all stood in the hall holding each other, crying. Joseph had become such an important part of our lives. I had a good marriage and my family and my children loved him. The kids called him dad and gave him a place in their hearts.

The scene in the hospital was a repeat of the first time Joseph had been so ill. Friends came to wait with me, comfort us, and to give blood. Prayers were offered during the four-and-a-half hours he was in surgery.

Joseph's mother was so upset, she couldn't stay at the hospital. The rest of us waited, pretending to be brave. Finally our vigil was over. The doctor came out of surgery to speak with us.

"Joseph had a rough time, but we found the trouble. It was a main artery in this stomach. We removed it and part of his stomach," he said.

A load the size of a small mountain dropped away from me.

"Will it happen again?" I asked.

"It could."

"When can I see him?"

"He is in recovery right now. We are still giving him blood. It took nineteen units to save his life. The nurse will let you know when you can see him."

Prayers do have wings and reach their destination quickly.

"Thank God he's alive," I breathed. I was elated and lifted by the good news and at the same time, I was weak from the sheer terror of the ordeal. My body felt heavy, my bones so weary and rubber-like. This latest in a series of challenges had taken its toll on me. What would it do to Joseph?

As I feared, this time Joseph's recovery was even slower. Our partners in the manufacturing business decided to sell, since Joseph would not be able to run it for a long time. The company was sold back to the original owners. Things were not falling into place when we most needed order.

After Joseph recovered, we bought a weatherization company and hired Vern and Jerry, Sharlene's husband, to work for us.

As the economy deteriorated more and more, and people lost their jobs, Sharlene and Karla came to work for us also. For a while most of our family was out of work which put a lot of pressure on all of us.

Sharlene and Karla both had a baby during this time. Karla and Ken had a little boy, named Kenney. (We considered Karla and Ken's children as our grandchildren. Karla was more like my daughter than my sister). Sharlene and Jerry had a baby girl named Rebecca. That made us grandparents of five beautiful children. In spite of the pressures and difficulties, we enjoyed many blessings.

## 25

An urgent call from Kelton's case worker, Robyn, brought Joseph and me to a meeting at the group home. We sat in conference with the administrator of the home, Kelton's trainer, and Robyn. It was required by law that Kelton was present at these meetings.

The trainer reviewed Kelton's programs. He reported the performance score was low, and our son was uncooperative. Kelton sat quietly on the sideline while they discussed him as if he were part of the furniture.

"He knows how to wash dishes, vacuum, and other things," I told them, "but when he becomes bored he won't stay with a task. He also needs to be put back on B vitamins. I know that would settle him down," I said.

"I've already explained to you, Mrs. Johnson, that we have to have doctors orders to do that. Our doctor does not see a need for vitamins," said the administrator.

Everything I said fell on deaf ears. As the meeting continued, the administrator brought up Kelton's visits home.

"I think he is visiting home too often, and Mrs. Johnson is not giving us enough notice before she picks Kelton up," the administrator's voice droned on.

In order to pick up Kelton for his visit at home, we had to call the day before. Only once had I called the same day, and the worker at the home had given me permission. The rest of the times, I had followed the rules.

I didn't agree with her about fewer visits home. I felt Kelton needed to know his family loved him. The quiet weekend time twice a month helped Kelton cope with the rest of the week. However, after much discussion, I agreed to decrease the number of his home visits.

Why was it so difficult to convince people that I knew what my son required? I had raised him, worked with him, laughed and cried with him. Kelton needed space, and I knew there was little privacy in a group home. His roommate, Berl, followed him everywhere, talking all the time; and several other residents were around him as well. No wonder he was not progressing.

I returned home very disturbed. Things were not right, but I knew he had to start solving his own problems. I just hoped he was being treated fairly.

His number of visits home decreased. We did not see Kelton for four weeks. He had lost at least 25 pounds since he has been in this group home, and he was dressed in old clothes which I had not seen before. I hardly recognized my own son.

The merry-go-round never stopped. I went to the school to talk to his teachers. Kelton was giving them a rough time by being defiant, yelling back at the teachers, and not really learning much. They were also concerned by the changes in Kelton.

I arranged another meeting with the school administrators, Kelton was present, so was the administrator from the group home, and Robyn from the Health Center. Joseph came with me. We discussed the various school problems. After the meeting, I put my arm around Kelton. "How are you, honey?" I asked, touching the back of his neck.

"How are you, fine," answered Kelton.

Beckie, the owner of the home group, came up behind me, and asked if she could see me. We walked out into the hall. Joseph followed a little behind her.

What followed was hard to believe.

"You really should not touch the back of Kelton's neck, he is a man and that just causes him problems," the woman said. She must have reached deeply into the sewer of her mind to come up with this innuendo.

"What?" I said as my mouth fell open.

"That's why I don't like Kelton to go home, you're always touching him, you should know better," she flapped on, unconcerned with my reaction.

I was stunned as I listen to her. This woman hinted at a sexual relationship between mother and son. I was going to be sick to my stomach.

Joseph must have seen the red danger signals flashing in my eyes, and contorting my face. He stepped in front of her, "Let's go," he said as led me out the door.

"Did you hear what that woman said to me?" I asked him.

"Yes," he answered. "She's sick."

"Let me go back and hit her—just once," I demanded.

There had been lots of conflicts over Kelton, many uncomfortable situations and difficulties, but never anything like this. I could not believe it. I had discovered a long time ago that when 'normal' teenagers get into trouble, people said "Boys will be Boys." Let kids like Kelton make a mistake, and they are quickly labelled misfits with behavioral problems. Instead of finding ways to help them grow and adjust, these kids were shunned and dumped as so much unwanted ballast.

I told Robyn what the administrator had said to me. Robyn was taken back by this ugly insinuation as well, and promised to keep a close watch over Kelton, so I would be informed of what went on with Kelton. I was grateful I had one ally in this battle.

At another meeting—I could hardly bear to be in her presence—a few months later, Beckie announced that she wanted Kelton removed from the group home. Robyn reasoned with her, asking her what the problems were.

"He is hitting the staff, and he goes into the bathroom and won't come out. He won't follow rules," she complained Before the meeting was over, Beckie had me in tears. I wanted to know what had happened to Kelton's clothes, radio and other items he was missing.

"The fellow I just fired must have stolen them," she said. How convenient, I thought.

"What about his money, where is it?" I questioned.

"I don't know," she said.

"Well, someone should take some responsibility to find out," I said. I was angry.

Finally it was decided Kelton should have another chance.

"I know if the administrator would take the time to find out what is bothering Kelton, he would be okay," I told Robyn.

"She has fired all her staff and is running the home herself," Robyn said. "She isn't supposed to be doing this. I just hope she will soon replace her help."

"You mean there is no trainer anymore?" I said, alarmed. I wish I could just bring him home.

"Well, she said she was going to hire another one soon. I'll look into it."

Two months later I was at work when Robyn phoned and said the administrator had called and again wanted Kelton removed from the home.

"I will pick him up at five when I get off work," I said. "Is that soon enough?"

"Yes," Robyn replied, "he gets home from school about three-thirty, that will give him time to pack his clothes." she said.

"What happened?" I asked.

"He hit his roommate. I'm surprised he hasn't long before now," she said, "that guy would drive me crazy."

"Well, why didn't she change roommates?" I complained. "I don't feel she has given Kelton a fair chance." Personally, I thought, she was not fit to run a home like this.

At five o'clock, Joseph went to pick up Kelton. Since the administrator and I didn't like each other, he had suggested I stay home.

When Joseph arrived at the home, Beckie said Kelton wasn't there.

"Where is he?" Joseph asked.

"He told me he wanted to go to the hospital, so I called the police and had them take him there," she stated.

Joseph could not believe what he was hearing. "Which hospital?" he asked.

"The State Mental Hospital. Kelton signed himself in," she said triumphantly.

"Kelton hates hospitals," Joseph told her. "You knew we were on our way, why have you done this?"

"I just wanted him out of here," she announced, as if another hour would have made a difference.

Joseph picked up two small boxes of clothes. "Where is his suitcase?" he asked.

"That's all there is," she said, as she walked away.

Joseph hurried to the State Mental Hospital. There he was informed that Kelton could not be released to Joseph. Kelton was his own legal guardian, so he would have to sign himself out after an investigation. Reluctantly, he came home and told me the news.

"How can she do that?" I raged.

I immediately called Robyn and she promised to see what she could do.

Nothing can compare to the helplessness one experiences when dealing with institutions and the unyielding mind of bureaucracy. And nothing, but nothing equals the fury of a mother fighting for her child.

I had a great fear of Kelton ending up in an institution. I had fought neighbors, doctors, and educators to keep him home. Beckie knew Kelton would sign anything he was asked to. I recalled that the last time he left a group home he had to go to a hospital for his ulcers. If Kelton had said "go to the hospital" it had been a question, not a request.

I shook with anger. It wasn't any of her business, nor was it within her rights to call the police and have Kelton taken to a mental hospital.

I paced back and forth until Robyn's call finally came. She said Kelton would have to spend the night at the hospital, and tomorrow there would be a meeting about the situation. She would call me then. "You can go see him this evening," she told me.

When we walked into the state hospital the front desk was empty. We stood there waiting. People walked by, lost in their own worlds. A man dressed in a robe, about my age, approached me. He reached out and touched my arm, "Take me out of here," he begged. His eyes were dazed.

"I can't," I answered. "I'm sorry." He walked slowly away.

Just then an orderly asked us what we wanted.

"We are here to visit Kelton Steele," I said. He looked through a card file and said, "Oh, yes. Go through that door, you should find him there."

The hospital smelled of drugs and confined bodies. I shivered and Joseph put his arm around me. We entered a big room filled with people. We looked everywhere for Kelton. Finally, Joseph saw him sitting in a corner wearing a light green shirt and pants that hung loosely about him. Kelton had been drugged. He just sat there like a vegetable. He didn't even act like he knew us.

"We are going to get you out, Kelton," I told him as tears streamed down my face. Kelton just stared into space, not knowing or caring what we said.

All of a sudden all the years of effort, struggle, tears, and prayers passed through my mind. For what? Is this how it was going to end? I couldn't stand it. I fled from the hospital.

I immediately called Robyn.

"You don't have any legal rights to get Kelton out," she said. "He signed himself in, and he is of age. He will have to sign himself out."

"How can he do that?" I cried. "They have him so drugged he doesn't even know us. I want him out tonight."

"There isn't anything I can do until tomorrow. But I promise I will do everything I can to get him out. I know Kelton does not belong in there."

I spent a sleepless night and a very long day with the minutes ticking by slowly, before Robyn finally called.

"Kelton will be released tomorrow," she said. "You can pick him up at three."

"Why not now?" I demanded. What in the world was wrong with now?

"He had to see the doctor, and the paperwork has to go through," she said.

"Thank you, Robyn. I know without your help we wouldn't have been able to get him out without a bigger battle," I told her gratefully.

"Try to get some rest," she advised. "I'm so sorry this has happened."

"I want to press charges against that insane woman. Tell me how to go about it," I asked. We had not had any luck with group homes, and I wondered what special brand of sadists set themselves up as keepers of the less fortunate, the mentally limited ones. They'd get away with murder—murder of the human spirit at least.

"You can contact *Guarding Advocacy and Protection* (G.A.P.). It's an organization working for the rights of retarded citizens." She gave me the number.

I called at once and told them what had happened. The person I spoke with said she would call me back the next day.

My life was made up of hope for tomorrows and promises for next days, which would turn into more tomorrows and a string of more promises for the next days. But for the moment, there was nothing, just pain and frustration. I wonder what it was like for Kelton?

Tomorrow did come. Finally. We took Kelton home—what there was of him, that is.

He retreated to his room, coming out only to eat, and eat he did. We couldn't fill him up. It wasn't long before he was gaining his weight back, while I filled with renewed strength and courage. It was especially troublesome for Joseph, but I had faith that our marriage would make it through.

G.A.P. did nothing to support Kelton's rights. The girl phoned back stating that she felt their organization could not get involved since they worked with the group homes all the time. Working with whom? For what purpose? What a courageous stand to take. Fortunately, people who sit on fences, eventually have to face the consequences of their uncomfortable perch.

The mental health center promised to schedule a hearing. "Looks like she is going to get away with it," I told Joseph. I could just hope not many other unfortunate people would come under her careless care and suffer as we all did.

Kelton was not happy when he went back to school and we could understand why. There wasn't anything there for him at all. But he had to attend for the rest of the school year before he was eligible for a work program.

One day Kelton must have had enough. He hit the school teacher, which got him expelled. Finally the school district, tired of me and our problems, signed the necessary papers for Kelton to enter a sheltered workshop program.

We attended the hearing conducted by the mental health center. The result was disheartening. I was very disappointed that nothing was done about the administrator of the group home, except that she had to hire help to operate the home, which was a blessing. I realized just how helpless the handicapped are. They have very few rights and their concerned families have little more.

Robyn left the center to go back to school. Now I had to deal with a new case worker. I had learned to rely on Robyn and appreciated her genuine interest in Kelton and the never ending challenges we faced. I was not looking forward to this change.

We were both pleased and surprised when the high school made an exception to let Kelton graduate early. It opened the way for other handicapped students in the school district to follow. Many students were not learning in the special classes and needed to be working.

Kelton was delighted to have a job. He worked right down the street from our business. We took him to work in the morning and he walked to the office to ride home with us after work. His job was assembly work, making boxes and doing other repetitious jobs. He achieved a high performance record.

"Do you like your job?" Mark asked Kelton.

"Yes! Like work!" he replied happily.

"What do you do?" Mark continued.

"Make lots of boxes," Kelton said quickly with a sly grin.

"How do you make them?" Allen wanted to know.

"Fast," Kelton said as he walked away. End of conversation.

It is difficult to understand why communication is so hard for Kelton. He knows all the words to say, but can't put them together for use in a conversation. Early one morning as a still fog lay over the streets, we drove slowly trying to see the white line down the middle of the road. Kelton started to speak, then stopped himself and sat rigidly, every nerve and muscle on edge. We drove along, silence humming in my ears. My mind filled with memories, for it takes less time to remember things than to live them.

There had been so many times when driving Kelton to one place or another that we could have talked, yet we rode along always in silence. I usually talked to him anyway, knowing it would be a rare moment if he replied.

A sense of urgency gripped me. Kelton was nearly 20 years old. Was time running out to teach him to speak better? Would he get too set in this pattern?

"Kelton," I asked, "Our life together has been like this fog. We can't see what is ahead of us and we get frightened. I can't see what is ahead for you, Kelton, and I get frightened. Somehow we need to lift the fog that keeps you from talking. When you won't talk, it keeps you from having and doing so many things."

Kelton studied me. A veil seemed to come over his eyes for a moment, then he delivered his ultimate silent speech to me.

Do you understand my concern for you? I thought to myself I stopped the car at his workplace. "See you tonight, Kelton."

"See you," he answered.

I could no longer delude myself into thinking that one day Kelton would become accomplished in the art of conversation. The times when he did speak were few and far between—and usually under stress. I knew he would have a rough time adjusting to independent living as long as he didn't communicate. There must be something else I could do to answer this age-old problem of Kelton's.

Whenever Joseph drove Kelton to work, he would tease him. Many times Kelton responded normally to Joseph's teasing. This was a good form of forcing him to communicate. In the car, he couldn't run away. Some of the teasing was verbal and some was touching him. I think it helped Kelton not to be so sensitive.

I called the mental health center again, and they told me about a girl named Karen who did tutoring for the school district. The district would pay for her services while Kelton was under 21 years of age.

I was encouraged that he would get some special classes in speech, and delighted when I met Karen, a dedicated and creative teacher.

"Kelton, this is Karen. She will be your speech teacher," I told Kelton cheerfully.

"Teacher," Kelton repeated.

"Hi, how are you?" Karen asked as she reached out her hand to Kelton.

"Hi, how are you?" Kelton answered shaking her hand.

"Let's get started, Kelton," Karen said as we walked toward the family room.

"Get started, yes," Kelton repeated.

Kelton loved the individual attention, and he liked Karen. She had a little trouble with his touching her, but she was able to handle it well.

Karen and Jan, another Salem trainer, had been trained in the Judevine method. At the Judevine Training Center in St. Louis, Missouri, children with communication problems have found help, and their families have found hope. The Judevine Center was founded in 1970 to disprove the notion that an institution is the only solution for autism, and to provide help through meaningful individualized programming.

They have proven that autistic children can learn and can replace their own disorganized behavior with constructive healthy behavior. The Center offers an answer to those who find communication with the real world a difficult and bewildering experience. The more Karen told me about their work, the more excited I became.

"There is a class offered this summer," Karen said.

"It's usually attended by teachers and the parents of the children. If the class is not full, I'll talk to Jan about you and Kelton attending."

As summer approached, my expectations were high. I believed this might be the answer to my prayers. I grew excited as I observed their teaching mode. For the first time in twenty years I saw a method that resembled what we had done with Kelton years before.

Karen moved quickly from one subject or activity to another, and constantly reinforced acceptable actions. Some of the things I had been doing were right according to this method, other things were not.

First we received classroom instruction, then we began to work with our own and other children individually. We observed them in groups, then tried to teach, following the instructions of our teachers.

We were videotaped and an instructor was present to help. Later we watched ourselves on video and discussed things we should have done, and things we did right.

Kelton enjoyed the classes and I felt it helped him. But it was only a small start. He required a lot more. We needed to break down his resistance of interaction with others and nurture the growth of healthy social behavior. The Judevine training was attempting to accomplish this.

The summer training ended too soon, but we were able to get one of the instructors, a young woman named Joyce, to continue with Kelton's speech therapy, and I would work with him at home. He started talking a lot better when cued, but resisted using complete sentences unless prompted.

To be born with normal intelligence and to have no instinct for communication is a devastating handicap. Kelton could not join in which always led to isolation. Normal babies are born with the ability to translate sounds into meaningful patterns, to learn quickly to read facial expressions, and to use these skills to make themselves understood. Autistic people do not instinctively communicate with others. Everything has to be taught, all social behavior and all language with its grammatical structure. These people have few skills for everyday living.

Our son was not a loner by choice. His attempts at communicating and socializing were poorly rewarded and he found it easier not to try. It has caused him great unhappiness. I realized this one night when Mark and Allen had some of their friends over for a party. Kelton was invited. We dressed him up and practiced what he would say. Kelton was excited about the event. He helped me prepare the food and clean the house.

When guests started arriving, Kelton greeted everyone, he served the punch and sat down by a girl. I watched, hoping this would be a success for Kelton. He sat silently. Soon the girl spoke to him; he repeated her. She moved away. He remained there for awhile, then got up and followed her and sat beside her again. In a few minutes she escaped.

I said to him, "Kelton, would you like to pass around the cookies?" He came to help.

Later in the evening, Kelton made another attempt to talk to someone, but the person quickly moved on. The boys showed a movie, and Kelton stayed for most of it.

I noticed he was missing from the party. I found him outside.

"Kelton," I called softly. He didn't answer, but sat down on the edge of the porch and rested his chin in his hands. I acted on impulse and, going to him, held him against me. For a moment, he let me hold him, then he pulled away.

"Did you like the party?" I asked.

"No like the party," he answered. There was a note of sadness in his voice. I tried to cheer him up.

"You did a good job serving everyone, Kelton. I was very proud of you!"

Five minutes passed while we sat there, my heart breaking for him. We sat gazing at the moon, listening to the sounds of laughter from the party. When he spoke next, there was real emotion in his voice as he suddenly looked at me and stated simply, "Need a friend!"

Long after everyone was asleep, Kelton wandered about, listening to the night sounds. Unable to bear his emotion, he walked restlessly around the yard. I stood on the upper deck and watched him as the moon sank to a shadow far down in the sky. It was one of the last warm nights of summer, and soon I was aware of a light rain failing.

"Come in Kelton," I called. "I'll make some hot chocolate." He turned and walked toward the front door. I went downstairs and turned on the kitchen light. Kelton came in and sat at the snack bar. He was tired, a shadow appeared on his cheeks. His blue eyes had a weariness I hadn't seen before.

I talked to him cheerfully. "Hey, Kelton, summer's over and who knows what this winter will be like? You have lots to be thankful for parents who love you, lots of people care about you, Kelton. You just have to keep trying."

"Keep trying," he answered as he drank his cocoa.

My thoughts turned to all the happy days Kelton had spent with Mark and Allen as children. He accepted them and found companionship and love. Now they were growing up, making new friends and creating their own world, leaving Kelton behind. Kelton was not competitive, and with his lack of awareness, he could not understand that his brothers had outgrown him. It made him feel deeply inadequate. He would adjust, but it would take time.

When Allen learned to drive a car, Kelton begged for a turn to drive. I let him steer the car. He did a perfect job of keeping the car in the right lane—in fact, he really did a better job than Allen.

Once when we were out driving, Allen made too wide a turn, nearly hitting another car.

"Kill us!" Kelton yelled. "Let me drive." For a long time after that, Kelton wouldn't ride when Allen was behind the wheel.

I continued teaching Kelton how to drive, but I explained to him that he could not drive unless he could pass the examination. I gave him a book to study. He looked at it and walked away. Later I found it torn in tiny pieces in the garbage. Neither of us ever mentioned driving again. He had driven a motorcycle and I knew he could drive a car, but it was not possible. Someday I knew he could be taught to operate a fork lift and other machinery.

Kelton reacted to the disappointments in his life, but he still found it difficult—impossible—to explain himself, so that his behavior was not understood by any of us.

We looked for suitable employment for Kelton. His appraisal of his self-worth was measured by his work. The sheltered workshops had a hard time getting contracts, and there was little work for him at times. Besides, he was bored with the sameness of the projects.

Kelton walked into my office at work one day. He paced around nervously, then kicked a display and said, "I have a brain."

He walked out and traveled the eleven miles home on foot. Kelton seemed doomed to spend his life in frustration, climbing one mountain after another but never reaching the lofty heights of contentment.

For the next three years he lived at home. During this time we kept looking for appropriate employment with proper supervision. We realized he needed to learn functional communication, ongoing speech development. Also, he needed self-help training, and social development. He required friends and love. Where were we going to find these things for him?

On Kelton's twenty-second birthday, we gave him a birthday party, and invited only family and friends he knew. Almost immediately he caught on to the spirit of the party. He loved the cake with all the candles and even liked his presents.

"Make a wish and blow out your candles, Kelton," Sharlene encouraged him.

"Wish," Kelton answered as he sat there looking at all the burning candles. A twinkle came in his eye, he laughed and blew out all of his candles.

After everyone left, I asked, "Did you have a good time at your party, Kelton?"

"Yes," he answered happily. He gathered up his presents and examined them. He put a cassette in his new tape recorder and turned up the music.

He looked at his slides through the viewer. I marveled that he had not run directly to his room, but was sharing a happy moment with me, not wanting the day to end.

After that, we planned more things to do for Kelton. Mark and Allen thoughtfully included him in their activities. They still had to keep him from touching girls, but his behavior improved a lot. They were able to take him to movies, bowling, and to the mall. There were times when he couldn't go with them, and I would find him crying in his room, or he would disappear on his bike.

One day when we drove up the driveway, a police car was parked there. An officer got out and walked toward us.

"Are you Joseph Johnson?" he asked.

"Yes," said Joseph. "What's wrong?"

"Kelton has been racing the cars on the freeway," the officer replied. "He has been picked up before for this. We are afraid he will get hurt."

"We will talk to him," I assured him.

"He waits at the entrance to the freeway, races the cars until they pass him and then goes back to race another car," he explained our son's latest escapade.

After cautioning us again on the dangers lurking at the highway, he policeman left, and we went to talk to Kelton.

"I guess we will have to put up the bike for awhile," I said, and Joseph agreed.

Kelton did not like having his bike put away, and in a few days we noticed the tires on his bike were flat. We never knew for sure if he let the air out or not, but I remembered all the times he broke things that wouldn't work. I wanted to forget the past and give him the benefit of the doubt.

Kelton was attempting to function normally in the everyday world, but we were constantly reminded of how different he was and of the enormous effort it took to live in a world where no concessions were made, where he was expected to conform.

Kelton and other autistic people whom I have met, share a basic problem of having no instinctive feel for communication and a lack of social awareness. Although Kelton has learned to be verbal, conversation on an everyday level is absent or irrelevant and repetitive.

Some people believe that autistics can't learn to make a living, can't think or can't have goals for a normal life. This just isn't so. Many autistic people now are finding employment and work opportunities.

Most of these people began working at local sheltered workshops to learn some of the skills necessary to succeed on the job—things such as promptness, working under supervision, cooperating with peers, working productively, and interacting appropriately with others.

They are paid on the basis of their productivity, in accordance with minimum wage. Later, they are moved to more demanding jobs in the community. Employment increases the autistic person's confidence and self-image. They act and feel more adult, which carries over to their work performance. In some parts of the country where such programs are initiated, instructors are having great success, according to Autism Society of America (1234 Massachusetts Ave. N.W., Washington D.C. 20005).

# *26*

The days flowed into seasons, and the seasons made up the years. All I had to do was to look at Mark and Allen to recognize time's passage.

This summer day was a special day for us. The boys were leaving home for a while. I went to their room that morning to see they had packed all they would need for their journey. Allen and Mark both stood up when I entered, towering above me. Where had the years gone? Both young men had their suitcases packed without my help, and were ready to leave.

I took their hands in mine and said good-bye to them in this private moment. Allen's tall leanness accentuated his height. Mark's eyes held excitement, and it occurred to me that they had experienced very little excitement and adventure of their own in their lives. There was a gentleness about Mark's face, but a firmness of the jaw. He was almost as tall as Allen, but huskier.

"Kelton wants to go with us," Allen said quietly.

"I wish we could take him!" Mark added, his eyes meeting mine. They started to talk about their trip. "The train leaves in two hours. We better get started soon," Allen reminded us.

While Joseph and Mark loaded the car with the boy's luggage, I went to look for Kelton. I found him in the backyard watching a squirrel running up and down a tree.

I smiled at him. "Kelton, we are leaving to take Mark and Allen to the train station. Do you want to come with us?"

"Yes!" he said, running to the house.

We got into the car and honked the horn for Kelton. Soon he emerged from the house carrying his suitcase.

"No, Kelton," Joseph said gently. "Leave your suitcase here, you are going to see the boys off on their trip to see their Grandma Steele. You are going to go with us in the car when we go to pick them up later on."

He returned to the house and reappeared, minus his suitcase, apparently willing to accept the fact that he could not ride on the train with his brothers. I did not see any kind of resentment in his demeanor.

Three weeks later, Joseph, Kelton and I traveled to Colorado to the Steeles' golden wedding anniversary. We had a beautiful time. We brought Mark and Allen home with us. Kelton had enjoyed the trip very much. He still had to fight being left out and struggled with his inappropriate ways of relating to others. He followed the girls around, and did not talk much. No one complained about him. He was accepted just for who he was. All in all it was a good trip.

Often several weeks would pass quietly. Kelton went about his business and I breathed with relief. No sooner did I relax then something would happen.

We were at my sister Elma's house one night when we received a phone call from our neighbor, telling us the police were looking for us.

"It must be Kelton," I said. "He is out riding his bike today."

Joseph called the police and was told there was a drunken driving charge against Kelton—riding his bike.

"Kelton doesn't drink!" Joseph said laughing out loud.

"I know," said the policeman, "But he was swerving back and forth, and this lady reported a drunken driver on a bike and we had to follow it up." Of course, Kelton was not drunk and the police released Kelton with no charges.

We all had a good laugh, but realized how very little freedom Kelton had because his actions were not appropriate for his age.

For the past year he had been riding the bus home from a sheltered workshop. One night he failed to return. I called his work.

"Kelton is in the hospital," the man said.

"Why?" I asked anxiously. "Did he have an accident?"

"No, he ate some poisonous berries while he was waiting for the bus. A policeman saw him and rushed him to the hospital."

"He picks those berries all the time, but he doesn't eat them. They're bitter," I added.

"I thought the policeman had acted a bit hasty but Kelton wouldn't tell him if he ate them or not, so the officer had no choice but to take him in to be checked."

Joseph and I arrived at the hospital only to have to wait again. They were pumping Kelton's stomach we were informed, and after a while of pacing the floor and moving around from one chair to another in restless anticipation, we were able to see him.

"What happened, Kelton?" I asked him. Again that silence.

"Sick!" he finally stated.

"That's what happens when you eat poison berries," I informed him.

"No eat berries," he yelled, startling me.

"Why didn't you tell them that?" I demanded.

"Oh, he did," the nurse said, "but we weren't sure he understood, so we pumped his stomach anyway."

Great.

I nodded uneasily. How many thousands of times had we all done this to Kelton? Even when he talked, we were never sure.

"No wonder he doesn't talk," I told Joseph. "It doesn't do any good!"

I worried about my child, my winter's flower. Feelings of uncertainty about Kelton's future never ceased. Without Joseph and me around, who would bail him out of situations created by misunderstanding? Who would come to his rescue and bring him back into the safety and comfort of compassion? I prayed that he would become independent so he could handle the ways of a world not of his making.

Before I knew it, summer had fled and the colors of fall had left the landscape to make room for winter's green. The holidays were around the corner. Christmas has always been a big affair at our house and this year, all of my children and their families: Sharlene and Jerry and their three children, Vern, Lynell and Kevin, Allen, Kelton, Mark, Karla and husband Ken and their two children (who call me Grandma because they don't have one), plus my sister Elma and her husband and her family, were going to be home for Christmas.

After some of our children had moved out and established families of their own, we had a new family tradition. Christmas Eve was established as family night, and we all gathered at our house. I cooked a huge turkey with all the trimmings, and after dinner Santa Claus came with a stocking filled with goodies for each one. After Santa left, we exchanged gifts It was a joyful evening.

Kelton caught on to the excitement and helped with the preparation of the meal. He had always liked being around the kitchen. He peeled potatoes, set the table, and chopped vegetables.

"I wish the other kids were as much help as you are Kelton," I told him. "I'm really proud of you. You are good worker."

"Good worker!" he smiled, hurrying to put a salad in the refrigerator.

"I hear Santa Claus is coming tonight, Kelton. Only this time he is going to come in the house and give you your stocking. Will you come upstairs and help Santa hand out Christmas stockings?"

"Help Santa, yes," he answered. I breathed a silent prayer that maybe this year he would take part in the Christmas activities we all cherished.

Kelton loved all the food, and helped put it on the table. Everyone was talking at once about Christmas and whether Santa would really be coming.

"I don't know," I said, "but we did write and ask him. Right, Kelton?"

"Right," he answered,

Dinner was chatty, noisy and wonderful. The food was delicious, everybody held their sides after the generous meal, groaned and confessed to having eaten too much. But that's what holidays are for!

After dinner, we went to the upstairs family room for the next event. Our Christmas tree was seven feet tall, loaded with twinkling lights, sparkling ornaments, and laced with tinsel. Kelton had even helped decorate the tree it this year. The pile of presents under the tree grew as each family added their contributions to Christmas giving.

We gathered around the tree full of anticipation. John and Ken, my sisters' husbands, picked up presents and called out the names, and Kelton distributed the gifts for awhile until he got a few presents with his name on them. Then he sat down to open them.

"What did you get, Kelton?" Karla asked.

"Get music," Kelton answered.

"It's a harpsichord! Boy, that's great, you can learn to play it," I added. Kelton looked at it, then laid it aside to open another present. Papers rustled, bows and ribbons were everywhere as eager fingers tore into packages, and shouts of joy and thank-yous rang out.

"Everybody listen!" I shouted over the din of voices, "I can hear Santa Claus."

Santa burst up the stairs, ho-hoing loudly: "Merry Christmas, Merry Christmas!" Joseph was right behind him, carrying Santa's load of Christmas stockings. What happened next threw us into gales of laughter, and would add to happy memories and genuine amusement for all the Christmases to come.

His arms full of packages resting on his big tummy, our hired Santa's pants fell off.

Kelton laughed the hardest. Santa hastily repaired the embarrassing moment and went on cheerfully ho-hoing, as Kelton shouted gleefully, "Pull off your pants" several times to everyone's amusement.

With his dignity restored and his pants securely fastened, Santa sat in his chair, and the grandchildren squealed in delight as they went up to Santa to get their stockings.

When Kelton's name was called, he just sat there.

"Merry Christmas, Kelton," Santa said. "Here is your sock."

"Go get it, Kelton!" Lynell urged.

Kevin had a camera poised to take his picture. Kelton walked up to Santa and touched his beard.

"Hair!" laughed Kelton.

"Sit on Santa's knee," Kevin said. "I want to get your picture."

Kelton sat on Santa's knee, keeping an eye on him. We all clapped for Kelton. It was a joyous occasion. Our son was participating and not running away. It was also the first Christmas that he liked all his presents.

After everyone left, Kelton and I were cleaning up. " Did you have a good time, Kelton?" I asked.

"Good time," Kelton repeated.

I gave Kelton the Polaroid picture of himself sitting on Santa's knee.

"This is for your book, Kelton. Here are more pictures. You can pick out some if you want to."

Kelton picked them up and looked at them. But when he went to his room he took only the picture of himself on Santa's knee.

Christmas Eve was over too soon, but the warm glow of the evening stayed with me for a long, long time. My gratitude was not just based on Kelton's participation in this treasured family gathering, but it embraced the presence of Joseph and my family and the love and sharing among us. Life was full that night.

The holidays had come and gone and Kelton continued to work at the sheltered workshop. If he was given enough work, he was content, but when he went to class to learn new skills, he became disruptive. He was making a desperate attempt to communicate that he wanted to work.

I put on my armor and went to battle again, I explained to the people in charge that Kelton's self-worth depended on his working. When he was given more work, he calmed down.

The following year was easy on all of us. Kelton was very stable, living by the rules, going bowling and to movies with Mark and Allen. But he had no life of his own. He was alone and lonely.

One afternoon, we had planned a meeting with his caseworker and two people from work. When his visitors arrived, I went upstairs to fetch him. I knocked on his bedroom door and heard his voice, rather muffled, saying, "Come in."

He was lying on the bed, his face hidden in a pillow. "Kelton, Mike and Lori from work and your case worker, Nancy, are here to see you Come on down and join us," I encouraged.

"Why don't you serve them the lemonade and cookies you made?"

Kelton got up somewhat reluctantly. I could see he had been crying.

"Are you okay, Kelton?" I asked.

"Okay," he answered and followed me downstairs, where he shook hands with his company and then went to the kitchen, bringing back the refreshments, he had prepared earlier.

During the meeting it was suggested that Kelton would do well at Oaks, a residential training center which prepared its clients to live in their own apartments, handle money and generally take of themselves.

From what I had heard, Oaks, a federally funded group home, was well monitored and had a good reputation.

"How old is Kelton now?" Nancy asked, looking through her papers.

"He was 23 in June," I answered.

"He has been quite stable for the past six months or more, hasn't he?" Nancy continued.

"Yes," I replied. "He's ready for a change. He has grown a lot lately, and has become an adult. He is showing us he is more responsible and eager to do more with his life."

"Well, I'll look into Oaks and see if there is an opening coming up," she said.

I saw the wistful look in Kelton's eyes. "Do you want to live at the training center, Kelton?"

"Yes," he answered.

Now I understood the reason for his tears earlier. He was terribly lonely and wanted to have friends of his own and affection. He was safe and loved at home, but he knew he needed something more in his life. I wondered if he was remembering past humiliations and fears from his previous experiences in group homes.

I concentrated on keeping my fears in check and not to let them influence my decision against entrusting my son's well being into the hands of strangers. I asked a lot of questions about the center. Nancy assured me of the quality of Oaks program and staff. I wanted no repetition of the nightmare horrors we had gone through before.

Nancy also informed us Kelton would be working with a new case worker. Her name was Gail.

"Every time Kelton gets to know someone, they change workers," I told myself grudgingly.

In the next month, Kelton went several times to Oaks to visit overnight. His visits were a success. He was excited each time he went to the center and asked when he could live there.

The center had a large staff and Kelton would benefit from a music specialist, sex therapist, recreational specialist, physical and mental health nurses and a trainer to help him prepare to live independently—on his own.

Finally word came that there was an opening at Oaks, and our son prepared to leave home once again.

"Please let this be a good experience for him!" I prayed all day long.

When I walked into the living room, Kelton stood there holding on to his suitcase, anxious to move on.

"I see you are ready to go!" I said. "Did you remember everything?"

"Yes," he answered.

"May I look?" I asked. Kelton handed me his suitcase and left the room.

I was busily going through his things, when he returned with his electric razor in his hand. He remembered!

"Well, it looks good and ready, Kelton. Are you excited?" The lump in my throat was growing.

"Yes, he said. "Have friends, time to move out."

"I love you Kelton," I said with tears filling my eyes. I paused, not knowing what to say next. Then I heard it, softly, but clearly. "I love you, mother," he said soberly, touching my shoulder lightly. I had never heard him say these words and my world filled with light and my heart sang.

I noticed how clear his eyes were and how flushed his cheeks with the excitement of his new adventure. I seemed much more anxious about the whole affair than he.

"Well, Allen will be leaving for college next year, you are leaving this year, and we only have Mark for two more years, and then all our children will be gone from home. Will you come and visit us, Kelton?" I asked.

"Yes!" he answered picking up his suitcase, "Time to go."

In silence we rode to the center. My mind retraced all the years of the fighting and struggling we had been through to get Kelton to this point. The child who had lived on the roof of his house, had become the adult who would soon be living in his own apartment.

"The people at the center said that within a year or so you will be in your own apartment, and they are recommending a better job for you, It's an exciting time. This next year, you will be learning to budget your own money, cook your own food, go places on your own. But you've been doing that for years, haven't you?" I said.

"Yes," answered Kelton.

"But now, they will help you learn to do it better," I assured him.

Joseph and I drove Kelton to the center and saw him to his room. We would see him three weeks later for a home visit.

"I'll call you, Kelton," I said. But he was already putting his things in his room.

"Why are you crying?" Joseph asked me as we drove home.

"Kelton has survived all the hardships he has suffered, but

I feel so thankful for some help at last. I feel this time he will make it." I answered.

"All the problems are not over," Joseph reminded me. "Society can be cruel and unfair, and Kelton will have to struggle every day of his life to try to conform."

"I've promised myself not to worry about him," I said trying to control my tears. "But it's hard."

Joseph pulled the car over and put his arms around me. "We'll take one day at a time. Remember what you have taught us all: yesterday is past and tomorrow isn't here. All we have to do is live today. Be happy for Kelton, he's getting his chance."

I took a deep breath, dried my eyes and smiled. It had been a rough journey, but I wouldn't have missed the trip. The sun was setting, painting a magnificent array of colors on the sky. The breeze played upon the clouds, building castles and cliffs. The sun shone through puffs of white, making their edges golden.

Across the road, a farmer was burning his fields, and as we came closer, black and gray clouds of smoke billowed high into the air.

I sat in silent awe as the masses of white clouds met the black clouds, forming a battle ground. For a while they didn't mix, but held their positions. Frustration and hope. The battle to create self and give significance to life.

*So many feelings and words*
*Lie in my heart, unused.*
*Remnants of past rainbows,*
*Melodies of golden memories.*
*Past experiences painted*
*On the canvas of life.*
*Some of joy, some of heartache,*
*I momentarily measure*
*The great lessons each has*
*Taught me,*
*Realizing that I have yet*
*An ocean of learning*
*Always receding before*
*Me.*

# AFTERWORD

It is now 1997. Kelton is in an excellent federally funded program called I.T.H. which provides supervision, training and recreation. He has a job and lives in his own apartment, Kelton has been to the State Fair each year, and there are regular field trips to the beach and the city. Kelton goes to dances, he bowls and takes part in a variety of activities.

He enjoys much more freedom than he would be allowed in a group home. He may have his ups and downs, but basically he functions well in this environment. They tried to assign him room mates, but he is happiest living alone. He loves to come home for visits and interacts well with the family.

Several healing techniques are developed each year. Parents are the fundamental source of information. The journey with Kelton and other people with limited abilities whom I have worked with, have opened my heart and put me in touch with the spirit and led me to the discovery of many gifts.

I have gradually moved away from believing in the healing affects of traditional drugs and medicine, and explored the mind/body healing method. Medicine is desperately in search of new ways to heal. Drugs, I've learned, are often only a cover-up of symptoms, have disastrous side affects and cure nothing. I also realize drugs have their place.

There is not a wall between mind and body. We have placed our own limitations as a result of conditioning from the past. The old programming—the old belief system—must be changed if healing is to take place. We all have our own inner healer.

Joseph and I have established the Rapid Eye Institute. Through inspiration and research we have a model of therapy that releases stress so the body can heal itself. Rapid eye technology approaches the neural distortion (stress) at the cellular level.

Studies have shown neural pathways in the brain become distorted under trauma and physical pain. By duplicating a natural process of eye movements (which happen in REM sleep) in an alpha state while awake, the body discharges energy that has held the distorted program trapped.

Work and research with rapid eye technology is being explored with autistic children. So far the therapy seems to work with those who will cooperate. Parents and other family members benefit greatly from the therapy. Fear, guilt and other stressful emotions are released and do not return.

The Rapid Eye Institute provides therapy and offers a training program to become a certified therapist for this process. We are excited with the wonderful results we have achieved.

For more information, write or call: Ranae Johnson, Ph.D., 3748 74th Avenue SE Salem, OR, 97301, (503) 399-1181.

## A Comment from Anson Bell, Director of Spruce Villa, Inc.
## Salem, Oregon

Kelton has taken full advantage of the various services offered by Spruce Villa, Inc., where he is living. He entered the federally certified portion of this program in 1984. Spruce Villa, Inc. is a ten-bed home which provides 24-hour supervision for the residents and is backed up by a professional staff consisting of a psychologist, social workers and others.

Kelton is independent and either walks or takes a city bus to work and places of recreation. He is an eager participant in household chores, as well as group activities, such as Special Olympics, bowling and facility-sponsored social functions.

In July 1986 Kelton was able to move into his own apartment in a complex for handicapped and non-handicapped tenants. He has his own bedroom and shares the kitchen and living room with one other person. Staff is available for the tenants, but people living on their own must be able to take care of themselves to a large degree.

Kelton is one of our lawn care crew's most productive workers. He is independent in the use of power tools as well as the servicing of the equipment. He is dependable and completes tasks in the required time allotted to a handicapped worker.

The future for Kelton looks bright. Because of his (past) problem with autism, he will probably require fairly consistent supervision in order to offset his tendency to be a loner. Kelton has a good attitude, and his willingness to accept responsibility will present him with interesting opportunities to enhance the quality of his life.